EVERYONE LOVES A FAIRY STORY . . .

Long Ago and Far Away
"LONG AGO AND F[...]
of the bestselling and [...]
This tale has all of M[...]
. . . .Adult fairy tales are very popular because [...]
classic works of Ms. Rogers."

—*Affaire de Coeur* (5 stars)

Once Upon A Time
"This novel has everything a romance reader desires
. . . A beautifully poignant fairy tale."

—*Affaire de Coeur*

"A bewitching, magical love story that will whisk the
reader into an ethereal land of enchantment."

—*Romantic Times*

"Marylyle Rogers provides her fans with a tremen-
dous and enchanting reading event. The author mas-
terfully and brilliantly juxtaposes the fairy world with
that of the Victorian realm in this enjoyable read."

—*Romance Forever*

Happily Ever After
"Marylyle Rogers is a magician. The remarkable Rogers blends medieval, time travel, and fantasy into a
great novel that audiences will savor for years to
come."

—*Affaire de Coeur*

"Another groundbreaking romance of lyrical grace
from a fabulous storyteller. A spectacular, utterly irresistible love story full of magic and joy. Ms. Rogers
waves her magic wand and the result is pure enchantment. . . . Romance fans will never forget it."

—*Romantic Times*

ST. MARTIN'S PAPERBACKS TITLES
BY MARYLYLE ROGERS

ONCE UPON A TIME
HAPPILY EVER AFTER
LONG AGO AND FAR AWAY

Long Ago and Far Away

Marylyle Rogers

St. Martin's Paperbacks

LONG AGO AND FAR AWAY

Copyright © 1997 by Marylyle Rogers.

ISBN: 0-312-96314-9

Printed in the United States of America

St. Martin's Paperbacks edition/October 1997

St. Martin's Paperbacks are published by St. Martin's Press, 175 Fifth Avenue, New York, NY 10010.

10 9 8 7 6 5 4 3 2 1

To Irene Goodman with earnest appreciation
for her patience and unwavering support.

Prologue

Inside a splendid castle that glowed with the white brilliance of moonlight a celebration was underway. A prophecy had been fulfilled by the daughter of Comlan, King of the Tuatha de Danann, and his human wife. Lissan had risen with the May Day dawn of 1900 but by accidentally invoking fairy magic had literally fallen through time to land in the year 1115.

There, by her actions, Lissan had preserved the security and health of both her beloved, Rory O'Connor, and the Kingdom of Connaught. Now in this magical haven they and those closest to them were being feted by an array of golden beings while enticing melodies flowed from pipes, harps, timbrels, and other instruments rarely seen by human eyes.

While others were diverted by an amazing variety of entertainments, a dark child held the king's attention. Her eyes, so dark a blue they were nearly black, never faltered in steadily meeting his penetrating scrutiny. Comlan was impressed by the solemn girl. Here was bravery, a valued trait and rare—particularly in humans.

"Your mother's name was . . . ?" Comlan quietly inquired of the young one who earlier in the recently settled conflict had been courageous enough to enter the fairy ring and summon him to rescue his daughter from humans intent on burning her as a witch.

"Cleva," Hildie answered, never thinking to question his purpose while with wide eyes gazing up at the wondrous figure so close. Though not their first meeting, she remained awed by King Comlan and all among his wondrous, mysterious kind.

Comlan slowly nodded before continuing in pursuit of verification for an important detail.

"Was it your mother who claimed you are descended from my sister, the Lissan for whom your stepmother was named and the one who in shedding her magic powers created the fairy ring?"

Sad memories of a happy time lost clouded Hildie's eyes but she promptly nodded. "Many times before an illness stole Mama away near two years past, she told me the tale of the fairy princess from whom we are descended."

Hildie broke their visual bond by glancing

downward to blindly study the amazing floor formed of a strange, translucent marble that seemed to glow from within.

"Did you know . . ." Comlan began while with a forefinger gently tilting the child's chin upward until again their gazes met. "That there is a way to be certain whether or not 'tis true?"

" 'Struth?" Breath audibly caught in Hildie's throat. Desperately wanting to know and yet afraid long-nurtured dreams would be crushed, she pushed vague fears aside to bravely speak, albeit a single word issued on a disconcerting squeak. "How?"

"When a fairy's power is shed"—Comlan was further impressed by the clearly apprehensive child's courage—"it leaves behind a mark. Throughout time every descendant of like gender bears that same mark."

Hildie bit her lip hard, hoping . . . hoping . . . hoping . . .

"Once my sister surrendered her powers for the sake of her mortal beloved," Comlan softly stated, "a small shape appeared on the back of her neck— a lopsided heart."

Instantly, Hildie swept a wealth of dark hair forward and bent her head, revealing her nape and the small shape of a lopsided heart that it bore.

"You are my niece, my human niece, although separated by many mortal generations." King Comlan lifted the child to give her a warm and fatherly embrace.

Suspecting their relationship would be proven, Comlan had already made arrangements for the safekeeping of this child. Thus, when Queen Amethyst called for his attention, Comlan summoned one of his warriors to step forward and entertain the young girl. Kieron, both trustworthy and amusing, accepted the charge.

Despite this incredibly handsome being's brilliant smile and easy manner, Hildie was wary of him and only cautiously complied as he led her to join the vast sea of amazing figures dancing in strange patterns. But with roguish charm and quick laughter Kieron soon lured Hildie's adventurous nature to appear and tempted her to join him in steps intricate but easily learned.

Kieron was intrigued by the dark and serious child so utterly unlike any in his world. When King Comlan first told him about this girl likely descended from the long-deceased Princess Lissan, the prospect of too much time in the boring company of a human had left Kieron reluctant to accept the royal commission to stand as her guardian and friend. However, the rejection of his king's request would've been difficult and foolish, if not worse. And now that he'd seen and talked with his charge, the duty seemed not so bleak nor difficult to bear.

When a change in tempo signaled the end of one dance and start of another, Kieron tugged his small and merrily laughing partner aside.

Hildie watched amazed as an instant later Kieron produced from some unseen source two goblets sharing the sheen of pearls and filled with the welcome refreshment of a delicious fruit elixir.

"Hildie," Kieron quietly called for the child's attention. When unusual eyes of deepest blue turned to him, he offered what was likely to be the best link to aid him in protecting the child. "I have a gift for you—a very special pet."

"Pet?" Hildie's dark eyes suddenly gleamed with silver sparks. She had always wanted a pet of her very own but Morag, her unpleasant and unofficial foster mother, refused to have another animal cluttering a keep that already hosted a great many hunting dogs.

"What kind?" A shadow crossed Hildie's face as she cast a dubious glance toward the golden and intimidatingly handsome man unaccountably willing to waste his time with her. Her gaze quickly dropped from eyes an impossible shade of aqua and darted from side to side as if daring disappointment to strike. "Where is it?"

"Here," Kieron answered and as he spoke a small fox suddenly appeared in his arms.

"A fox?" Hildie was surprised and delighted by the dainty creature of auburn fur and black-tipped tail.

"Not only is she tame," Kieron explained as he lowered the animal into the child's welcoming hold, "but she possesses a very special talent. If ever you have need for my help, send her and fetch me she will."

Already in a place of wonders and impossible

realities, Hildie didn't for a moment question Kieron's claim although she couldn't imagine bothering this awe-inspiring being with her petty woes. She could take care of herself. Still, instead of asserting that ability, she instead quietly asked, "What's her name?"

Kieron gave the child a gentle smile. "You'll have to give her one after you've both returned home to Ailm Keep."

As he spoke, Kieron's attention was caught by King Comlan's motioning him to bring Hildie back and rejoin the evening's festivities.

CHAPTER 1

Ireland, 1127

Despite the warmth of the May sun, Hildie shivered. It was a response caused by neither pleasant coolness in the shade of towering trees nor even the slightest chill in gentle spring air. No, the sound of someone behind and noisily moving closer delivered cold proof of her failure to escape unwelcome company.

Hildie's honest attempt to avoid a persistent suitor had been thwarted. Hoping to elude Rolan Shanahan's prying and far too personal eyes, she had brought her small half sister to this favorite glade for a picnic. Here she'd shared with five-year-old Amy a simple meal and played silly games until the child fell asleep in her lap. But now it seemed certain that Rolan was approaching. Must be he since only a fool would march so heedlessly through forest undergrowth and Rolan, at least two years her junior, was undeniably that.

As the lone son amidst a sizeable family of sisters, Rolan had been doted upon. Unfortunately he accepted liberal but unjustified praise for truth and looked even more the buffoon by wearing self-importance like a badge of honor.

Determined to ignore her uninvited companion for as long as possible, Hildie blindly studied the sleeping child's riot of golden curls. Suddenly air motionless an instant before gusted from behind, sweeping the thick cloud of Hildie's ebony hair forward to leave her nape exposed.

" 'Tis true!" Horror shook the words gasped by a strained male voice. "Holy Mary deliver me from Satan's child."

If her magical friend were near, Hildie would think him playing a prank, but Kieron wasn't here. She turned to cast a scowl over her shoulder at the vain adolescent who gaped for scant moments before awkwardly spinning to flee. The next instant he was blundering through forest foliage like a graceless ox.

It was clear that Rolan had heard rumors concerning her distinctive marking . . . and accepted without question the gossiping biddies' utter misinterpretation of its source. More reason to name him a fool. But then—Hildie chided herself to be more charitable—there were few beyond her father's inner circle who either knew or would believe the truth behind the tiny, lopsided heart resting on the pale cream of her nape. Even her father still had difficulty accepting its meaning since the mark actually was, as whispered by many, physical proof of a mystical heritage—but *not* the demonic parentage that Rolan so feared.

With eyes a blue as deep as any midnight sky, Hildie glared into forest shadows that had swallowed up the fleeing youth. Her father and stepmother, Lissan, would be disappointed by Rolan's craven flight . . . but she wasn't! The prospect of a lifetime in the boorish toad's company was repulsive.

Hildie longed to choose her own path, live by her own rules. But she had to confess it was already too often a fact that she only abided by the restraints others would impose when it suited her. Oh, she was careful to listen with a pleasant smile and due respect to her father and Lissan—before doing what she deemed best.

Because her loving parents knew and leastways tolerated her independent spirit, Hildie silently questioned how they could expect her to be content with a mere mortal as mate. In the next instant a pang of guilt struck with such unexpected force that her arms unconsciously tightened around the child cradled within. The better, more pertinent question was how could she be a daughter so ungrateful when allowed far more say in the choice for spouse than any other female of her age and station?

Hildie shifted uneasily on the glade's soft padding of lush grasses as if physical movement had power to ease emotional discomfort. By acknowledging the uselessness of the action she reluctantly admitted that the current predicament rose from her stubborn refusal to yield irrational dreams.

Despite the priest's oft repeated admonishments against the sin of a willful nature, Hildie continued to nurture the weak hope that she could bring a halt to the seemingly endless line of persistent suitors by steadily following one simple course of action. Surely, if she consistently rejected all formal proposals, other prospective but unwanted mates, like Rolan, would flee in terror of her reputed link to unearthly powers. Then, though still unable to claim the only male she coveted, leastways in the end—old, gray, and alone—she would be left in peace.

In reality, Hildie knew the dream was doomed so long as the rich prize of an alliance with her father, the most powerful lord in Connaught and mentor to its king, could be gained by acquiring her for wife. Even were she a snaggle-toothed hag, no family of good birth which boasted an unattached male would fail to pursue such a valuable union.

Although squinting up into bright sunlight, Hildie sensed a gathering darkness as if storm clouds were threatening fair skies. Did it portend a dismal future in which there remained the inescapable duty to choose a husband . . . a human husband.

Oblivious to the steady gaze of a child she hadn't

realized was awake, Hildie's lips tightened. Hers was an unattainable fantasy and yet she refused to surrender precious dreams to be content with a mundane fate. Despite her parents' earnest hope that she would outgrow an impossible infatuation, how could she settle for a mortal when she knew another far, far more—

"Kieron."

Startled to hear the name constantly in her thoughts spoken aloud, Hildie gave her ebony hair a brief shake while her gaze dropped to its source— the little girl in her arms but no longer asleep.

"Kieron," Amy repeated, dark eyes sparkling while her tiny finger pointed to a spot just beyond Hildie's shoulder.

Dark lashes fell for a moment and a faint smile appeared as Hildie surrendered her attention to an incredible, golden being. Kieron stood very near. Hildie assumed that she had failed to instantly sense his presence only because he'd already dominated her thoughts so completely.

"Greetings, elfling." Kieron's deep voice purred as he bent to tap a fingertip on the little girl-child's dainty nose.

Hildie's smile tilted awry. "Elfling?" she asked, instinctively questioning this use of the pet name Kieron had previously reserved for her.

"I've been lonely since *my* elfling stopped calling out to me." The gentle mockery in Kieron's tone implied a jest and yet he spoke what for him was an uncomfortable truth.

Despite an initial reluctance when first charged by his king to stand as guardian to Hildie, at their first meeting Kieron had been intrigued by the dark and solemn waif. Then, while years passed in her world, he'd watched the serious girl mature in a process which to his delight had dimmed neither her fiery spirit nor sense of adventure.

Made sensitive to Kieron's ever-shifting moods by her feelings for him, Hildie easily understood the unspoken question behind his words. He wanted to know the meaning of her silence. However, it was a different curious issue that first captured her attention and inspired a dubious sidelong glance. Not even the contrary nature of fairy could justify the patently false claim of loneliness made by this male ever relentlessly pursued by a legion of females in his world.

When the obvious disbelief on Hildie's face showed Kieron what path her thoughts had followed, his wry smile deepened with self-derision. He had been at least as disconcerted as she now seemed to be on discovering himself longing for the company of any particular female, far less a human, and least of all this one by oath fated to be as sister to him!

To calm the uneasiness prompted by this response, Kieron tried to convince himself that it was merely a product of the mortal years during which he'd been responsible for Hildie. He bolstered that theory by choosing to ignore the fact that such a measure of human time represented little more than one fleeting moment in the vast life span of his kind.

Thinking Kieron's mockery intended for her, Hildie hastened to end the long silence by tentatively offering the wordlessly sought explanation for their long separation.

"I grew up." Hildie despised lies but could hardly confess to having stayed away in dread of betraying how besotted she was with him.

"Fearing you wearied by my youthful follies—" Hildie broke their visual bond, worried that while standing so close Kieron's amazingly acute senses might read the truth of her emotions for him and too likely be repelled. "I wanted to prove to you that I'd outgrown them."

Hildie was certain that a childhood of playing the fool ever calling Kieron to rescue her from silly scrapes was shameful enough but an infinitely worse possibility loomed. She'd spent months earnestly striving to avoid the devastating sight of incredible aqua eyes darkened not with disgust but with pity. Pity for the adoration of a poor mortal utterly lacking his own golden race's ethereal perfection.

Her reluctant admission warmed Kieron's stern expression with a breath-stealing smile whose power Hildie had first recognized at their introduction more than a decade past.

"Outgrown them? But why?" Kieron's quiet laughter gently rolled across the peaceful glade.

"Your intrepid adventures were a constant delight."

"Oh, aye, intrepid." Hildie grimaced while refusing to meet the lure of his gaze, still fearing what he might discover. This was no time for confessions. Not now, nor likely ever would she dare reveal how often she had played the role of pint-sized lady in distress just for the delight in being rescued by her hero. Never mind that she could easily have escaped from most situations all by herself.

"Intrepid?" Hildie hastily repeated, hoping to mask her uneasiness. "Like when I climbed the fairy ring's oak to save that fool cat . . . only to have him leap safely down and leave me trapped high above?"

"I thoroughly enjoyed rescuing you then and every time." The quiet tenor of Kieron's voice made it impossible for Hildie to doubt his sincerity. "Your multitude of predicaments always posed an unanticipated array of uniquely entertaining challenges . . . and you know how highly my kind prizes the unusual and even more the unexpected."

Uncertain how to respond, Hildie's gaze dropped to the curiously watching child in her lap.

"Besides . . ." Without hesitation Kieron seized this perfect opportunity to broach the purpose of his visit. "It's admiration for all of your fearless adventures that has brought me to you now."

Kieron's announcement startled Hildie into glancing up to meet his steady gaze.

"In return for the many times I delivered you from minor predicaments, I have come to beg of you a similar boon."

"Tch." Hildie gave her head a brief, indignant shake. "I am no longer so easily gulled as once I was." And to her mind Kieron was clearly teasing her again. It was a pursuit in which he had time and again taken gentle delight. This suggestion that she—a mere human—could possibly be of aid to one of his wondrous powers must be a jest.

" 'Struth," Kieron immediately protested. "There is a task which only you can—"

"Ouch!" Hildie abruptly yelped. The sharp tug on her black locks was no less insistent for having been delivered by a toddler's hand.

"Amy go home." The child was tired of being ignored, and her eyes, a blue as dark as those belonging to both her father and Hildie, were unwavering in their quiet demand. "Go home."

Sapphire gaze lifting to the sky, Hildie found the sun had fallen below the western forest's deep green silhouette and although the copper streaks of sunset glory had yet to appear, clearly they were near. Hildie was horrified by this proof of how late she would be in returning with her charge to safety within the keep's protective walls.

Following the line of Hildie's glance, Kieron understood the source of her dismay. He immediately swirled his cloak around the pair. Then, within the span of a single heartbeat, he transported them to a site on the woodland's border where trees opened onto Ailm Keep's tilled fields.

Sunlight glided over auburn fur as Seun bounded from the dark line of trees at their backs. Sighting the fox who'd earlier scampered away in chase of a butterfly, Amy impatiently wiggled until Hildie lowered the child's feet to the ground.

"Lady Hildie—" A distant call pulled the dark colleen's attention from the toddler hugging a long-suffering pet. "I pray 'tis you!"

Dark head lifting, Hildie peered toward the source of this hopeful plea. An aged and nearly blind guardsman hobbled toward her across rows of new-sprouted crops so anxious to reach her that he spared no thought for the damage left in his wake.

"Praise the Saints! You've been found!" Despite labored breathing, Duff still continued. "Your father sent the whole of his garrison on a quest to fetch you back home."

Hildie's brows arched. Her return was later than planned but, with Kieron's aid, not so late that search parties ought to have been dispatched.

"An important visitor has entered the keep." Duff gave her a coy grin. "And I do believe that 'tis for you he's come."

"Who, Duff?" Considering the near constant stream of suitors that had begun with the arrival of fair weather, this simple fact wouldn't raise such a stir unless the visitor was someone important. . . .

Hildie nibbled her bottom lip, an old habit

picked up long ago from watching her idolized stepmother and revived whenever she needed to steal a moment either to collect her thoughts or contain her temper.

Apprehensive, Hildie took a deep breath and repeated the question likely soliciting an unwelcome answer. "Who is it that's come?"

"Lord Morven, the master of Dunbarrough Keep." Duff was plainly torn between his excitement at being the bearer of this announcement and his lingering distaste for any native of Munster.

It seemed to Hildie as if her heart had just plummeted to her toes. She saw the purpose behind Lord Morven's arrival as clearly as must Duff. Though a stranger in Connaught, Munster's most renowned warrior had undoubtedly come seeking her for bride. And, worst of all, this potential groom holding considerable power in the neighboring and often enemy kingdom could not easily be rejected.

"You must make haste, Lady Hildie," Duff urged, "Lord Morven is presenting his suit to your father even now."

Wondering what Kieron thought of this unhappy development, Hildie peeked over her shoulder. But, in a further demonstration of the contrary nature of fairy, her magical friend had departed as abruptly as he'd earlier appeared.

Inside the soaring stone tower of Ailm Keep, the great hall was host to an uncomfortable scene.

While an odd assortment of inhabitants surreptitiously watched, its lord and his wife faced a stern visitor nursing a sense of outraged affront.

" 'Struth, the accord between your people and mine is of grave importance." Rory O'Connor politely nodded a dark head toward his guest, at the same time exercising considerable willpower to restrain growing annoyance with this man who leaped too hastily to faulty conclusions. Rory bridled his tongue by focusing on one critical fact. Not only was Lord Morven a powerful warlord but master of lands joined to Rory's own by the bridge spanning a deep ravine marking their border.

Despite strained and lingering tensions an uneasy truce had held throughout the twelve years following a serious conflict between Connaught and Munster which had ended with the death of Morven's uncle Mael. And, as much as Rory rued the need, he knew how important it was to maintain the two kingdoms' precarious peace—an issue greatly complicated by this man's proposed alliance with Hildie.

"But my daughter's delayed return is in no way a slight to your honorable offer of marriage." Despite Rory's best intentions, a pointed comment escaped through gritted teeth. "How could it be when we received no advance notice of your visit?"

By her husband's rare lapse in tact and the muscle twitching in his jaw, Lissan knew Rory's patience was wearing perilously thin. She immediately waded into the conversation with soothing words intended to calm the meeting's troubled waters.

"I'm certain our daughter will soon return, Lord Morven." Lissan awarded the frowning visitor a gracious smile of unmerited warmth while noting with distaste that he had hair as bright a red and was plainly as unpleasant as his predecessor at Dunbarrough Keep.

"But for now surely you'd appreciate a private moment's rest before all of Ailm Keep gathers for the evening meal?"

Returning his hostess's sweetness with a sour grimace, Morven inclined his head in stiff assent before stomping after the eavesdropping servant summoned to direct him to a waiting chamber.

No sooner had their uninvited guest been led off to the promised chamber than an aging member of the garrison hobbled proudly into the hall with Hildie and her young charge in tow.

"I found them, my lord," Duff brightly announced, an action complicated by the breathlessness caused a man of advanced years by his hasty climb up an outer stairway which turned back on itself twice before reaching the keep's entrance.

"A feat for which you have my gratitude." Rory gave a gentle smile to this faithful guardsman who lent earnest effort to every chore. "And you've earned a rest before the day's final repast."

As Duff withdrew, beaming over his lord's praise, Rory motioned for Hildie to join her parents in the lord's private chambers at the tower's highest level.

Silently climbing through the gloom of a stairway lit only by intermittent slants of fading daylight falling through narrow arrow slits, Hildie mentally braced herself for news certain to follow. The prospect was bleak. She was certain her parents knew that if left to her, she would choose to refuse Lord Morven's offer. And yet, as had not been the case with the many earlier requests for her hand, Hildie was painfully aware that this proposed alliance was far more important and not so easily rejected.

Hildie's expression was solemn by the time they reached their destination, a large chamber lent luxurious comfort by gifts from the Faerie Realm upon her father and stepmother's marriage a dozen years past.

"Lord Morven journeyed here from his impressive home some distance beyond the bridge," Rory began, attention resting on the young beauty stubbornly refusing to meet his gaze. "He has come on a mission holding the dangerous potential for overtilting the delicate balance of peace between our two kingdoms toward war and renewed bloodshed."

This was even worse than anticipated. Hildie's heart thumped with dread while she fixed an unjustified glare on the intricate pattern of birds and flowers carved into the chest behind her parents. She'd realized that refusing the lord from Munster would be more difficult than shooing away a pesky adolescent like Rolan, but she hadn't expected to hear that her action could jeopardize their kingdom's security.

The uncomfortable silence lengthened until Hildie glanced up at her waiting father—nearly two score and five yet still a strong and handsome man with thick, dark hair untouched by silver.

Not until certain of his headstrong daughter's complete attention did Rory continue, determined to ensure that she fully comprehended the import of this ominous development.

"With his proposal to claim you in wedlock, Lord Morven delivered a formal letter from his liege, King Muirtrecht." From the edge of his dark tunic Rory slipped a folded parchment free.

"It, too, advances the union as a physical symbol of Connaught's alliance with Munster. . . ." Penetrating dark eyes squarely met others of like hue with unspoken caution not to view so serious a matter lightly. "And it most skillfully implies a deadly price for refusal of his loyal noble's suit."

Considering their visitor's testy nature, Rory suspected the man would take delight in meting out punishment for any perceived slight. In truth, he suspected the famous warrior would be avidly watching for the faintest excuse to launch an assault.

CHAPTER 2

In a small room one level below the lord of Ailm Keep's chamber, Hildie abruptly turned over. That action rocked a sturdy bed even before she punched her pillow—hard.

The unwelcome guest from Munster had joined the keep's inhabitants in the great hall for an uneasy evening meal. A seemingly interminable length of time had passed while in near silence a parade of courses was delivered and empty platters removed. And throughout, beneath the uncomfortable facade of pleasant hospitality a vibrating strain could almost be heard. Indeed, the tension had grown so taut that the dinner's end had come as a relief to not only those at the high table but also to all who served or sat along lines of trestle tables stretched out below the dais.

Lord Morven hadn't spoken a single word directly to Hildie but his cold, near colorless eyes rarely strayed far. To her it was plain that behind his supercilious mask he was skeptically judging her worthiness as wife . . . as if it were a position she coveted. Hah!

Hildie tossed about to again lie on her back and glare up into gloom relieved only by the faint strip of moonlight drifting through an arrow slit in the wall above her bed.

While Hildie found the notion of being landed with the immature and cocky Rolan for spouse depressing, it was nothing compared to the disgusting prospect of having Morven foisted upon her. And not simply because the red-haired lord was her father's age (which he was). Nor, she reluctantly admitted, could distaste for a repugnant appearance be claimed when, though not notably attractive, his features were well enough aligned.

Nevertheless, Hildie vehemently told herself, she couldn't, wouldn't marry Lord Morven. She shivered with distaste for mere possibility of intimacies shared with him.

But what choice did she have when so much depended on her acceptance? Dark eyes clenched shut against the inevitable answer: None. She had none. . . .

Hildie forced herself to stare again into shadows above while with another unhappy truth cautioning herself to accept bleak reality. What did it matter whether she wed Morven or Rolan or some other nameless suitor when balanced against the immovable barriers between her and the only male with whom she'd welcome such bonds?

To Kieron she was no more than an amusing example of an inferior race, like some cute pet or precocious child. Sadly, even if by some miracle Kieron could take her feelings for him seriously, neither his king nor her father would approve.

Though her papa put up with the fairy breed for the sake of his beloved Lissan, Hildie was well aware that he'd stand fast against any suggestion of the stronger alliance in a daughter wed to one of their number—no matter her own ancestral link to Tuatha de Danann.

Hildie stifled a growl of protest and was glad that she had when a muffled sound reminded her of the toddler sleeping on a small cot very near. Purposefully lowering thick lashes, she willed herself toward the misty world of dreams and had nearly succeeded when a very real hand closed around her mouth.

Startled, Hildie gazed up into the handsome face of this welcome intruder—an incredible figure with an aura akin to the moon's subtle glow.

"Shhhh." Forefinger pressed against closed lips, Kieron's silent command was clear. Hildie promptly nodded, and he released her mouth to gently lift her into his arms.

Cradled near, face buried against his throat, Hildie remembered the many past times he'd whisked her in an instant to some distant site. Where were they going now? In a heartbeat she confessed it didn't matter so long as he held her close. In that same heartbeat the journey ended as abruptly as it had begun.

With feet again on firm ground, Hildie found herself amidst peculiar, totally unfamiliar surroundings, and facing a wall apparently of solid stone. She looked up but could see nothing above— neither ceiling nor stars and moon. . . . Startled by this strange destination, she flashed her companion a curious glance tinged with more trepidation than she'd willingly admit.

Kieron's only response was a reassuring grin. This he flashed to Hildie even while leaning to one side and tucking his fingertips into a slight crease in the rock.

As the wall shifted, a low grating noise echoed through the unseen depths. Hildie would have stepped back if Kieron hadn't wrapped his arm around her shoulders and held her steady.

Sensing his elfling the victim of a nervousness rare to her, Kieron urged her through the portal. From there they descended a seemingly endless flight of shallow stairs that curved around and deeper, ever deeper.

When at last the ground leveled out and they came to a halt, Hildie peered anxiously about the damp, musty cavern whose limits were lost in blackness darker even than a moonless night. This eerie place was oppressively silent. Hildie swallowed hard and, despite the courage on which she prided herself, instinctively leaned toward the only source of light—Kieron's magical glow.

"There's no reason to fear," Kieron quietly reassured Hildie. "We're inside the mountain beneath King Comlan's castle."

Embarrassed by her momentary cowardice and wishing to hide any further hint of uneasiness from the penetrating gaze of her secret beloved, Hildie immediately launched her most favored weapon of defense—questions.

"Why did we walk down those steps?" Long familiar with the rule that forbade fairy answers given without human questions first asked, Hildie had often used it to her own advantage. "Why didn't you simply whisk us here?"

Kieron's white smile flashed while his deep, mocking laughter echoed through the vast cavern. He was pleased to find the sweet colleen still adept at waging this gentle form of warfare.

"Because," Kieron answered, "even the Tuatha de Danann's powers cannot pass through walls of natural stone."

Hildie frowned. "Natural stone?" What other kind was there?

"We can whisk ourselves and others through human built barriers of stone or into hollow hills where caves are formed of earth and lesser rocks." The gentle humor in Kieron's response warmed Hildie despite the chill of surrounding air. "But never those which were naturally formed in ancient times."

"But why are we here?" Adventurous spirit bolstered by her magical friend's unwavering support,

Hildie promptly asked the most basic question. "Nay, why did you bring me to this place in the middle of the night?"

Kieron ignored the second to answer the first. "I told you this afternoon of an important task that only you can perform."

Despite eerie surroundings, this claim left Hildie as skeptical as when first asserted. Again she wondered what kind of action she could possibly take that he or any other of his kind couldn't do easier and better?

Kieron answered her unspoken query by pointing through the gloom to a dimly seen and odd arrangement of stones—not tumbled but carefully placed in a close-fitting, circular pattern. Hildie squinted, trying to more clearly see the strange markings laid across their smooth surfaces.

"Can you read what is written there?" Kieron asked, a dark thread of unaccustomed strain woven through the deep textures of his voice.

Slowly shaking her head, Hildie moved nearer to the curious structure.

"Lissan taught me to read and write our language—both as it is now and as it will be in the future—but this bears no resemblance to either."

Hildie's stepmother, Lissan, had once begged her own father, the Faerie Realm's king, to fetch a trunk full of books back from the future into which she'd been born. King Comlan had delivered that chest to Tuatha Cottage here in 1115.

When Kieron wryly nodded in response, his

golden hair seemed to glow brighter. He had neither reason nor desire to investigate the relief
found in her response. But he had wondered, even
feared, the possibility that people in the far distant
mortal centuries yet to come might decipher the
ancient language.

"Just as Lissan's teaching illuminates a window
on times to be—" Kieron offered a cryptic explanation that posed more questions than it answered.
"The light of this script reveals an infinitely more
ancient past."

"But the markings . . ." Hildie motioned toward
the strange characters deeply etched into granite—
a horizontal line intersected by carefully placed
slashes above, below, or through.

" 'Tis Ogham," Kieron softly said. "And used by
the Sidhe who in that far distant past were the first
of my race."

Curiosity already increased by Kieron's first ambiguous statement, as he'd no doubt intended, Hildie asked, "Can you read it?"

Silence grew while Hildie waited for his response. She was surprised by his hesitation and,
while ostensibly staring at the engraved marks, cast
a sidelong glance toward the companion far more
intriguing.

"Parts." With this succinct answer Kieron prevented any need to admit how in youth he'd been
too impatient to devote the attention required for
the mastering of these cryptic patterns. In the next

instant, his mercurial nature produced a roguish grin and wry statement.

" 'Tis a tale repeated so oft that all inhabitants of the Faerie Realm know it well."

"And now you mean to share it with me?" Though accompanied by a winsome smile, Hildie's words were less query than polite demand.

Potent grin flashing white again, Kieron complied. "In the long, long ago when the world was young, uncontrolled forces moved aimlessly across the earth's surface both creating and destroying without purpose or reason."

With the kindled fires of inborn curiosity stoked to new heights, Hildie listened closely.

"Confusion reigned . . ." The intensity of this mortal colleen's attention struck sparks in the depths of Kieron's aqua gaze. "Until the ancestors of my breed imprisoned the powerful Dragons of Chaos—clearing the way for humans to impose their own forms of restraint upon nature."

Hildie waited expectantly for Kieron to continue. When it was clear that he meant to say no more, she quietly appealed for a specific explanation.

"What has this tale of a mystic past to do with me?"

Neither speaking nor meeting her gaze, Kieron stepped past Hildie and moved around to the circle's far side before bending to closely examine the markings on the stone at his feet.

"Here is the warning which states that once folly freed, only a Seunadair can reharnass the turbulent fury of the Dragons of Chaos before it destroys both your world and mine."

"Seunadair?" Hildie quietly repeated the peculiar term while moving to stand at his side and peer intently at the markings he lightly touched. "Is that why you were amused when I named the fox you gave me Seun?"

Again Kieron's grin flashed. "I was amused that you chose so appropriate a name for your pet— Seun, the term for a charm of protection."

Because it was obvious that Hildie found this an insufficient response, Kieron relented. "A Seunadair is one who possesses the powers of enchantment . . . powers able to drive the Dragons of Chaos into retreat and impose unbreakable restraints upon them."

"But surely they're not free." Hildie stated it as a fact and hoped Kieron wouldn't hear her misgivings. Though still more than half convinced that all of this was a prank he meant to play on her, she was familiar enough with the ever changing, inexplicable currents flowing throughout the Faerie Realm that she couldn't be certain.

"There are signs . . ." Kieron answered with a solemnity rare to him. "Aye, though the signs are faint and scattered, they expose an intensifying threat, warn of an imminent escape by the Dragons of Chaos." His ever penetrating gaze seemed to bore even more deeply into Hildie's dark eyes. "The Seunadair is urgently needed."

These alarming words succeeded only in deepening Hildie's bewilderment. "What possible use could you have for me when clearly you must find this wondrous being?"

Aqua eyes held Hildie firmly in their thrall while Kieron slowly answered. "*You* are the Seunadair of which the stones speak."

"Me?" Hildie gasped incredulously, sapphire gaze dropping to the circle of stones. "I have no magical powers." She hastily backed two paces away as if the lines of Ogham had become hissing adders. "I'm not even fairy."

"Ahhh," Kieron persisted, "but you are niece to the king of the Tuatha de Danann." He paused until dark eyes lifted to him, ensuring her serious consideration of what followed. "And this inscription speaks of a special Seunadair—one possessed of a magic not of fairy born."

"Nay." Hildie fervently shook a cloud of black hair as if fierce denial would make it so. "I cannot possibly be *that* Seunadair—"

With this, Hildie's third repetition of the term, a deep rumbling welled up from the bowels of the earth. Initially a slight vibration, it grew in shuddering power until even the closed ring of stones ominously shook.

Hildie was allowed no moment to fear the event's consequences before Kieron swept her up into his arms and dashed up the stairway. Once beyond the portal, he tucked her face into his shoulder and in the next instant deposited Hildie atop her abandoned bed in Ailm Keep.

Sitting bolt-upright, Hildie made a rapid visual search of the chamber empty save for a sweetly sleeping Amy.

Had Kieron truly whisked her into the Faerie Realm's nether regions? And had the Dragons of Chaos shaken the earth in their quest for escape? Or had it all been merely a vivid dream born of wishful longing to be with an impossible love?

Face expressionless, King Comlan turned from the bright and cheery heart of his castle and motioned Kieron from the great hall into the small chamber branching off on one side. Once they were closed in privacy, he turned to the younger male with a stern question.

"With what unthinking knavery have you occupied your night?"

Bright aqua eyes blinked. Kieron was both startled by the question and, due to his mercurial nature, oddly delighted by the surprise. Although more adept at sensing the emotions and thoughts of others than even most of his kind, his elder and far more experienced monarch stood impervious to any attempt to pierce an icy mask.

"Did you believe it possible to invade the inner sanctum of my home undetected?"

Kieron instantly named himself a fool, scowling beneath the assault of an unfamiliar and uncomfortable pang of guilt.

The visit had been a witless action but to Kieron the prospect of confessing its purpose to his long-suffering king was infinitely worse. How could he admit to committing the wrong merely to reestablish his link with the enticing human colleen? It was particularly difficult when he knew his king would believe the silence threatening that link only a natural process in human development, and one that Kieron ought to encourage.

"Sire." Kieron evaded the challenge of confessing each misdeed by simply recanting the whole. "I pray your forgiveness for this penitent subject."

"My forgiveness is easily granted," Comlan solemnly met his companion's plea. "However, I fear that a higher price may be demanded for your transgression in delivering Hildie, a human, to the site of greatest peril to the continuing existence of all."

"Then the Dragons of Chaos are real?" Kieron's words were less question than statement of confirmed truth.

Comlan slowly nodded while at the same time motioning Kieron to sit. He knew that many among younger generations of the Tuatha de Danann, parted from the deed by millennia rather than centuries, doubted the tale of their forebears triumph. But he had thought this favorite among their number too wise to accept the common claim that 'twas merely an old legend invented by long-past boasts and embellished with retelling to become no more than simple entertainment.

In his leader's unexpectedly open expression, Kieron read disappointment—and its source. "I'm shamed to admit that I didn't believe ... until in apparent punishment for my casual intrusion a power greater even than that which our fairyfolk wield shook the circle of stones at my feet."

" 'Struth the intrusion of you and your companion was responsible for the ominous tremors rising from the deepest core of this realm." To this chilling agreement Comlan meaningfully added an even more daunting statement, "That quaking opened a crack in the sealed gate you so carelessly approached."

"What action can I take to undo my wrong?" With his earnest query, the seated Kieron leaned forward.

"*You* can do nothing to see it undone." There was a complete and revealing lack of emotion in Comlan's deep voice. "Nor can I."

Beneath a cloud of anguish for the gravity of his misdeed, Kieron sank back in his chair and stared blindly at the tips of supple leather boots.

"However, though we cannot know how critically the gate has been weakened ..." Comlan's words won Kieron's attention. "My grandmother passed on to me the consolation of an ancient remedy which may now stand us in good stead."

Because Kieron was well aware that the woman of whom his king spoke was Queen Aine, the previous monarch of the Faerie Realm and once a being of amazing powers, hope sparked in aqua eyes.

"As a child she was told by the ancients themselves that any breach might heal itself . . . if left in peace to mend."

Kieron's bright smile flashed but his king remained solemn.

"Toward that crucial goal," Comlan quietly stated, "I must have your word that you will not repeat your unsanctioned visit."

With unwavering intent in aqua eyes Kieron rose to his feet and extended an arm toward his king while gladly giving the requested vow. "You have my oath on all I hold dear that never again will I foolishly tempt such catastrophic harm."

After the two shook, forearms joined, Comlan motioned for the younger man to lead the way in rejoining a merry gathering in the much larger great hall beyond.

An invisible observer continued to hold himself immobile until the two glowing beings departed. Ardagh was pleased with himself and pleased with a delightful opportunity for revenge unknowingly provided by enemies.

Ardagh had been shunned by his own kind since his failed attempt to halt the onward march of Christianity at Athlone on the banks of the River Shannon. But he had turned this unpleasant experience to his own advantage. While purposefully ignored by others of the Tuatha de Danann, Ardagh had learned a skill that he alone possessed. Though natives of the Faerie Realm could make themselves invisible to humans, only he could hold himself unseen even amidst the magical breed.

To develop and refine his unique talent, he'd had to give up his once cherished scarlet robes and love for dramatic entrances and exits but deemed it a small price. Particularly now after that ability had allowed him to overhear a private and most revealing conversation between Comlan and Kieron.

Ardagh saw that by wielding what had been learned, the first steps might be taken in a delightful scheme to bring an end to all who had wronged him—fairy and human alike. And it would be the more delicious if the daughter of his worst mortal foe were the instrument of destruction.

Alone and no longer bothering to hide, Ardagh's uptilted brows took on an even more devilish slant as he gleefully grinned and whisked himself to the security of his own home.

CHAPTER 3

Despite reluctance to greet the new day, Hildie had forced herself to descend spiraling stairs and now paused in the arch opening to an already over-filled great hall. The presence of a stranger welcome to none smothered the reassurance she normally found in the simple sameness of muffled banter and trenchers scraping across tabletops. Hildie's unhappy reverie was broken by her father.

"Hildie—" Rory fought to hold his tone utterly flat but his daughter heard its tightly restrained impatience.

Spine straightening and lips resolution-tightened, Hildie promptly moved toward the dais. Although Lord Morven merely watched in silence, she clearly heard his reproach for her indefensible crime of having twice kept him waiting.

As Hildie took her seat at the high table between father and unwanted suitor she was all too aware of an unnatural quiet broken only by the crackle of hearth flames fed by a young houseserf.

Kindhearted Lissan took pity on her stepdaughter and attempted to lessen the strain with a steady flow of quiet words on unimportant matters.

Ever delighted by his softhearted wife's skill and deft touch at smoothing the rough path through all manner of trying situations, Lord Rory gladly aided her cause.

"Lord Morven, are your lands in Munster a promising site for the successful pursuit of wild boar?"

"When the season is right." Lord Morven's cryptic response came with a slow, disdainful nod, an action that caught and reflected sharp gleams of firelight in his red hair.

That this man reputed to be a great warrior talked of hunting boar in the spring further lowered him in Morven's esteem. And yet he had to admit that the lord and lady of Ailm Keep's ability to maintain composure no matter the provocation was amazing—and an inauspicious start for the attempt to succeed with his hidden schemes.

Lips twisting in a derisive smile, Lord Morven inwardly acknowledged secret facts. His monarch honestly sought the proposed union as physical confirmation of an alliance between kingdoms. But Morven's intentions toward the headstrong beauty (clearly loath to sit at his side) were vastly different.

Hildie exercised considerable willpower to keep from publicly recoiling from the man whose steady gaze she felt as if it were a vile insect slowly crawling over exposed skin. To maintain a mental distance, she tried to focus on her previous night's adventure. And, she defiantly told herself, it truly had been an adventure no matter whether a literal experience or the vivid dream she'd nearly convinced herself it must've been.

"My duties must soon take me off to distant farms to make certain no irreparable damage was done by the earth's trembling last night." Rory directly addressed his disgruntled guest. "I would be glad of your company, if you would care to share a day's ride in the sun?"

The mention of trembling earth jerked Hildie's attention back to the high table's conversation. Her father's matter-of-fact statement that the ground had moved meant her time with Kieron must have been real. Her heart soared only to abruptly hurtle back down into dismal climes under the weight of an unavoidable truth. If she'd actually been with Kieron, then the terrifying legend of the Dragons of Chaos was equally real. Not a reassuring possibility.

Hildie barely heard Morven stiffly decline his host's offer. She was too intent on trying to convince herself that the earth's tremor had merely influenced the flow of an already vivid dream and had no deeper meaning. . . .

"Lord Rory—" A booming voice abruptly silenced the hall. "As your loyal supporter, I demand Lady Hildie's hand be given my son."

Hildie's gaze flew to the source, a husky figure blocking the entrance. It was Rolan's ruddy-faced father, the head of the Shanahan family, whose loud words had seized the hall's full attention. She was horrified by this further complication added to the already nasty morass threatening to drag her down into its unsavory depths.

Her alarm deepened when the beefy man rashly added, "Reject a Shanahan and lose the allegiance of your most productive farmer—and most valuable supporter."

Rory O'Connor's handsome face froze against the quick succession of a rude intrusion, injudicious demand, and foolish threat. Yet it was the contemptuous Lord Morven rather than the keep's master who responded.

"It would be more prudent for your lord to see his daughter betrothed to his equal—me, the lord of Dunbarrough Keep in Munster. And," Morven sneered, "be assured that rejection of my honorable offer will demand the payment of a much more devastating price—rivers of blood and the shattered peace of two kingdoms."

"Silence!" Rory thundered while slowly rising with ominous restraint to glare down on both a still-seated Lord Morven and the elder Shanahan. "Be warned that I will not tolerate uninvited visitors in my home who not only presume to know what decision I should make but actually dare to speak about me as if I weren't here."

Face mottled by an unattractive flush, Shanahan

started to contradict the accusation but went mute as the full force of his lord's piercing gaze turned to him.

"Shanahan, you may stay as my guest but only if you first acknowledge my sovereignty over this place . . . and *you*."

Shanahan diffidently nodded before sharply turning to motion for his son to join him in taking the last open seats—at the end of a trestle table furthermost from the dais.

It isn't over, Shanahan inwardly fumed. *I haven't lost, not yet*.

While the hall's company slowly returned to their interrupted meal and hushed conversations, another watched unseen.

A vastly satisfied Ardagh grinned from his perch in the rafters overhead. This was better and even better.

His schemes could only be delightfully enhanced by the revival of an old conflict between the mortal kingdoms of Munster and Connaught. He hadn't dared dream of pleasures to be found in a rebellion among O'Connor's own.

By midafternoon, Hildie was ready to wreak mayhem on all of the male gender. It was difficult but she held a forced smile on tightly compressed lips while sitting uneasily in the family's private solar flanked by Lord Morven on one side and the Shanahan men on the other.

Hildie's own father had departed just as he had

said he must. The visiting of outlying farms to assess possible damage was, she realized, a necessary duty. But still Hildie felt abandoned to negotiate the treacherous waters churning between glaring suitors alone.

The veil of civility restraining open battle, flimsy at best, looked to be in imminent danger of falling into shreds. Hildie suddenly found it difficult to tame a wicked imp tempting her to give it a healthy tug and then watch unwanted visitors wreak havoc on each other.

"Hildie." Lissan quietly summoned the younger woman's attention. "In the flurry of our unexpected guests' arrival, I nearly forgot that I promised Donal he could spend the night with Eamon." She grimaced regretfully. "I dare not abandon my duties to take him myself. Thus, I pray that you'll see him safely to Tuatha Cottage?"

Hildie grinned. By the fact that she knew no such promise had been made (though her little brother would no doubt welcome the treat) it was clear that Lissan had recognized the tension perilously near a breaking point. But then, Hildie reminded herself, considering her stepmother's sharp senses that was only to be expected. She had mistaken Lissan for a fairy princess on that morning long ago when they'd first met—before even the golden woman herself knew that it was true.

"I'll check and see if Donal is ready to depart. We must leave soon if I'm to go and return before dark." Hildie wished she had bitten her tongue to

prevent the escape of words certain to be inter-
preted as a request for escort by the very people
she wanted most to escape.

"My Rolan will assuredly be honored to accompany you on the journey." Shanahan rushed to
make the offer before Morven could speak.

Fuming at herself for making such a foolish mistake, Hildie forced a brittle smile and rose, shaking
her head in vain hope that they'd accept it as a
polite refusal.

"Nay, my lady." Morven rose, too, but rather
than noticing Hildie's wordless refusal, he glared
at his ruddy-faced competitor. "No need to trust a
farmer for protection when a proven warrior
awaits your command."

"Your concern for my daughter's safety is commendable—but unnecessary." Lissan's soothing
voice firmly smothered the sparks of male discord.
"Lord Rory long ago charged one of Ailm Keep's
finest warriors with the duty of serving as our children's protector."

Grateful for this deliverance, a bright smile returned to Hildie's lips. Not only had Lissan saved
her from unwelcome companions but had chased
ill-humor away with overly extravagant praise for
Grady who, though slavishly loyal, was too easy-
going to ever be deemed a great warrior.

When in response to their hostess's words, Lord
Morven started to argue and Shanahan noticeably
bristled, Lissan was quick to add a honeyed promise as sop to sensitive pride.

"My husband will be home long before Hildie can possibly return from her mission, and I know he intends to counsel with you both on the important issue at hand." Lissan's warm smile gently tilted into a mock pout. "I fear Lord Rory would not be well pleased to discover you absent."

While Lissan held the disgruntled men's attention with warm smiles and flattering words, Hildie slipped silently away.

CHAPTER 4

By nodding and flashing a grin over her shoulder toward two boys dutifully waving from the cottage's open portal, Hildie released them to pursue adventures more exciting than wishing her Godspeed on the return to Ailm Keep. The pair—one as dark as she and the other as fair as his mother's fairyfolk—immediately disappeared.

"Thank you for bringing Donal to visit us." Maedra smiled at the young woman she strongly suspected had welcomed the excuse to escape the company of unwanted suitors. "My Eamon thoroughly enjoys your little brother's visits."

Hildie's attention shifted to the delicate figure who had accompanied her several paces into the neatly tended herb garden that lay just beyond the small home's doorway.

"I gladly came at my stepmother's suggestion." Hildie indirectly confirmed Maedra's assumption that kindhearted Lissan was responsible for this pleasant turn of events.

With a conspiratorial smile, Maedra agreed. "Assure Lissan that we'll see Donal safely home on the morrow. Unless you . . ."

Hildie's grin flashed again. "Much as I'm likely to long for such a respite, my father is almost certain to be thoroughly annoyed when he learns how I slipped away today, making any chance for a repeat performance doubtful."

"I fear you are right." Maedra's smile gently tilted awry. The lord of Ailm Keep was an admirable man—strong, just, and loyal—but hardly noted for his tolerance of actions he deemed foolish. And no one acquainted with Lord Rory could fail to be aware of how sorely his patience was tried by Hildie's continued rejection of her many suitors. Frustrated by his daughter's procrastination, he would never easily accept anything likely to further prolong her seemingly endless dithering over the choice of mate.

"If I'm to have any hope of reaching the keep before dusk," Hildie continued, bright spirit undaunted, "I'd best be on my way."

Grady had waited outside while Hildie visited with Maedra. Now as his lady stepped outside, he brought their horses from the cool shadows of a lean-to stable built against the cottage.

"Safe journey to you," Maedra warmly wished the dark beauty who mounted her plump, little mare while the dainty fox who accompanied her everywhere patiently waited and watched. "I know that Liam will regret having missed your visit."

Hildie smiled down at the incredible female who had put aside extraordinary powers to live a mortal lifetime with a human mate. Still, even without those powers she shared the golden perfection of her Tuatha de Danann breed, as did her son.

Because of her own distant tie to the Tuatha, Hildie was wryly amused that the one thing on which both Lord Rory and King Comlan agreed was that children born of marriages between their races would never be told of their split heritage.

Lending earnest attention to his duty as guard, Grady cautiously led his lovely charge into the dense forest's familiar gloom. Hildie trusted her overvigilant guide and happily relaxed. She allowed herself to take delight in the cool shadows, soft perfumes, and gentle hues of wildflowers that coyly peaked from the woodland walls of dense green.

Atop a docile mount that would steadily plod its way home to Ailm Keep's stable without her hand on the reins, Hildie permitted thick lashes to drift down. She savored these quiet moments of peace and revived the simple pleasures of a childhood game by blindly identifying the source of various scents. First heady fragrance of wild rose, then jonquil's tangy odor, and next a faint hint of—

Suddenly a brawny arm roughly jerked Hildie from the saddle. But accosted from one side and slightly to the rear, Hildie's ankle was painfully wrenched by the force with which her foot was twisted from the stirrup. She landed hard, face-down across the bare back of an unfamiliar horse.

"Grady!" Hildie's desperate cry came out a muf-fled squeak from behind the hand firmly clamped over her mouth. Though wildly struggling to win free, she caught a brief glimpse of the hooded fig-ure bounding from the forest while swinging the cudgel that knocked Grady from his mount.

After her guard fell to the rutted path, uncon-scious, Hildie's screams no longer posed a threat to the foe who promptly released her mouth. In-stead that captor then focused his energies on lash-ing Hildie's wrists together against the small of her back. She instantly took advantage of this action which unintentionally granted her the chance to is-sue an assuredly more effective call for assistance.

"Seun, fetch Kieron."

The fox immediately became a blur of auburn fur rapidly disappearing into the thick foliage border-ing a well-worn path, but Hildie barely had time to note her obedient pet's departure before a truly unexpected savior appeared.

Mounted on a powerful destrier, Liam thun-dered down the path toward the scurrilous scene of villains daring to assault his lord's daughter. As he swung down another round of violence erupted. Wielding a stave with unparalleled skill, he knocked the wretch holding Hildie captive to the ground with one end, then with the opposite sent Grady's assailant reeling.

When Hildie's fallen captor struggled to rise and hurl himself at Liam, she twisted wildly and slid from the horse's bare back. Though she landed in an ungainly heap, it felt like a victory. And, interrupted before bonds were securely knotted, she was able to shake her hands free of thick twine. Scrambling to her feet, she immediately slapped the horse's flank, sending him off on a mad gallop.

The sharp sound of her palm striking hide came just as Liam finished laying his opponent low for a second time. While he glanced toward the bolting horse, the two foiled kidnappers demonstrated amazing agility by joining their only mount's hasty flight into the twilight woodland's deepening shadows. Liam promptly pursued but soon returned, a look of disgust marring his usual amiable expression.

"They disappeared—" He met Hildie's questioning gaze directly. "Not even a trail of crushed vegetation left behind."

Hildie nodded. Because they both had experience of such matters there was no need to voice uncomfortable but clearly shared suspicions. Only beings in possession of unworldly powers could move across the earth without disturbing its surface.

Before either could further investigate, Liam's eye was caught by an incongruous item lying amidst the green blades crushed by a recent struggle. He moved to retrieve a bronze brooch. It was richly enameled with the pattern of a convoluted

Celtic knot adopted by the Shanahan family as their own symbol.

Liam was relieved by this distinctive ornament's apparent proof that the culprits behind the attempted abduction of his lord's daughter were merely human and turned his attention to the unconscious guard. Though unfocused, Grady's eyes were open and blood once flowing freely from the wound on his temple had slowed and begun to congeal.

"Hold steady," Liam soothed as he bent to carefully lift the groaning man. "We'll take you back to Tuatha Cottage where Maedra will tend your wounds while I escort Lady Hildie safely home to Ailm Keep and her waiting family."

Liam's proposed plan was logical since the cottage was much nearer than the keep but Grady's lips firmed into a mutinous line. However, before he could protest the decision, he dropped again into a deep, unnatural sleep.

After placing their patient gently across his horse, Liam helped Hildie into her saddle, then mounted his own steed.

Although Liam had welcomed the evidence of a seemingly mundane source for her assailants, Hildie was not so easily convinced. Why would the Shanahan family, why would *anyone* seize her and risk Lord Rory's ire? And her father would be furious!

The thought of her father's anger reminded Hildie of how tardy she would be in reaching the

keep. An unhappy prospect considering how displeased her father had been when she'd failed to
make a timely return from her picnic with Amy. A
moment later guilt struck her for having allowed
personal issues to take precedence over concern for
Grady's injuries.

Going slow for the sake of her wounded guard,
much time was required to accomplish their return
to the cottage and more was given to see him comfortably settled under Maedra's gentle care. Thus
when at last they reached Ailm Keep, the sun had
long since deserted the sky while, as if in deference
to Lord Rory's dark mood, the moon had yet to
rise.

"Seun—" An exasperated Kieron called after the
small animal leading him down a forest path.

Again and again during human years come and
gone the fox had guided him to a young Hildie in
need of rescuing. (Not that he hadn't been aware
of how easily she could have freed herself from
most perils—it was a game they'd both enjoyed.)

This, however, was different. Never had any of
Hildie's earlier pleas come at night nor had Seun
ever before led him over such lengthy stretches of
mortal ground. These two factors left Kieron to
wonder if his spirited elfling had devised a new
game that began by playing this prank on him.

Seun came to an abrupt halt. When the animal
nosed dark-stained grass, and set up a soft, mourn-
ful howl, Kieron sank to his knees at her side.

Reaching out, he plucked several blades. A close examination confirmed his worst fears. They were covered with blood . . . *human* blood? Hildie's?

Leaping up, Kieron issued an immediate command to the dark beauty's pet, "Find Hildie!"

Head tilted, the fox sadly gazed at her master for long moments before lowering a soft, auburn body to rest on stained grass while filling the night with plaintive whine of her quiet cries.

Although night had fully descended and the evening meal long done, Ailm Keep's great hall remained crowded when an ominous hush fell with the first sight of the young mistress.

Unnatural silence ruled in that long delayed moment when Hildie, disheveled from rough handling earlier endured, limped into the chamber unexpectedly escorted by Liam rather than Grady.

Liam further deepened the intense curiosity of onlookers by leading Hildie to a position opposite her father's central place on the dais. Next he reached across the high table to carefully place an item directly into his lord's hand. With the action, Liam softly murmured a few succinct words meant for his leader's ear alone.

"Shanahan!" Though tightly restrained the depth of condemnation contained in Lord Rory's single word seemed to shake the vast chamber.

Hildie watched as her father rose to tower above others still seated on the dais and at trestle tables below. Along with the attention of many others filling the large chamber her dark gaze remained steadily focused on him.

"What wicked demon escaped from the fires of hell possessed you to attempt the abduction of my daughter?" Lord Rory demanded in a voice more threatening for its deadly quiet control.

The keep's master moved down the dais with the lithe grace of a predator preparing to strike. By the time Rory halted directly behind his accused supporter, the man appeared so stunned by the charge that a normally ruddy face had gone deathly pale.

"You must know that so vile a deed courted not Lady Hildie's affections but my outrage." The sharp snap in each of Rory's words felt to Shanahan like the lash of a whip.

"I had naught to do with that vile crime!" The one blamed met his lord's piercing eyes unflinching although his unnaturally ashen face abruptly burned ruby bright.

"How could it be true?" Shanahan continued to heatedly refute the accusation. "How when both Rolan and I have been right here since the midday meal which we shared with all in this room—including you and your daughter?"

"Nay," Rory snapped back, "how do *you* account for the presence of this pretty piece at the site where Liam and the culprits struggled?"

With slow care Rory deliberately placed an enameled brooch on the tabletop a scant distance from one of Shanahan's meaty, faintly trembling hands. The bronze piece gleamed brighter for a background of pristine whiteness provided by the double layer of linen tablecloths.

"Since both my son and I are wearing ours, I cannot—nor ought be expected—to account for how that piece appeared where it was found."

Beyond an initial brief glance at the brooch, Shanahan refused to falter in meeting his lord's steady gaze. Knowing too well how highly Rory prized courage he dare not fail.

"I suggest only that it is important to remember how anyone may have copied the symbol which my family adopted for its own." Shanahan broke his visual bond with Rory to lean forward and stare pointedly down the table toward Lord Morven and coldly add, "Mayhap for the purpose of seeing my son and me unjustly accused of this wickedness?"

"I resent your implication," Morven snarled, chair scraping over the dais's bare planks as if preparing to leap to his feet and demand either an apology or the satisfaction of a blood feud.

"Hold!" Rory commanded. "Ailm Keep is mine. The crime was perpetrated against me, not either of you. Thus the punishment, the vengeance is mine to seek."

The protagonists sat mute, jaws clenched in icy animosity while unspoken warnings flashed in Rory's dark, penetrating eyes. "I forbid the pursuit of senseless reprisals in my home."

Although Morven and Shanahan yielded, the room's tension lessened not one whit. As Rory's belligerent guests settled into morose silence, he berated himself. Plainly the assault on his daughter had disrupted his usual cool reasoning to such an extent that he'd succumbed to the witless folly of attacking before investigating all facts. To take a step toward repairing that error, Rory turned to his daughter.

"Hildie, surely you saw some portion of your attackers? Leastways some familiar detail?"

"I wish that I had," Hildie earnestly responded, dark tendrils of disarrayed hair brushing her cheeks as she slowly shook her head.

Uncomfortably aware of a curious audience, Hildie longed for some way to explain her strange impressions—to herself most of all. How could she rationally describe men with blank faces, not merely expressionless but utterly lacking any spark of life? Were they beings conjured by magic? Not an actual fairy but an apparition fabricated by their powers? She didn't know if it was possible and yet . . .

But why would one of their number want to take her captive? What purpose could it serve? Besides, though Kieron and others of the Tuatha de Danann delighted in playing pranks on gullible humans, Hildie knew beyond question that Kieron had never permited any action likely to cause her pain. The dull throbbing of her ankle was proof that the attempted abduction had resulted in precisely that misfortune.

* * *

As the stone tower of Ailm Keep and its human inhabitants at last succumbed to the calming peace of sleep, an unseen presence left well pleased by the progress of his designs.

In nearly the same moment that Ardagh departed an unexpected visitor arrived to stand protectively over the bed of a dark beauty drifting through the gentle mist of dreams. . . .

This night, as so often before, Hildie's slumbers were invaded by the welcome fantasy of an impossible event—a golden hero opening powerful arms and gently sweeping her against his broad chest. A slight smile of delight curled the sleeping maid's lips while in her dream aqua eyes glowed with the reflection of ardent vows of endless devotion. And then, after Kieron fervently whispered her name, he would claim the passion of a gladly shared kiss.

Hildie— Having soundlessly uttered her name, Kieron was startled when his elfling's lashes lifted. He'd come only to be certain that she was safe and had promised himself to leave the instant that his goal was achieved. But now the lure in dark, unfocused depths of her eyes proved more potent than even the enchanted wiles of his own kind.

Following a dream-ordained path, Hildie wrapped silken arms around Kieron's strong shoulders, twining her fingers through cool gold strands while lifting to press her lips against his mouth.

Kieron was unprepared to withstand the beguiling colleen's innocent onslaught, and under the untutored yet passionate fire of her chaste kiss his honorable intentions fell to ashes. Arms closed about her slender form, he lifted Hildie full into his embrace. Firm mouth brushing across the berry-sweet nectar of hers, he gently probed and tenderly coaxed until he had heated the kiss she'd initiated as an inexperienced child into a devastating merger of souls.

Hildie's heart went wild. Loving the intimacy, the taste, the masculine scent and the feel of Kieron's big, hard body blazing sensations swept over Hildie, stealing breath and turning bones to water. As she melted even closer against Kieron's strength, a soft, aching moan slipping from her tight throat, she sank ever deeper into the devastating but irresistible well of smoldering desire.

The sound of Hildie's hunger sent Kieron over a vague precipice into that same well of fiery heat. Yet, as he arched her delicate body tighter into the curve of his hard form, he was shocked to full awareness of his wrong. The unexpected and far too dangerous pleasure in the delicious feel of lush curves separated from him by no more than the fine-spun cloth of his tunic ignited a host of warning beacons in his mind.

Though the Tuatha de Danann disdained boring consistency in near all ways and delighted in their mercurial natures, oaths earnestly given were held inviolate. And yet by his actions here he had seriously jeopardized the solemn vow given his king.

'Struth, this should *never* have happened. More importantly, it must *never* be repeated.

When Kieron abruptly lifted his mouth, Hildie cried out against the loss. Heavy lashes rising, she gazed with palpable hunger into a mesmerizing glitter in the aqua depths of his eyes.

Annoyed with himself for falling weak to forbidden temptations and, irrationally, with her for so easily luring him off kilter, still Kieron couldn't prevent himself from visually feasting on his tantalizing elfling with impossible longing.

When forced to fight a powerful urge to claim more, Kieron sensed his self-control in peril. He disappeared in an instant leaving Hildie to again wonder if their moments together had truly happened or if it had been merely another vivid fantasy born of hopeless love for a being who could never be hers. . . .

CHAPTER 5

The soft mists that arrived with the next dawn lingered. By midafternoon they'd settled the gentle balm of leastways a temporary respite over the whole of Ailm Keep.

Lord Morven had begun the day by declaring an intention of going back to his home in Dunbarrough Keep. That flat statement was immediately followed by the announcement that he would return in three days time and would then expect the master of Ailm Keep's decision on the proposed alliance. Lying unspoken yet clearly heard beneath these words was the threat of what price the lord from Munster would claim for the possible insult of his suit's rejection.

Lord Morven lost no time in leading his entourage beyond the staunch palisade barrier of upended logs closely joined together, top ends of each sharpened into a dangerous point. They soon disappeared into the forest beyond.

Although their journey would carry them in the opposite direction from the Munster contingent, Shanahan, his son, and supporters soon rallied together for their own leavetaking.

From the narrow parapet high above, Rory had watched the welcome retreat of Lord Morven and lingered to see the dutiful departure of his own people. They moved through the bailey wall's iron-bound gates intent on returning to outlying farms where they had responsibilities waiting to be resumed, duties too long ignored.

Those who justly remained in the keep were grateful for even a brief period of peace. It was a harmony that continued when Liam and Maedra arrived not long after the departure of competing suitors. Coming to return Donal to his parents, they were accompanied by their son, Eamon, and a sheepish Grady sporting the fresh bandage affixed to his wounded head.

In a great hall still hosting too many overly interested onlookers, Rory greeted the newcomers and directed them to join himself and his family in the private solar above.

Regretfully acknowledging that too surely another day was destined to pass with minimal productive work accomplished and few duties met, Rory led the way up a winding stairway built into the width of the keep's stone wall.

They gathered in a chamber at the top of the next

flight, one level down from the lord's bedchamber. Once inside with the door closed against too many curious eyes and ears beyond, the men joined their leader at a small table to quietly review the previous day's attempted abduction.

"Did you truly see nothing familiar in those who attacked you, Grady?" Rory questioned his guardsman, hoping with little expectation of success for news of some tiny, telling detail that would betray the culprits' identity or leastways lend some hint of a promising track to pursue.

Grady frowned under the discomfort of finding himself trapped between guilt for having failed in his duty to protect Lady Hildie and shame for having observed no useful clue.

"I caught only a brief glimpse of the figure snatching Lady Hildie from her mount before I was hit from behind."

"And you, Liam?" Rory shifted his attention to the second man, a trusted friend and supporter. "You also saw nothing familiar in those with whom you fought hand to hand?"

"As I reported yesterday," Liam acknowledged with a bleak smile.

"That then," Rory said, eyes hard as black granite and mouth tightened into grim lines, "leaves us with only the brooch—"

"But the Shanahans *didn't* lose that brooch. They were both wearing theirs." Grady instinctively defended the two men whose farm neighbored the one his family worked. "Surely you must see that anyone could have made a copy."

"I fear not," Rory ruefully disagreed although he would've welcomed any proof to judge as innocent the pair who owed duty to him. "A replica could be produced neither quickly nor easily."

Rory knew it wasn't necessary to point out that the Shanahans' competitor from Munster couldn't possibly have known before his arrival at Ailm Keep that he'd have reason for such an item, far less what its design should be.

"I think we should study the brooch in question more closely," Liam suggested, anxious to refocus their search and locate some useful piece of information, even the flimsiest of shreds. "Mayhap it possesses hidden secrets to share."

Nodding acceptance of Liam's practical proposal, Rory rose and moved to retrieve a miniature, iron-banded chest from the deep ledge of the narrow window cut through a thick stone wall. On returning, he placed the wooden box in the center of the table, detached a ring of keys from his wide leather belt, and separated out the smallest.

Once the chest was unlocked with its lid laid back, Rory delved inside and withdrew a tiny, kidskin bag. This item he carefully uptilted and gently shook . . . and then again more firmly . . . and again.

The sack was empty.

Grady gasped, "Where's the brooch?"

"Indeed, where?" Rory flatly echoed the unpleasant question while holding the bag's open end close enough to peer inside.

Rory's gaze shifted to solemnly meet Liam's equally disgusted stare while inwardly he devised plans. Soon he would seek a meeting with the king of the Tuatha de Danann. Though unwilling to discuss the likelihood with his own followers, Rory felt certain that the brooch's seemingly impossible disappearance could only have been accomplished by one possessing the Tuatha's uncanny powers.

Because the men spoke in hushed whispers others in the chamber heard little of their dialogue. Lissan sat on one of a pair of matching chairs drawn near to the fire with a drowsy Amy curled up in her lap. The flames were welcome amidst a stone keep chilly despite the spring season.

Maedra had claimed the vacant seat placed close enough to encourage quiet conversation while Hildie perched on a stool nearby and at their feet young boys played quiet games.

Leaning forward to hold delicate hands toward bright warmth, Maedra solemnly said, "Dangerous currents have been roused and are beginning to flow across the countryside."

Lissan responded to this soft statement with a hesitant smile. Maedra was a treasured friend who had put mystical powers aside for the sake of Liam, her human beloved. But still the dainty female spoke and doubtless thought in the enigmatic patterns of a race never easy with anything of a certainty one way or another. And thus aware of

Maedra's inbred discomfort, Lissan assumed this strange talk of dangerous currents was Maedra's convoluted method for broaching the subject of the failed crime.

"We are fortunate," Lissan ventured an irrefutable observation. "Liam returned home in time to foil the wretched knaves foolish enough to attempt the wrongful deed."

By this response Maedra recognized both Lissan's misinterpretation of her meaning and the gravity of her own error. Maedra all too clearly realized that her preoccupation with a growing concern had dangerously misled her. She had nearly opened the door into secret matters which should have remained sealed away and certainly never shared with any human . . . not even a half-fairy like Lissan.

Privy to both sides of this conversation, an uncomfortable Hildie suspected that for the first time she knew more about actual events than either of the two older women. Maedra spoke of unworldly currents while Lissan feared human predators. Only Hildie knew the truth behind the very real and increasing threat rising from Dragons of Chaos nearly free.

"Sit." Face a stern mask, Comlan imperiously waved toward one of two chairs facing each other across a small table.

Despite the dubious glance he cast the seat amazingly uninviting despite its soft cushions, Kieron reluctantly obeyed. Twice now during too short a span of time he'd been called to face his sovereign in the privacy of this lesser chamber branching off from the Faerie Castle's great hall. And this time he was even more deserving of censure.

"I received a distressing report of an attack that should never have occurred." While issuing this ominous statement, Comlan chose to remain standing, towering above his seated supporter. "It was *your* duty to ensure that no harm befall Hildie."

How, Kieron wondered . . . No, *who* had made this report and by what means had they learned of the attack? Few in the Faerie Realm wasted so much as a moment's thought on events in the mortal world, far less to bother carrying tales about the boring human race to their own king.

Abruptly aware that he had injudiciously left his king to wait while silence stretched too long, Kieron spoke.

"You often remind us of an all-important and fundamental precept." Kieron instinctively offered the first defense that came to mind even though pitifully weak. "Fairyfolk must never interfere in the lives of mankind."

Comlan found in this response both satisfaction with the younger male's acceptance of a crucial restraint and irritation that he had so skillfully used it against his sovereign. But then, as if in proof of his breed's mercurial nature, the king of the Tuatha de Danann erupted into laughter.

" 'Struth," Comlan said, on taming his amusement into a broad grin. "But, as you well know, when you accepted the commission to stand as Hildie's guardian, the oaths you gave ensured that any action necessary to enforce her safekeeping would be judged as exceptions to that principle."

"Aye," Kieron promptly responded, acknowledging his wrong and annoyed with himself for the initial craven instinct to shirk justified censure. "I ought to have been alert enough to prevent the deed. In truth, I deeply wish I had been. But instead I must confess that I was unprepared even when Seun arrived summoning me to Hildie's defense."

Face again expressionless, Comlan slowly nodded acceptance of the belated apology. His acute senses read sincerity in the repentance of his mortal niece's oath-sworn guardian.

"Fortunately," Kieron added, "Maedra's human mate was successful in defeating Hildie's assailants. Liam then escorted Hildie safely to Ailm Keep. She is home and well."

"And how do you know this to be true?" With the question, Comlan settled into the vacant chair across from his companion.

Kieron shrugged with a wry grin. "I was concerned after Seun came to fetch me and yet was unable to lead the way directly to Hildie's side. Thus, I visited her there."

Brilliant azure eyes narrowed as Comlan pointedly asked, "In her bedchamber . . . at night?"

"The hour was late in mortal time," Kieron conceded. "But it also afforded me the best opportunity of finding Hildie alone. Only while the keep slept did I have a chance to talk with her and be certain she was unharmed."

Comlan was clearly unconvinced that this excuse justified the deed—a suspicion deepened when under his steady gaze the younger male shifted, betraying uneasiness despite his centuries of experience in shielding all emotions.

Vividly remembering the kiss exchanged, Kieron feared his king's piercing eyes could see a guilt he couldn't hide since, because guilt was uncommon among fairy, he possessed no practice in dealing with the ill effects of its discomfort.

"Take care, Kieron," Comlan gravely cautioned. "Hildie is destined for a human mate and a lifetime in the mortal world. You must do nothing to interfere with the natural development of her affections for one of their kind."

"But she kissed *me*." Kieron instinctively defended himself, only recognizing his words for the revelation they exposed after they slid too easily off his errant tongue.

"And you, of course, did not respond?" Comlan wryly challenged this foolish excuse too hastily and rashly given but didn't pause long enough for Kieron to answer.

"I admit to being disappointed." Comlan feigned exaggerated regret. "Apparently our gossip exchange isn't the ideal of reliability I've always assumed. Can't be when it would have everyone believe that you are a lady charmer of vast experience. Surely such a male would be well able to withstand the innocent wiles of a chaste human colleen?"

Ignoring his king's gentle barb, Kieron made an awkward attempt to deflect the difficult question about the forbidden kiss.

"Seun arrived, as so oft before, summoning me to Hildie's aid but the animal could only lead the way to a meadow. Still, it was there that I found grass stained with human blood." Kieron wanted to refocus attention on the failed abduction's danger to Hildie.

"As 'tis by your royal command that I guard the colleen, how could I do less than dare all to be assured of her safety? And how could I turn Hildie away when she reached out for my comfort?"

Comlan's one-sided smile greeted this reasoning, but he saw no purpose in disputing its details. Instead, he offered an ambiguous statement.

"I've learned two things from my observations of Hildie—she fears little and possesses quick wits."

Comlan's mocking smile deepened when Kieron promptly nodded agreement. "In truth, Hildie's wits are quick enough to have soon learned the way to bend you to her will . . . no easy trick, and a skill that it would seem I must ask her to teach me."

Although sharing his race's preference for constant change, for the first time in his long existence

Kieron wished for certainty—certainty in knowing his ruler's true opinion.

Only faith in King Comlan's never-wavering honor reassured Kieron that he had been forgiven for wrongly whisking Hildie into the cavern beneath their Faerie Realm's castle. He had no reason to be sure that the same boon had been or would be granted for his error in falling even temporarily weak to the temptation of Hildie's innocent lures.

"Would you have me surrender my position as Hildie's guardian?" Kieron made the offer in honest contrition despite the pain that separation would bring. The next instant the bleak prospect of life after this loss was swept away by a sudden surge of unexpected hope. If released from his vows to stand as her guardian, would the heaviest barrier between them be lifted as well? Might there be a future—

"Nay." Comlan slowly shook bright hair, nearly sure of the unfortunate source for a belated sparkle in aqua eyes. "Hildie relies on you to bolster her seemingly indefatigable courage."

Under the pain of instantly crushed hope, maintaining an impassive expression was nearly impossible, but Kieron succeeded and listened while his sovereign steadily continued.

"I will refrain from chastising you for wrongs I don't doubt you recognize as clearly as do I." Comlan sent Kieron a long, penetrating stare. "And yet, I must again remind you that by oaths given, though it may be difficult to continue viewing Hil-

die merely as a charming child, you can be to her
no more than an affectionate older brother."

Kieron stood silent and unmoving before the
leader whose calm declaration permitted no excuse
for misinterpretation. Aye, King Comlan's crystal
clear reminder left no room for Kieron to doubt
what was still required of him . . . even though he
had just begun to realize how very hard it would
be to continue keeping that promise.

"I have one suggestion toward further securing
Hildie's safety," Comlan said. "It's a stratagem I
employed for tracing the human I was most anxious not to lose."

Kieron realized his king was referring to the human he'd wed, their Queen Amethyst.

"Present Hildie with an amulet of any design or
making . . . but after casting over it a spell of finding. Though not an easy charm to either fashion or
perform, unlike the living pet you gave, so long as
she carries the amulet on her person, you'll always
be able to locate her."

Comlan chose not to suggest a repetition of the
error he'd made by adding to the original spell of
finding a further spell of protection. The latter had
led to complications that he'd rather see Kieron and
Hildie avoid.

CHAPTER 6

After the keep had settled for the night and Amy drifted on the innocent clouds of childhood's deep sleep, Hildie sat cross-legged atop her own bed. The gown she had worn during the failed abduction attempt was spread across her lap while by the light of a lone candle she worked to repair linen skirts torn in the struggle to resist.

Hildie pulled her needle through pale green fabric to skillfully complete a final knot just as a low rumbling more felt than heard intruded. Sapphire eyes instantly lifted to the taper on a chest within arm's reach and widened. While the rumbling deepened an intricately designed candle holder that Kieron had given her to honor a past birthday moved as if an unseen hand had slightly uptilted the smooth surface beneath. As it slid toward the edge Hildie's hand shot out. Her quick action prevented open flame from tumbling down to ignite dry rushes strewn across the floor's thick oak planking.

The next instant Hildie sensed an impossible movement. Stone towers didn't sway—not even in gale force winds. And tonight the air was calm, the skies were clear.

The earth had moved! Just as it had while she and Kieron stood facing the peculiar stone structure in the cavern beneath the Faerie Realm castle. Were the Dragons of Chaos breaking free?

No! Hildie sternly told herself she would never accept that such creatures were more than legend. Hah! An inner voice immediately mocked her attempt at self-delusion. When she had seen and experienced too much to wonder at either magical beings or events, how could she question the existence of the dragons? Hadn't she already been part of a legend coming true after Lissan fell through time to fulfill the White Witch's destiny?

Hildie pensively nibbled her bottom lip. It was a sad fact that there were skeptics in her world who had begun to doubt even their own memories of fairy, doubts encouraged by the priests' insistence that any and all examples of inexplicable powers were the wicked work of the devil.

"Come." The quiet call beckoned with welcome reassurance.

At the sound, Hildie thrust the green gown aside and threw herself into Kieron's waiting arms without a moment's hesitation.

"It's happening again...." Hildie's anxious

whisper began in the bedchamber but ended in the moon-silvered forest glade where Kieron had whisked her.

Hildie could almost be grateful for the quake's excuse to be again wrapped in Kieron's arms and snuggled closer. She loved the feel of his warm strength, the powerful muscles tensing where her breasts flattened against his broad chest. Heart running wild, she rose on tiptoes and lifted her mouth toward his.

Though deeply aware of why this must not happen, Kieron was irresistibly drawn to the enticing vision of the winsome virgin—piquant face overwhelmed by clouds of lustrous hair and trembling sweetness on tempting lips. Tantalized by her fresh, wildflower fragrance, he sank into the fathomless longing in sapphire depths and was lost.

Kieron's firm mouth brushed achingly across hers until it went pliant. Savoring Hildie's honeyed wine, he deepened the kiss with a warm assault that parted her soft lips, allowing him to search for forbidden delights within.

As the kiss settled into devastating intimacy, a tiny, inarticulate sound welled up from Hildie's core. Gladly surrendering to a blaze of sensations, her hands opened and instinctively moved up, relishing the muscled planes beneath.

Kieron went motionless beneath Hildie's touch, finding perilous delight in her enticing caress. In that same moment he was all too conscious of lush curves that in their last embrace had imprinted a seductive brand on his chest. Memory of that dangerous pleasure stabbed him with shame for having then, and again now, put at risk the solemn vow he must uphold. Kieron abruptly pulled back and gently set his elfling aside.

"Why?" Hildie plaintively asked while clouds of hurt replaced the sparks of passion in her dark gaze. She tried to move closer again but was restrained by hands preventing her body from brushing against his.

"This cannot be—cannot ever be." Despite frustration with himself for so easily surrendering to her innocent wiles, as Kieron cupped Hildie's shoulders to hold her tempting form safely away, his touch gentled into something far too nearly a renewed caress.

"But why?" Hildie wistfully repeated the question. Head tilting to one side, sending a cascade of ebony hair forward, she waited for his answer although inwardly afraid she already knew the sad truth. She could never be a rival for the golden beauties of his world.

Although Hildie thought she knew what Kieron would say, she was stunned by his completely unexpected response.

"I can never be more to you than an older brother." Kieron's slight smile held not a drop of humor.

Because he would willingly sacrifice much to prevent Hildie even the smallest measure of distress, Kieron wished he could, but didn't for an instant, believe his fiery elfling would meekly accept the position of little sister.

The scoffing glance Hildie cast him made her opinion of Kieron's claim crystal clear. She had never before and could not now or ever think of him as a brother.

"How can you even say such a thing?" Hildie heatedly demanded.

There was no hint of Kieron's usual merry nature in the stoic mask he'd donned. "Because that's the way it *must* be."

"No!" Hildie stubbornly shook her head with such force that black tendrils whipped her face. "I will never see you as a brother, nor will I ever be convinced that you think of me as a sister.

"Moreover—" Hildie fervently pursued her argument. "In what just passed between us, the passionate embrace we shared, there is proof that we are not, cannot be siblings!"

"By the oath I took," Kieron flatly responded, "it is my duty to see that such an embrace is never repeated."

Knowing precisely how willful Hildie was, even as he spoke Kieron recognized how difficult it would be to continually refuse the beguiling colleen's purposely wielded charms. The next instant he chastised himself for wrongly blaming his innocent elfling. Particularly after all he'd done to see their bond strengthened, even risking his king's ire by daring to invade the Faerie Realm's inner sanctum.

Kieron could only hope that Hildie didn't see how his wrongful actions, repeated tonight, made an obvious lie of any claim he might make of a wish to be only her brother.

"Oath?" Hildie's attention settled on this term as unexpected as his talk of a sibling relationship. "I don't understand? You gave no oaths to either me or my father."

Wry smile reappearing, Kieron said, "As a part of the Tuatha de Danann, rare are the human oaths given that would be binding."

Hildie scowled. From her experience with the Tuatha de Danann she would swear that, despite a love of pranks and all things uncertain, they truly were an honorable race who always held their promises dear.

"Don't misunderstand." When Kieron threw his head back, bright hair caught and amplified reflected starshine even as his deep laughter filled the glade. "I meant only to jest about your race's strange and unfortunate habit of casually making wagers with careless vows."

Kieron had purposefully chosen his words knowing Hildie would be amused by his use of the term *strange*. It was the word she'd so often teasingly used to describe him.

"You surely know that any oath, light or burdensome, which is seriously spoken by any of my kind must be honored . . . whether given to fairy or mortal."

"Tch, tch." Hildie clicked her tongue in disapproval—not of Kieron but of her own foolishness in not immediately realizing that his ever-shifting mood would seek to change the tenor of their conversation.

As if to prove her assumptions, Kieron abruptly turned solemn. "The weight of the vow to stand as your brother and protector which I gave to my king, your uncle, is the heaviest and most serious I have ever given. It is an oath that I *must* keep no matter the cost."

"But why?" Hildie was stunned to learn of the Faerie Realm monarch's involvement in this unhappy situation. Had she been wrong in thinking of her stepmother's father as a friend? "What reason could there be for you to swear such a ridiculous thing to King Comlan?"

"When he asked," Kieron answered, "I agreed to stand as your guardian."

"But that's not bro—"

Kieron waved Hildie's question aside. He knew there was no reason for this human maid to understand the practices and customs of his world, and he gave a cryptic explanation.

"In my world the rite of guardianship over a mortal involves accepting grave responsibility and requires the vow to stand first as father, then brother, and lastly son."

"Son?" Hildie gasped. Brother was bad but this was even worse.

Kieron's flashing grin returned. " 'Tis only our way of saying that although the candle of life burns much more quickly in human time, a sworn protector from the Tuatha de Danann will remain ever constant in kinship."

"Constant?" Hildie's brows arched. First he'd called her people strange and now he had used this term that was an anathema to the Tuatha. She could hardly believe Kieron had even allowed the word to pass through his lips.

Kieron nodded, acknowledging the dark beauty's surprise. "Aye, 'tis something we abhor—which emphasizes its importance as a measure of our commitment to the promise." Unable to prevent himself, he brushed fingertips over the smooth satin of her cheek. "It means I will always be here for you, whatever or wherever the need.

"Aye, here I will be—" Though his face remained expressionless, Kieron forced himself to drop his hand and add what he most dreaded. "—Even though one day you will take a mortal man for mate and bear his children while I become a distant memory from your youth."

"No-o-o . . ." Hildie softly cried, reaching for the precious goal denied.

Kieron caught small hands in both of his much larger ones and gently but firmly held Hildie back while raising the one subject certain to shift her attention.

"I came to you tonight because the shaking earth was a fresh warning of perils rising from below and growing stronger."

Letting forehead fall to rest atop the joined hands

Kieron clasped in his own, Hildie forced the anguish born of their conversation into hiding and tried to focus on the matter he'd come intending to discuss with her.

"By time spent in the cavern beneath my king's castle, we've already weakened the gates holding back the Dragons of Chaos." The repression of an urgent desire to nuzzle ebony ringlets crowning her bowed head lent a further thread of strain to Kieron's deep velvet voice as he added, "Now we must undo our wrong . . . *my* wrong."

"No, not just your wrong." Hildie immediately glanced up to deny him complete culpability and accept her portion of the blame.

"'Struth, I am the one at fault, the one responsible for the whole disastrous misdeed." Kieron's slight smile was full of self-mockery. "Had I not led you to the very gate itself, no harm could've been done."

"But the Dragons of Chaos were already breaking free," Hildie loyally argued. "You said there were abundant signs and portents . . ."

Under the unintentional stab delivered by her reminder of false claims made to win her company, Kieron's self-derision deepened.

"No matter the cause . . ." Kieron again attempted to return both her attention and his own to the challenge ahead. "It is time for us to subdue the Dragons of Chaos and reseal the gate's rift against further harm."

"How?" Not for a moment did Hildie doubt her

incredible companion possessed the answer. And, because of that trust, she was the more completely dismayed by his response.

"You, the Seunadair, are the key." Not even color-stealing moonlight could rob Kieron's solemn aqua eyes of their hue.

"But I have no magic," Hildie instantly argued with undeniable logic. "No way to tame Chaos. What could I possibly do?"

"The answer is written on stone." Kieron's potent smile flashed but bore a bleak edge. "However, because our return to the cavern's ring of stones is forbidden—even were I skilled at interpreting Ogham—we couldn't read its counsel."

Having no solution for their quandary, Hildie continued to gaze expectantly at the glowing figure—her friend and protector but *never* her brother. Hildie's faith was not betrayed.

"Thus," Kieron continued, "we must seek the advice of others. My king mentioned something to me which holds leastways a shred of promise. His grandmother, Queen Aine, told him about how she as a child talked with the ancients."

Kieron gazed steadily into Hildie's dark, unwavering eyes and continued, pleased to think that she had followed his reasoning.

"Queen Aine herself listened to Sidhe memories of the fierce battle waged against the Dragons of Chaos. And by that she must surely have learned how the victory was won, how the gate was closed to imprison their dangerous enemies beneath a sealed ring of stones."

When Kieron paused, Hildie tightened fingers still clasped in his hands, anxious to hear more. He must think Queen Aine's experience held clues to the solution they sought.

"Having told her grandson this much..." Kieron yielded to his elfling's intense curiosity. "Would Queen Aine fail to share the information most vital to her realm's security with the descendant destined to succeed her to the throne? Never."

"But..." Hildie tentatively approached a possibly delicate question. "As King Comlan blames us for cracking that seal, wouldn't we dare too much in asking him to share that infinitely more dangerous secret with us?"

" 'Struth, yet still there is hope." Kieron's honest grin flashed. "Queen Aine likely repeated the same tales and lessons for Comlan's younger brother, Gair. We must go to Prince Gair and petition his aid in the quest to see our harm undone."

Hildie wished she felt less dubious about this scheme for approaching a prince of the Tuatha de Danann rarely seen even among his own kind.

Recognizing his tender elfling's discomfort, Kieron found himself again prey to an unpleasant emotion nearly unknown among inhabitants of the Faerie Realm—guilt.

By his wrongful attempt to bridge the lingering chasm of silence that had stretched between them, he was responsible for entangling Hildie in this ominous situation. That he hadn't done it unintentionally was no comfort. It merely reinforced the importance of pursuing the most promising chance for assistance toward the objective.

"Prince Gair and his wife live in a home deep inside the hill that rises behind Tuatha Cottage," Kieron quietly told Hildie. "The same cave-abode once inhabited by his sister, the Princess Lissan responsible for the forever blooming fairy ring on the peak above."

Before Hildie could respond, Kieron whisked her to the top of that hill. Then at the foot of an oak growing from the middle of that circle of miraculous flowers he spoke.

"Stay here where you know you'll remain safe and unseen while I seek permission to enter Gair's hill-home."

Though long familiar with such wonders, still Hildie blinked when Kieron disappeared in an instant. Time stretched by anxiety lengthened. To occupy herself she settled on a green cushion of thick grasses beneath the tree's wide-spread limbs and gazed into the shadows of a forest crested by moon-silvered leaves and drifting mists.

Was there truly a way to subdue the peril inadvertently roused and nearly free? Knowing herself to be a mere mortal and no more, Hildie couldn't seriously believe herself to be the Seunadair able to wield magic so powerful ... or any magic at all. She almost wished she were, since only that enchanted being could end the danger.

It was truly unfortunate that the identity of such a being was apparently unknown even in the Faerie Realm. Hildie was so deep in troubled thoughts that she didn't realize Kieron had reappeared until he spoke.

"Gair and his wife, Mae, are waiting for us." Kieron lifted Hildie into his arms and tucked her face into his throat.

In an amazing abode filling a hollow hill, Hildie surreptitiously glanced at walls covered by intricate tapestries in subtle shades, walls that lacked either windows or doors.

"Welcome . . . niece." The speaker's smile was full of mockery yet genuine warmth as well.

Even while dropping an elegant curtsey, Hildie peeked at the golden, green-eyed male greeting her. As nearly King Comlan's mirror image, she would've known them for brothers even if Kieron hadn't already told her it was so.

"Ah, pay him no mind." The woman of brilliant red hair laughed, stepping forward to link an arm through her husband's. "When Gair is of a mind to tease, there's no stopping him."

"Hah!" Gair promptly responded with a playful tap on his wife's nose. "I wasn't teasing."

"Oh, I know, I know," Mae pertly flashed back. "As Lissan's human descendant, Lady Hildie *is* your niece . . . but still you *were* teasing her."

"Nay." Gair ruefully shook golden hair. " 'Tis my wife, Mae, who you must pay no mind. Though her heart is pure, she's far more of a mind to tease than even me."

Hildie was surprised. Kieron hadn't told her that their host's wife was human although by hazel eyes and brilliant red hair lacking any hint of fairy gold it was plain that the woman wasn't born of the Tuatha de Danann.

" 'Struth." Mae grimaced with sham remorse but a merry gleam was in her eyes. "I do see a bit of fun in everything—keeps life an interesting place to be. And that's most important when it continues nearly forever."

"She had a choice, you know." Gair lowered his voice in feigned affront. "Though I did save Mae's life, she could've chosen to remain in the mortal world and live only a brief human life span."

"Without you?" As Mae gazed up into her mate's handsome face, her cheery disposition broke out in a broad grin. "Never."

"Ah, there you have it." Gair planted a quick kiss in the middle of Mae's forehead before returning full attention to guests still standing near the cozy chamber's center.

"Kieron tells me your purpose here is far more important than a simple visit with new friends. So, come, sit awhile and let the four of us discuss this looming challenge in detail."

The two couples moved to where several chairs beckoned with the promised comfort in an assortment of soft pillows. As they all settled in a loose circle, Hildie's troubled thoughts returned. How could this pleasant visit lead to a reinforced prison for the Dragons of Chaos?

"I agree with your escort, Lady Hildie," Gair solemnly began. "From the description of the visit you shared to the Circle of Stones and the message written there, you are almost certainly the Seunadair of which it speaks."

Ebony hair cascaded over Hildie's shoulders as she sat forward. Though her soft lips opened with denial despite the recent wish made beneath the fairy ring's oak, their host's next words blocked her unspoken argument.

"Were you to proclaim yourself the Seunadair, we'd know that you were not." Gair's emerald gaze proved as penetrating as ever King Comlan's had been and Hildie's mouth closed beneath its force. "The fact that you so seriously doubt you could possibly be that legendary figure further supports the likelihood that you are."

While automatically nibbling her bottom lip, Hildie's hands twisted tightly together. There was no comfort in this news that even the true Seunadair wouldn't believe herself to be the one destined for such a fateful chore.

"That you fear a lack of both the power and the mystical words to cast a spell able to again confine Chaos, in no way disqualifies you for the task. Toward filling those two lacks I assure you of my full support."

Hildie's brows dropped into a worried scowl. How could even this incredible prince of the Tuatha help a mere human gain the magical powers assuredly essential for so serious an undertaking? She was startled when Gair answered, as if he had read every doubt in her thoughts.

"I neither can nor need to provide you with the necessary power when 'tis foretold that the Seunadair will possess no magic until the moment of greatest need arrives . . . but in that moment she will find no lack."

Instinctively, Hildie glanced up into Kieron's eyes for reassurance. The warmth in his slow smile caught her breath.

Having observed the intimate reassurance given, Gair stifled his own smile while leaning forward to gently unclench and claim one of the lady visitor's hands. His action summoned her dark eyes back to directly meet his gaze.

"In truth, the Seunadair will be imbued with all and more than required by a current flowing direct from a reservoir which the ancient Sidhe of the distant past stored up against that need."

Convinced of Prince Gair's sincerity, if not the truth of his claim about her part in the legend, Hildie nodded.

"By memories of my gran Aine's tales and warnings I believe myself able to aid in forming a spell for subduing and again imprisoning the Dragons of Chaos."

Hildie felt a small seed of hope begin to sprout in her soul.

"But—" Gair reluctantly added.

The prince's small audience heard an ill-boding in the pause—a silence as loud and dissonant as a cracked bell's clang.

"There is one detail of the legend seldom included in its retelling, a detail I fear you'll find disheartening." Gair's grip tightened on the fingers he clasped while Kieron gently took Hildie's free hand. "Even when in possession of a potent spell, the true Seunadair can succeed with her task only if she casts it while standing on a specific spot . . . a site not by legend revealed."

The faint light of predawn washed the sky and slanted through the narrow window of Hildie's bedchamber while, to prevent disturbing a sleeping toddler, Kieron whispered into his elfling's small ear.

"Never take it off."

Hildie glanced up from the dainty ring Kieron had gently placed on her middle finger to meet his devastating aqua gaze with a silent question in her own. Surely giving her such a personal gift was not the action of a brother?

Reading doomed hope on his forbidden love's face, Kieron quickly spoke to make its true purpose clear. "It carries the spell of finding and so long as it rests securely on your finger, I can easily locate you."

Falling back on a long-established tactic, Hildie tried to hide the depth of her disappointment with a question. "You expect more abductions?"

"I hope not . . . but should it happen, I'll be better prepared."

Fearing useless emotions would be clear in her eyes, Hildie closely studied the golden ring. The band was formed of delicate and intricately woven strands that held an exquisite rose with a precious sapphire at its heart.

Glancing up, she wasn't surprised to see that Kieron had already vanished.

CHAPTER 7

"Eamon, are you here?" Issuing from the shady side of an ancient and gnarled tree trunk, Donal's murmured words were far too loud to truly qualify as a whisper. And yet he was certain that he'd kept his voice quiet enough. With green eyes deepening to a forest hue, Donal defiantly told himself that if his friend didn't answer soon he'd start yelling in earnest.

This was their secret meeting place and, even when playing, they never raised voices loud enough to risk being discovered by adults likely to forbid them its joys. Their mothers insisted on carefully escorting them between homes for visits, but near a year past the two youngsters had found this giant elm halfway between. Now, whenever the weather was fine, they kept a pact to meet here every midweek. So where was Eamon?

"Eeeaamon—" Again Donal impatiently called, and called louder.

Despite his shrill call, Donal still glanced cautiously over his shoulder while stealthily circling the tree. He and Eamon had shared jolly times staging pretended battles here every week since the last snowfall. On this day it was his turn to play the brave knight of Connaught and Eamon's to be a blackhearted knave from Munster.

Was that why Eamon hadn't come? That thought startled Donal to an abrupt halt. Would Eamon prefer to simply stay home rather than take his fair turn at pretending to be the villain who must, of course, lose?

No. That wasn't at all the sort of thing his amiable friend would do, but . . . Deep scowl marring the smooth brow between dark hair and emerald eyes, he irritably kicked at a small twig.

"Shhh!" A soft thump emphasized the brusque command.

Something had landed right behind Donal. He spun about to face the grinning boy rising from hard ground cushioned by the past autumn's fallen leaves tangled in fresh blades of grass.

"If truly you were a knight of Connaught and I a warrior from Munster"—Eamon made a show of brushing fragments of crushed leaves from his clothing before finishing his statement—"then woe be to our kingdom for you would've lost."

"Hah!" Donal immediately protested. "You weren't playing fair."

"Playing fair?" As Eamon slowly shook his head in mock disillusionment, a few stray beams of sunlight wending through the woodland's thick ceiling of leaves glowed brightly over golden hair. "Think you that any knave from Munster might possess sufficient honor for that?"

Donal gave a slight shrug, acknowledging his protest's lack of right reasoning before saying, "Clearly not if judged by the one who just left Ailm Keep."

"You mean the lord whose own keep lies beyond our bridge?" While nodding in the vague direction of the span crossing a nearby ravine, curiosity sparkled in Eamon's hazel eyes. "The visitor who wishes to wed your sister Hildie?"

To Donal's surprise, before he could speak, Eamon waved any answer aside.

"Let's not waste time on such silly matters. I have something important to share with you!" Something really, truly exciting! The golden-haired boy loudly clapped his hands together. "I have made a great discovery."

Knowing the joy his friend took in pranks, Donal cast him a dubious glance.

" 'Tis amazing, peculiar ..." Eamon's enthusiasm was not the least bit quashed by the doubt in emerald eyes. "I swear it's true! I'll even wager my next two turns as knight that you have never seen anything like it."

The eager zeal of these claims roused as much suspicion in Donal as curiosity. And yet, since the fun of playing knight and knave was growing near as stale as week-old bread, he would risk being the butt of Eamon's jest for even the possibility of a fresh adventure.

"Show me."

In prompt response, blond Eamon led his dark-haired friend on a twisting course. They clamored over fallen trees, ducked under low-hanging branches, and avoided at least the obvious stumble-homes in verdant undergrowth.

As time passed and distance lengthened Donal grew bored with what seemed a pointless journey halfway to Tuatha Cottage. However, before he could ask how much farther they had to go, he bumped into his suddenly motionless friend. Anticipation flaring, Donal quickly glanced around.

They were still in the middle of the forest surrounded by towering trees, thick bushes, and climbing vines but no hint of anything more exciting, certainly nothing to justify the claim of a great discovery.

Donal was disgusted with himself for again playing the fool to one of Eamon's pranks. And too plainly that was precisely what he had done since, if this was their destination, it was nearer to being a sorry disappointment.

"There—" Eamon spun about to face his companion while triumphantly motioning behind toward the ground at his back.

Questioning the state of his friend's wits, Donal stepped forward and with a skeptical grimace allowed his gaze to follow the indicated path . . . and meet a startling sight.

Emerald eyes went wide with amazement.

It looked as if some giant had lifted the earth like a crusty tart and then with the disappointment of finding it hollow had hurtled it down to split open. Curiosity forcing wariness aside, Donal dropped to his knees at the jagged fissure's edge and leaned forward for a closer look.

Intent examination brought an even greater surprise. It was undeniable that their accidental find was in truth a rudely torn and doubtless unwelcome opening into a secret cavern.

Donal solemnly settled back on his heels before glancing up to meet the other boy's triumphant hazel gaze. "A cave?"

"Grand, isn't it?" Eamon hopped from foot to foot, dancing with glee and fairly radiating excitement over his discovery.

Apparently oblivious to these words, the serious, dark-haired boy's attention returned to the rent in the earth.

"How can this be when it's nearly flat around here?" Donal asked, absently waving toward their surroundings, heavily forested but lacking any real incline. He'd have sworn the ground was solid, too. "Only caves I've ever seen or heard about were in steep hillsides or in places where cliffs rise sharp up from the sea."

"So what?" Eamon challenged, annoyed by his

companion's lack of enthusiasm. "Why should its flatness matter?"

Realizing that he had disappointed his friend, Donal grinned in atonement and picked up a pebble left exposed by the earth's upheaval. He motioned for quiet with a grubby forefinger pressed against tightly closed lips, then tossed the small rock into the mysterious shadows below. Individually raised fingers marked the passing of time. One . . . two . . . three . . . The sound of pebble striking cave bottom came just as the fourth lifted.

"Can't be very deep," Eamon was quick to say, more in hope than confidence. "Let's meet again tomorrow and go exploring!"

Although ever the more cautious one, Donal immediately nodded . . . yet made a practical suggestion. "Exploring will be great fun . . . but it'll be more fun if we arrange to take tallow-dipped rushes along to light our way."

"Shooo!"

Absorbed in settling the details for their plans, the boys were startled by this intrusion of a raspy voice.

Spinning about, they faced a peculiar figure as inexplicable as the cavern they'd found. Once tall but now age-bent near in half, he had sharp features, oddly winged brows, and flowing white hair.

"Go away, you nasty little creatures." The stranger flapped his arms at them as if they were pesky birds invading a tenderly cultivated grain field. "Begone!"

"No! You go away," Donal boldly challenged. "My father is lord of these lands, and he'll hunt you down for trespassing."

"Humph!" Before the grumbling sound could fade, its source had disappeared.

The boys boldly stared at each other with fine bravado, anxious to hide any hint of alarm inspired by the fact that only a magical being could vanish right before their eyes.

"You can't tell your father about any of this," Eamon flatly stated.

" 'Struth." A dark head immediately nodded. "If our parents hear anything about that vile stranger or even your discovery, they'll make certain we never slip out alone again."

"Swear a pact by our 'sacred elm'?" Eamon thrust out his arm.

Donal grinned. The first game played at their secret meeting place had involved pretending they were Druids. And as Druids they'd declared holy all ground covered by the towering elm's shade.

The two boys heartily shook on the promise.

Unnatural quiet reigned over Ailm Keep's great hall while its lady glided into the arms of a powerful man not her husband.

Not until the golden woman stepped back, did Lord Rory move forward with an arm extended to the visitor. "Welcome."

The two leaders met, joining strong forearms in a sign of respect. Though each justly claimed control over this portion of Erin, no rivalry lay between them since the dominion of each existed simultaneously on different planes.

"An attempt was made to abduct my daughter," Rory flatly stated, dark eyes meeting the brilliant gaze of his guest. They were a mirror of Lissan's emerald eyes.

A small contingent of houseserfs lingered in the large chamber ostensibly toiling over afternoon chores. They made a well-practiced but false show of ignoring their master's conversation while stoking hearth flames, turning spitted meat, and scattering fresh herbs across the floor to sweeten its layer of rushes growing stale.

" 'Twas a foul deed reported in my realm as well." King Comlan nodded, remaining as expressionless as the solemn human he squarely faced. "I trust you have apprehended the vile wretch responsible for my niece's danger?"

"Would that I had," Rory answered, tacitly ignoring his guest's reasserted claim of kinship with Hildie, despite the many human generations separating them.

"In truth," Rory continued, "I requested this conference to seek your support in our search for these vile wretches."

Comlan's dark gold brows arched in silent query. He was well aware of the uneasiness with which his daughter's mortal spouse continued to view the Tuatha de Danann, never mind that this

96

breed was the source of half the blood in Lissan's veins.

"Why do you ask my aid?" Comlan didn't speak it aloud, yet they both knew the renowned warrior, Lord Rory of Connaught, was more than able to defeat any mortal foe.

Though acknowledging the unspoken praise, Rory's tight smile contained no amusement. As with anything relating to this mercurial king of the Tuatha de Danann, he wasn't certain where mockery ended and sincerity began.

"Deeds were done that I fear no one in my world could have accomplished . . ." Rory paused before adding, "Not alone."

Comlan nodded again, bright hair reflecting gleams of firelight. "Tell me first all you know about the circumstances and individuals involved." His respect for the human was reaffirmed as Rory stood boldly before him as few men of his race could. "And explain what it is that leads you to suspect that one of my people is involved."

Infusing the story with contempt, Rory succinctly told of the failed abduction, its two perpetrators, assaulted guard, and Liam's fortuitous intervention. He added how an apparently betraying brooch had been found.

But, before answering King Comlan's last request, Rory turned toward Lissan who carefully handed him a small, wooden item.

"I put the brooch, a very real brooch, into this chest and locked it with my own hand." By glancing down Rory directed the other male's attention to the miniature, iron-bound box. "I then concealed this in a secret place within my private chamber, a place known only to me and Lissan.

"In the first instance it would've been difficult for anyone to creep unseen into my private chamber. In the second, because the chest was securely hidden, it would've been nearly impossible to find. And yet neither of those reasons would've been enough to make me suspect that someone from among the Tuatha was involved."

Rory silently extended the piece in question toward Comlan.

"Somehow that important brooch was removed from this chest although it remained locked and apparently untouched."

Comlan took the small box from Rory's hands and examined it closely.

" 'Struth." Comlan's emerald eyes lifted to bond with Rory's dark gaze. "To get inside without the key, this would've had to be smashed open."

The fact that powers no mortal possessed had clearly been employed in this foul deed roused Comlan's seldom loosed temper. Yet before he could probe for further information, another problem intruded.

"Milord, milord!" A plainly flustered Grady burst into the hall.

"What is it?" Rory demanded of the guardsman assigned this morning to stand guard at the bailey gate.

"Lord Morven approaches and with him a host of heavily armed supporters." Grady's usually affable expression was weighted down into lines of dread by the prospect of the unwanted arrival.

"Be calm, Grady," Rory sternly directed although furious with himself for having allowed recent events to push awareness of this looming deadline from his thoughts. "If our guest from Munster returns, then my lady and I will welcome him. Now go back to open the gates the moment he hails you."

Lissan slipped her hand through the crook of her father's arm. Comlan gazed down into her strained smile just as Rory rejoined them.

"Lord Morven is the master of Dunbarrough Keep which lies across the bridge marking our border with Munster."

Comlan nodded. "The nephew who replaced Lord Mael there."

A slight scowl drew Rory's dark brows together. Somehow the Tuatha always knew as much or more about the ever-shifting complexities of human affairs than did any mortal.

" 'Struth, Morven replaced Mael," Rory agreed. "And unfortunately he has gone at least as far as his uncle toward threatening the uneasy peace between our two kingdoms."

Comlan's expression was impassive and his emerald gaze was chill.

"Father," Lissan broke a strained silence. "The man and his king demand that Hildie be given as bride in physical proof of the alliance between Munster and Connaught . . . or in blood they will claim retribution for the insult."

The immediate burst of green fire in Comlan's eyes matched the silver storm in Rory's dark gaze. For once the two were in perfect accord. But the sound of booted feet stomping up the wooden outer stairwell intruded.

Rory proffered his arm to Lissan, and she lightly laid her fingertips atop the deep blue linen of his sleeve.

As the keep's lord and lady strode forward to greet their uninvited guest, Comlan vanished unnoticed by humans intent on the visitor and wary of his purpose. However, though invisible to mortals, he lingered wanting to see what manner of being this Lord Morven might prove to be. He also hoped to observe possible clues toward unmasking Hildie's erstwhile abductor, as well as discovering that culprit's source of uncanny abilities.

"I have returned, just as I warned." Morven's strange eyes were so cold they seemed truly formed of ice. "And as forewarned, I have come for your decision."

Lord Morven strode forward to plant himself within arm's length of his host, legs braced and arms crossed over his chest.

"Will you give your daughter to me?"

The near empty hall was deafeningly quiet. Attention was so intent on the dramatic scene playing out before them that no one noticed a boy slipping into the hall.

Donal was initially relieved that he needn't face either the difficulty of inventing an excuse for his absence or method to avoid possible mention of the cave, far less the odd stranger. In the next instant his father's unexpected words drove thoughts of his own challenges into obscurity.

"I agree to a formal betrothal." Rory had spent so much time worrying about his oldest daughter's abduction that he hadn't devised a plan to neutralize Morven's threat. And by that unhappy lack he felt he'd truly failed Hildie.

"Then let us have done with it now," Morven demanded, swinging one brawny arm down to point at the floor between them.

Donal peeked between two unabashedly staring house serfs and was shocked to see the wretched knave from Munster belligerently standing to face the keep's master.

Rory slowly shook his head, as much in self-disgust as in a refusal that could be no more than a useless delay. Though he hadn't promised Hildie in marriage, he couldn't fool himself that this fact was an adequate excuse for his mistake in not planning for this confrontation earlier, not when a betrothal was as binding as nuptial vows.

"You must give Hildie time to prepare," Rory calmly reasoned.

Morven's color ominously deepened.

"In two days time—" Rory unwillingly placated

the other's increasing anger. "In two days time Lord Morven and Lady Hildie will be betrothed."

Plainly far less than pleased, Morven gave his bright head a sharp nod. "Naturally I will stay until that rite has been performed."

"Of a certainty, milord," Lissan forced herself to graciously agree despite her distaste for the whole situation. "The chamber where last you slept still awaits your return."

CHAPTER 8

The morning was bright as Lord Rory's people gathered in a simple wooden chapel adjoined to Ailm Keep. They had been honorably summoned to this sanctified chamber to bear unhappy witness while their master's eldest daughter was betrothed to the objectionable lord from Munster. Their retreat had left the courtyard deserted—save for one lone figure.

Alone at the bottom of the keep's exterior stairway, Hildie paused to glare at the outgoing path. Smoothed by the constant tread of many feet, it led around to an arched doorway and a destination that today she would give almost anything to escape. She had hoped, sincerely hoped and earnestly prayed that some miracle would prevent this dreaded rite but . . .

Hildie's destination was not far away and yet . . . She feared that the emptiness of the waiting route was an omen of her future in Munster—without Kieron. Holding pride close to strengthen her determination to meet the coming ordeal undaunted, Hildie squared her shoulders and bravely set forth.

A ghastly shock pounced from behind.

Wrongly believing herself safe within the security of her home's stout palisade, Hildie was stunned when powerful arms reached from behind to jerk her back against a massive chest. Her mouth instantly opened but the thick lump of cloth promptly shoved inside stifled a bloodcurdling scream.

"Quick!" Shanahan loudly murmured in a tone that was likely as close as he could come to taming his resounding voice into a whisper. "Tie that gag in place, and make certain it's secure, while I bind her wrists together."

As the father bent forward to focus on his chosen task, Hildie valiantly twisted her head from side to side, fighting to prevent Rolan from fastening two ends of a long strip holding her crude muzzle in place. She failed.

" 'Twas easily done." Rolan's announcement contained a full measure of his endless conceit. He wasn't afraid of her. And his father was right. The prestige to be won by his union with her left any superstitious twaddle about her origins of less than no account.

Worse, in Hildie's biased opinion, he took one step back and allowed his insolent gaze to move slowly over her curves. "Lovely . . . and *mine*."

"We've got to leave now!" Shanahan coldly snapped as he straightened from the finished chore of using rough weed-woven twine to bind delicate hands behind their captive's back.

Though rarely irritated with his only son and beloved heir, for this foolish a waste of time he sent the boy a chastising glare.

Taking advantage of the distraction caused by their minor skirmish, Hildie slowly turned to one side. After she had maneuvered herself into position, Hildie brought her shin sharply up to kick between Rolan's legs as hard as she could.

The arrogant youth instantly bent double. Although with his father close behind and the courtyard empty the action wouldn't secure her freedom, Hildie watched in satisfaction and belated gratitude for the graphic jests she'd overheard bored, alesotted warriors exchanging. Their words, exceedingly crude, were her source of information about the useful, debilitating power of such a blow.

Unfortunately, it almost immediately became clear that no matter the fervor of its delivery, the kick hadn't been as debilitating as Hildie had hoped. Though still hunched over, Rolan glared up into wide, dark eyes as he spat out words in a tone hovering somewhere between a groan and a hiss.

"You vicious bi—"

Hildie heard no more of the vehement curse since, despite his awkward position, Rolan swung one meaty fist upward to forcefully deliver a solid punch just below her chin. It instantly robbed her of all conscious thought.

"Be calm, son," Shanahan cautioned even while catching the woman falling backward into his arms. He hastily lowered Lady Hildie's limp figure to the courtyard's hard-packed dirt and then reached out to clasp Rolan's shoulders with callused hands. Giving his son a brief, sharp shake, he repeated the terse order, "Be calm."

The act of easing Rolan's anger with quiet words had a most peculiar effect on Shanahan. Face going ruby red and bushy brows settling into a fierce scowl, he erupted with the first harsh castigation that he had ever leveled on his son.

"Cuffing Lord Rory's daughter was the act of a simpleton! Fool boy, don't you realize that your witless violence will destroy any hope for approval of the marriage?"

That was precisely the problem. Shanahan shook his head in disgust. The boy seldom bothered to waste his precious time thinking.

With signs of his father's extreme displeasure so unmistakable, Rolan realized that he had truly stumbled into a hornets' nest this time . . . and the rudely disturbed insects were very, very angry.

The younger man's shoulders were abruptly released as without a word the elder Shanahan bent to lift and roughly hoist the unconscious woman over one thick shoulder.

"Surely . . ." Rolan donned his most ingratiating grin. With a boyish cajolery that rarely failed, he fully expected to win from his father an affectionate tolerance, if not outright forgiveness. "Lord Rory will see that we have only claimed just retribution by successfully performing the very deed for which we were wrongfully accused."

In response to this ridiculous argument—nay, to this wretched example of his son's complete lack of rational logic—Shanahan's frown deepened. He laid Lady Hildie facedown across his horse before swinging up into the saddle.

Unnoticed by either of the Shanahans, the stable door soundlessly opened, just a crack barely wide enough for one young boy to slip through.

It wasn't fair. Truly, it wasn't fair! Keith irritably kicked at a harmless pebble daring to lie in his path. Why should he be the only one forced to stay behind and work while everyone else, even that oaf Ian, had been ordered to spend the morning idly sitting in the chapel?

Nursing a sense of hurt injustice, he glared at the courtyard's dusty surface. So intent was Keith on ground pounded flat by the passing of many feet that he nearly missed the wicked sight that earned his opportunity for a moment of glory.

Burning tapers glowed on the metal rings within rings that were suspended from beams high overhead to lend the chapel a golden aura. Bathed in that gentle light a priest waited at the altar, the perfect image of pious serenity with his head reverently bowed over hands joined palms flat.

Long minutes dragged past, and those sitting below the altar grew increasingly uneasy. The chamber's once expectant hush became an uncomfortable
silence disturbed only by the sounds of shifting feet
and nervously cleared throats.

Rory glanced down to his wife, seated on the
right, and reassuringly squeezed her nervously
clenched hand. The depth of Lissan's worry had
first been betrayed by the glimpse he'd caught of
small teeth nibbling a tender bottom lip.

Next, by slightly turning a dark head, Rory
looked toward the supercilious man standing aloof
on his left. Lord Morven's fiery hair burned while,
in contrast, his sneering face had gone colder and
colder with every passing moment until now it
seemed formed of ice-coated stone.

Where was Hildie? Rory inwardly seethed. How
dare his daughter be tardy for yet another meeting
with Lord Morven? How when this one was by far
the most important?

All too aware that he was as worthy of blame as
Hildie, Rory berated himself. He had made the error of granting first her request for private time to
compose herself and next the boon of entering the
chapel alone. The sound of clenched teeth faintly
grinding accompanied his admission of folly in
leading his people to the chapel while leaving a too
independent daughter in the keep unattended.

A shrill call abruptly pierced the quiet chapel's
serenity.

"Quick, my lord, come quick!" Heard from beyond chapel walls an adolescent voice broke under the strain of panic.

Without hesitating to question which of two lords this desperate call was meant to summon, Rory dashed for the door. Every male in the building hastily followed in his wake while all the women rushed to crowd close behind.

As his master drew near, the sandy-haired boy rushed forward. His wildly flailing arms were unmistakable evidence of his alarm.

"Keith, what's wrong?" Rory caught the youngster's hands and quietly soothed his agitation with a promise. "Tell me and I swear I will immediately deal with the matter."

Suddenly aware that he was the focus of attention for the whole of Ailm Keep's inhabitants, Keith puffed up with pride. He welcomed this moment of importance and told himself that he'd earned it by having been excluded from a serious event.

"They took her!" Each word of this vehement statement was crystal clear and thickly layered with scathing condemnation.

"Took who?" Rory's penetrating eyes narrowed on the boy but his face remained impassive. Although inwardly acknowledging the obvious answer, he stole brief moments to resign himself to its sorry inevitability. He had the nasty feeling of having experienced this same event before.

"Lady Hildie," the boy answered, casting his questioner a glance laced with disgust. How could his master have missed so blatant a fact? "They took Lady Hildie."

The crowd was so engrossed in this dramatic scene playing out right before their eyes, that they were startled when it was a lord not their own who sternly demanded to know more.

"*Who* took Lady Hildie?" Lord Morven's voice was as frigid as if gale-blown from across the North Sea's endless ice floes.

Keith's attention shied away from the unpleasant and intimidating lord from Munster. Instead, he focused on his own while firmly announcing, " 'Twas the Shanahans who took her."

Lord Rory's gaze seemed to harden into solid black granite, unyielding and bitterly cold.

Misinterpreting the instant chill of his lord's gaze as doubt, Keith earnestly defended his claim. " 'Struth, I *saw* them throw Lady Hildie's body over a horse and ride away." For good measure, the boy fervently added, "I swear it is so."

"I believe you," Rory calmly reassured the boy. "Now show us where it happened."

Nodding a sandy mane of unevenly cut hair, Keith spun and without hesitation led the way directly to a site on one side of the keep's exterior stairway. Here he pointed to where earth rarely disturbed betrayed signs of the recent skirmish.

Bounced roughly up and down by a galloping horse, Hildie gradually awakened from her unnatural slumbers. Her first sight, a confusing sight, was of the ground below rushing past with alarming speed.

This time her kidnappers had succeeded!

Thoughts racing as fast as the beast carrying her, Hildie desperately sought some method of escape. Unfortunately, this time Liam wouldn't stumble across the villains. She knew of a certainty that he was among the many waiting in the chapel to watch her betrothal. And even her magical ring was of little use since Kieron wouldn't know to exercise the spell of finding until he learned of her taking.

Don't be a moonwit, Hildie silently berated herself. *Calm down!* To these admonishments she added a stern caution to both calm her pounding heart and think rationally.

During the last attempt, after erstwhile abductors put her across a horse, she'd won freedom by throwing herself from its back. Of course, in that instance the horse had been standing motionless in one place. This beast was madly weaving an uncertain, dangerously erratic path through the forest. And tossing herself down now would too likely end in the pain of nasty bruises and broken bones. Such injuries would, in turn, truly keep her a prisoner.

"Whoa," the elder Shanahan called a halt. "We'll pause here, allow both ourselves and our mounts to drink from the stream."

Though Hildie purposely remained limp, head down over the horse's back, she peaked through the wealth of dark hair left free for the ceremony which had tumbled in loose tangles across her face. As her captors reined their stallions to a stop she caught glimpses of the small but fast-moving brook dividing a narrow glade. Lined by thick greenery, this opening in the forest beckoned with the promised comfort of lush grasses and an abundance of sweet-scented wildflowers.

She continued to feign an unconscious state when lifted from her uncomfortable position, then lowered to the ground's verdant padding. The Shanahans left her leaning awkwardly against a fallen tree trunk while they gave their full attention to refreshing themselves with cool water.

A swirl of soft, black cloth suddenly enveloped Hildie. She gasped but knew crying out would be futile. Her abductors were the only people close enough to hear. Still, Hildie immediately sensed that she was not being saved and that the being whisking her away was not a welcome rescuer. Kieron wouldn't rudely bundle her up this way, wouldn't hide himself from her. But if not Kieron, then who?

In the tense body held close by his still powerful arms, Ardagh sensed both alarm and curiosity. It put a cruel grin on his lips. This opportunity to upset Lord Rory's daughter, King Comlan's niece, was an unexpected yet delightful pleasure.

Leaving behind human fools oblivious to their loss, Ardagh whisked the dark colleen to the one place no human could follow and whose position was unknown to any other among the Tuatha. Although he had once scorned Gair for living in his sister's abandoned hill-home, since Ardagh's humbling fall from favor a similar hollow hill had become his abode—and assuredly the perfect prison for this mortal prey.

Deposited atop an exceptionally soft perch, Hildie began attempting to fight free of concealing cloth wrapped about her like a shroud. It was a battle proven unnecessary when the dark garment vanished as abruptly as it had appeared.

Stunned, Hildie's wide dark eyes quickly searched the chamber for the foul miscreant who had whisked her here and left her atop this high tester bed draped in incredible brocades.

She was alone. Alone in this place far too beautiful to be a mortal's abode—but whose? Certainly not Kieron's or King Comlan's or . . .

Ardagh grinned, taking wicked delight in Lady Hildie's bewilderment. She was a human and remaining invisible to her required no great skill. However, the trick allowed him to take joy in watching the pitiful mortal's futile struggle to make sense of mercurial fairy magic.

Proud of this haven adorned with all the fine luxuries which he had accumulated over a very long lifetime, Ardagh gleefully exercised his contrary nature. He soundlessly settled down to watch and listen, but not in a chair. Rather, he sat cross-legged in the middle of a small, intricately parqueted table to the left of his unwilling guest.

Then while with a midnight dark gaze Lady Hildie closely scrutinized her surroundings, Ardagh stoked the warming fires of enjoyment by carefully listing to himself the many successes he had already won or would soon see come to pass.

By stealing his *guest* away from fumbling human captors, Ardagh had succeeded in spiting two figures most deserving: the Faerie Realm king holding a position that rightly should be his and the mortal lord who had been at the center of his humiliating downfall on the banks of the River Shannon.

Ardagh took satisfaction in the prospect of all the deliciously nasty accusations and counteraccusations certain to follow once Lord Rory and his daughter's intended betrothed overtook the errant Shanahans. And better still was the near certainty of renewed enmity soon to be followed by bloodshed between the two mortal kingdoms he held in large part responsible for his downfall.

That the participants in this conflict could in no way be aware of how all the pain and even the deaths thus wrought were negligible compared to the total destruction which the Dragons of Chaos would wreak in ending the world.

CHAPTER 9

"Taken?" Kieron's bronze brows crashed together in disbelief for an instant before smoothing again under the comforting certainty that here amidst the bright amusements of the Faerie Castle's great hall Sean had merely repeated outdated gossip.

"Nay." With wry humor inspired by his own relief Kieron hastened to correct the speaker's obvious mistake. "Though someone *tried* to abduct Lady Hildie, they failed."

Sean scowled. He didn't like having his tidbit of fresh and tasty gossip disputed. Particularly not when the one contradicting him seemed so amused . . . at his expense.

" 'Struth, those who had attempted to steal Hildie away were foiled." Recognizing the other man's irritation, Kieron ruefully added, "I myself talked with Hildie after her return."

Giving golden hair a quick shake, Kieron chided

himself for having been so openly upset by the claim. Such a revelation of honest emotion was disgraceful for any member of the Tuatha. Inwardly, he admitted to having clearly erred with a mistake that knocked awry his skill in easily donning false masks. It was further proof of the folly in permitting distaste for the repugnant fact that his precious Hildie was at this very moment being legally bound to a human male to overcome his usual control.

"I fear, Kieron," a voice full of regret spoke from behind, "that it is Sean who has the right of this matter."

Kieron swiftly turned to meet his king's unwavering gaze. The steady purpose in emerald eyes destroyed any hope that Sean might simply be misinformed. The once repelled flood of alarm for Hildie's safety returned along with a dispiriting undercurrent of shame. He had, for the second time, failed in a guardian's oath-sworn duty to protect his sweet elfling.

While Comlan's head slightly tilted, his intense, penetrating stare and serious expression were a wordless reminder of the precaution he'd suggested Kieron should take.

The amulet!

Kieron's brilliant smile flashed a moment before he vanished in pursuit of complete privacy. Once in solitude, he would focus on the ring with the full force of his will and thus transport himself instantly to its location.

* * *

"There, my lord, there—" An excited Grady emphatically waved down the kind of clumsily laid path only someone in desperate haste would foolishly leave behind.

Rory gave a quick nod of thanks to the loyal guardsman who had found this trail briefly lost after fording a stream. He then motioned his party of rescuers to follow him down the path marked by crushed grasses and broken twigs as it wove between trees and through thick undergrowth. Suddenly, on rounding the trunk of a massive oak, they broke into a narrow glade and found the culprits they sought.

Neither of the Shanahans were mounted but rather sat disconsolate on the banks of a stream. Confronted, they jumped to their feet in a panic to flee . . . too late. Several of their fellow warriors from Connaught swung down to quickly catch the pair and force them to kneel before their lord.

"Beg forgiveness, lord." The elder Shanahan immediately pleaded for leniency while his son bowed so low his forehead nearly rested on the earth. "We couldn't bear to see Connaught's lovely lady bound to that knave from Munster."

Although Shanahan's words had begun as a penitent whine, they ended on a venomous roar which in turn brought a vicious snarl from Lord Morven.

Rory's temper snapped. Determined to see that this witless confrontation be allowed to escalate no further, he sharply intervened. Rory issued a harsh demand for the answer to a question driving straight to the heart of their reason for being here.

"Where is Lady Hildie?"

Face flushing ruby-bright, Shanahan's head instantly dipped as low as his son's. How could he respond with honor when the truth was certain to only make matters worse?

"Shanahan!" Rory's single, harsh word held the power to force an answer.

"Lady Hildie was unconscious when we laid her against that tree—" Unwilling gaze jerked up by his lord's inflexible demand, Shanahan waved toward the oak's huge trunk.

"After we finished watering the horses and ourselves—a very brief time, I swear—we turned to find her gone."

"Gone?" Rory's sharp voice sliced cleanly through the glade's tense silence. "Gone where?"

Rory tempered his instant of delight in the possibility that his daughter had simply walked away with awareness of how unlikely it was to be true. Not that Hildie couldn't have done it. He had no doubt that she was both courageous and capable enough. However, Rory did sincerely doubt that any escape could have been so easily accomplished.

That another shared this opinion was evident when a sneering Lord Morven almost simultaneously asked, "Are you so lacking in right wits that you failed to follow her path?"

"We would have, had there been one to follow,"

Rolan snarled, joining his father's verbal self-defense for the first time.

"No path?" Morven scoffed, perversely welcoming the Shanahans' misdeeds and personal insults for their further excuse to pursue his own plans . . . plans that would have proud Connaught humbled, crushed beneath the cudgel of Munster.

"See for yourself—" The belligerent elder of the two pursued and overtaken scrambled to his feet, waving aimlessly at surrounding vegetation. "The only tracks here are those left by our horse and the hooves of *your* steeds."

Narrowed sapphire gaze probing the shadows on either side, Rory verified the truth of Shanahan's claim. But if no tracks had been left to logically explain Hildie's sudden disappearance, that left only the inexplicable power of fairy interference.

But why? And who among their number? Not King Comlan. But perhaps the one who had consistently watched over her for a decade and more? Nay, if Kieron had rescued Hildie, as she'd often insisted he had done before, he could and would have delivered her home in an instant.

No matter, Rory's expression darkened. Though it seemed obvious to him, he could hardly expect Lord Morven or even any among his own people to believe that otherworldly forces were to blame. Particularly not after he had spent the past decade refusing to publicly acknowledge even so little as the mere existence of the Fairy Realm.

Distastefully studying a host silent too long, Lord Morven's anger grew apace with his impatience for this man, this supposedly great warrior who dawdled when action was required. Using the logic of this negative judgment he made an abrupt decision. At last the appropriate moment had come for launching the most essential and vital step in his strategy for conquest.

"I have endured too many insults in this kingdom," Morven announced, voice so clear and loud it pierced the glade's renewed quiet. His reproachful glare lingered to slide down over Lord Rory like corrosive acid. "Plainly you never intended to honor the promise of a betrothal.

"Nay," Morven harshly expounded. "You have instead connived with your *loyal* supporters to trick me into believing that Lady Hildie was abducted. Aye, tricked me when, in truth, I have no doubt you planned to keep her safely hidden until I gave up on the match and departed alone."

Rory started to protest but stopped, unwilling to lower himself with useless denials when it was certain that this man didn't for a moment believe his own claim. Lord Morven had clearly postulated the daft notion simply to justify the actions he had intended to take all along.

"And leave I shall," Lord Morven indignantly added. "But I will return after consulting with my sovereign on his wishes regarding the extent of retribution to be exacted."

Rory and his supporters stood watching in

strained silence while the Lord of Dunbarrough Keep led his guardsmen back into forest shadows. No one observing this departure doubted that violence would be King Muirtrecht's response.

The whole of Munster's armed forces would surely descend upon Connaught determined to take the payment of revenge in blood.

Since the moment in which the dark shroud her captor had swirled out to envelop her had vanished, Hildie had gazed around a frighteningly beautiful place and found that she was . . .

"Alone." Hildie hadn't meant to speak aloud, but it hardly mattered in this empty place where her own voice was the only sound and it more heartening than crushing silence.

Unaware of an invisible observer lingering near, Hildie sat primly on the side of an amazingly comfortable bed and again took stock of impossible surroundings—a small chamber laden with incredible beauty. Artfully scattered across a polished stone floor were a multitude of thick rugs while pillows adorned with delicate embroidery were piled atop satin bedcovers and intricately carved chairs.

Dark eyes lifted from a ewer and goblets seemingly formed of translucent pearls which rested on an ornate table within arm's reach to again scan walls covered with detailed silk tapestries. Their lovely scenes were worked in an array of subtle hues the likes of which the mortal world had never seen. They continuously decorated walls lacking either windows or doors.

This abode was very like Gair and Mae's luxurious hill-home in that it also lacked visible portals or entrances of any kind, all unnecessary for those with fairy powers.

Was that the situation here? Did this place belong to a member of the Tuatha de Danann? Must be so ... yet how could it be when she had been taken by two very human abductors who she knew to be easily unnerved by the inexplicable? The Shanahans would never be brave enough to connive with any wielder of uncanny powers. Only think of Rolan's terror on glimpsing the mark of a lopsided heart on her nape.

"So, elfling, how did you get here?" A potent if wry smile appeared as Kieron's aqua eyes caressed the goal of his quest.

Hildie jumped to her feet and rushed to the welcome intruder, expression full of such glowing warmth that it betrayed both the width of her love and the depth of her relief.

Melting against Kieron, Hildie promptly answered. "I wish that I had any vague notion who deposited me here—or why."

Despite solemn oath, Kieron's arms instinctively wrapped around the sweet temptation he'd come to rescue once again.

"No matter," Kieron whispered into Hildie's ear. "The amulet I gave and you accepted brought me directly to your side."

Arms wrapped around Kieron's neck, Hildie straightened the fingers of one hand. She glanced gratefully at her golden rose and sapphire ring before returning her gaze to its source.

Kieron's half smile deepened even as he gently pressed his forbidden love's face into the crook between broad shoulder and warm throat while whisking her to freedom.

Under the weight of a rare and most uncomfortable self-reproach, the scowling Ardagh materialized. He sprawled in his favorite chair—a replica of Comlan's golden throne, the one he still believed should rightly be his own.

Irritation overwhelmed Ardagh's bloated pride in his ability to remain unseen even to the Tuatha. That skill had betrayed him by allowing the sort of witless error which in others he scorned as proof of a contemptible lack of intelligence.

How, Ardagh demanded of himself, could he have failed to research and consider every possible threat to his plans (no matter how remote)? With that failure he had made a serious blunder . . . but, he felt certain, not a fatal one.

By believing Seun to be Kieron's only aid in locating the lady captive, Ardagh had mistakenly thought the threat easily neutralized. He had cast a simple spell of confusion over the fox to prevent the animal from successfully following Hildie.

He, unfortunately, hadn't recognized her lovely ring for the amulet it was. And for that he had paid the steep price of losing the opportunity to thwart its powers and prevent a rescue of the one destined to play a pivotal role in his revenge.

Outside the shadows of dusk intensified while, after a day overfull of most unpleasant surprises, the lord and lady of Ailm Keep sat across from each other at a small table in the family solar. Firelight from a hearth cut into the width of a stone wall joined candle glow to cast into sharp relief the faces of the two deep in private conversation.

"The Shanahans swear that they were intent on slacking thirst and drinking from a brook when Hildie simply vanished without a sound." Reaching out, Rory claimed Lissan's dainty fingers and gently held them between his own large hands. "And I can swear to the truth that whoever stole Hildie away from the Shanahans left no tracks behind."

"Kieron?" Lissan stated it as a question but a flood of relief was already flowing through her. Lissan thought it clear that the Tuatha guardian her father had assigned to Hildie had again rescued the girl.

Rory could hardly fail to see bright relief banishing a concern that had clouded his wife's green crystal eyes. Still, despite his deep reluctance to rob Lissan of that comfort, he acknowledged an uncomfortable necessity. He must point out the unhappy facts making that possibility unlikely . . . and expose the glaring need for Lissan's help in seeking the support of someone possessing similar otherworldly powers.

"We both know that if it were Kieron who took Hildie from the Shanahans, she would assuredly be home with us now." Rory carefully held his voice so flat it lacked any hint of emotion.

Wielding a shield of unflinching, courageous spirit Lissan fended off the immediate assault of disappointment freed by words she'd no doubt were as unwelcome to her husband as to herself.

Deep regret cracked Rory's stern facade as he added more proof that Kieron was not involved. "It's been hours not only since the abduction but since I and my search party caught up with the Shanahans."

As Lissan nodded acceptance of unpleasant but irrefutable realities, her golden ringlets caught and reflected the flickering light of candles arranged on a silver platter nearby.

Because his wife and oldest daughter were exceptionally close friends, Rory knew how hard it would be for Lissan to admit the involvement of someone from her father's Faerie Realm in the crime against Hildie. But it was a fact that must be faced to win any hope for undoing the wrong.

"Although Kieron can have played no role in recent events," Rory began, "it is even more certain that another being wielding powers no human possesses must be a party to the misdeed."

A slight frown marred Lissan's smooth brow yet

she again nodded agreement while softly murmuring a proposed solution.

"I will go to my father, tell him of these further vile happenings, and beg his aid in saving Hildie from whichever foul knave among the Tuatha who dared abduct their king's human niece."

Rory responded with a grim smile. This plan was precisely what he knew must be done. Moreover, he knew that the plea was best made by Lissan who could emphasize the insult done to the king of the Tuatha de Danann by the wretch who had dared kidnap Hildie from her mortal family.

Sliding her chair back, Lissan rose to her feet. While Rory ordered that her mare be saddled and brought to the bottom of the outgoing stairway, she retreated to their bedchamber.

Once in that lovely room at the keep's highest level, Lissan hurried to a treasured, leather-bound trunk. She carefully lifted its arched cover and reached inside to lift out thick volumes written in a language unknown to the inhabitants of her husband's world, the language of the future.

Not until several neat stacks grew progressively more precarious as they towered above the trunk's edge did she uncover a much smaller chest. With a tiny key she unlocked and opened it to reveal her mother's precious unicorn brooch.

Lissan softly smiled. With this amulet she was armed against human foes and could safely venture into a night world all too likely filled with skulking foes. Aye, she could journey unimpeded to the fairy ring. And after stepping into its circle of forever blooming flowers, by arrangements made though seldom used in the twelve years since her marriage to Rory, an escort to her father's enchanted home would soon appear.

Rory helped his wife to mount her dainty mare and watched until she disappeared into the darkness beyond bailey gates. Retreating then to the keep's great hall, he greeted the guardsmen summoned and waiting to meet with him. Though they doubtless expected his focus to be the rescue of his daughter, Rory admonished himself to trust Lissan—and *her* father—while he prepared to defeat a dangerous threat.

It was his duty to protect the safety of the keep and all who lived on his lands. Thus, his attention must be given and plans must be laid to overcome the expected threat from Munster.

CHAPTER 10

"Home again," Kieron announced, mocking smile flashing as he lowered Hildie to sit on the welcoming comfort of her own bed.

Hildie had begun to resent the fondness in Kieron's voice. Fondness, as if she were an amusing child, was a pale imitation of the passionate declaration of love she longed to hear. She evaded penetrating eyes too likely to read her emotions by glancing beyond the bed's far side. The cot was empty—and revealing.

Aqua gaze following the same path, Kieron found the toddler's absence at this late hour equally disturbing. He had sensed a large presence in the great hall as he arrived at the keep, and the fact that Amy had been allowed to linger there emphasized the gathering's importance.

Assuming that the missing Lady Hildie was this meeting's subject, Kieron regretted his inability to immediately ease their concerns. He was convinced of Lord Rory's sincere desire to safely recover his daughter. But he was just as certain the mortal lord who had never been comfortable with the Tuatha de Danann would most definitely not be pleased to see one of their number materialize in their midst cradling the kidnapped colleen in his arms.

"Sweet dreams, elfling," Kieron gently whispered as he made to pull his arms back from the too sweet temptation she was.

Refusing to be so easily set aside, Hildie threw her arms tightly around his neck.

Unprepared and pulled off balance, Kieron tumbled onto the bed still wrapped in Hildie's embrace. Rising up on one elbow, Kieron gazed down into eyes gone purely black and was frightened by the strength of his own desires. Here like a most coveted but forbidden gift lay the fulfillment of fantasies heightened each time he had safely deposited the naively seductive beauty atop this bed.

Hildie twined fingers into his golden mane while her lashes descended to lie in dark crescents on creamy cheeks. Purposely sinking into the welcome balm of unthinking sensations, she urged Kieron back into her arms. Burying her face into the crook between his shoulder and throat, she nuzzled against firm skin that seemed to take fire beneath the caress. Then, surrendering to temptation, Hildie let her tongue venture out to taste.

That tantalizing touch set fire to the blood pounding through Kieron's veins. Fingers caught in ebony silk urged her head back until he could claim the teasing mouth with his own.

Eagerly yielding to the insistent possession of that deeper kiss, Hildie pressed closer. Desperate for this delicious play, sweet and devastatingly hot, to continue, she twisted against his warm, strong chest while a tiny, inarticulate sound welled up from her core.

The aching sound forced upon Kieron an unwelcome awareness of precisely what was happening—dangerously pleasurable and utterly wrong. Muttering something faintly violent, he clenched azure eyes shut, and struggled to subdue the raging flames of almost ungovernable hungers.

Kieron forced himself to pull sharply away from beguiling enticements near too great to withstand.

"Go, calm your family's fears."

An anguished groan escaped Hildie's tight throat as with this quiet command, the figure in her arms abruptly vanished.

"Daughter—" King Comlan was surprised but pleased to receive this guest whose visits to the Faerie Castle were extremely rare, thanks to her husband's tiresome discomfort with all beings and events inexplicable to human logic.

At the edge of a hall where magnificently arrayed dancers whirled across a polished floor of translucent marble Lissan paused, uncomfortable with standing as the center of attention for a large group of magical beings.

Comlan smiled indulgently on the beloved child whose golden appearance fit so smoothly into his world. Then, sensing Amethyst's growing anticipation, he rose and offered his arm.

As their king stood, sprightly music abruptly went silent and dancers went still while they watched him carefully lead his elegant wife down from the dais for a joyful reunion. Beneath the warmth of her parents' embraces, Lissan's uneasiness vanished.

Soon Comlan leaned back, motioning for the resumption of music and dancing while he escorted his wife and daughter into a small, opulent chamber on one side of the bright hall.

Lissan gladly accepted this change. Although the vast room left behind was host to a constantly changing array of marvelous entertainments, an abundant feast, and hauntingly beautiful music, she welcomed the privacy of this far more intimate apartment.

After the three settled into the pillowed comfort of matching chairs, Amethyst lost no moment in seeking news of the grandchildren so near and yet well beyond her reach.

"Is Donal still as raven-dark as his father?" A slight tinge of regret flavored the older woman's voice and wistful smile.

"Aye, Mama." Lissan knew that the joint decision reached by her husband and her father cast the only shadow on her mother's happiness in the Faerie Realm. It was their decree that Lissan's children never be told of their Tuatha heritage, never know their grandmother Amethyst. "Donal is very much his father's son ... even though he has my green eyes."

"And how is my little namesake?" Though the severing of bonds with her human family was the price to be paid for a nearly endless life with her beloved Comlan, Amethyst assuredly had the right to ask about the grandchildren she would never meet.

"Is your little daughter still the opposite of Donal, possessing your golden hair but Rory's dark sapphire gaze?"

Lissan nodded. "Our Amy is as fair as I am and just as willful, too, I fear."

As curious about the children as his wife, Comlan patiently waited, but once Lissan had answered these questions and many more, he felt free to pursue her purpose for this visit.

"Have you come with further news of your stepdaughter?" Comlan inquired, aware that Lissan couldn't know he'd already been informed of the successful abduction.

Lissan slowly nodded, recognizing this as the time to tell what had happened ... and make her plea for help in solving the inexplicable.

"The same pair wrongly blamed for the first attempt to steal Hildie away were observed roughly throwing her over the back of a horse and riding into the forest beyond our bailey wall."

"Didn't the one who saw this crime bother to

intervene?" Comlan's penetrating emerald eyes met their exact replica in his daughter's gaze and probed for unspoken meanings.

"Oh, yes," Lissan instantly answered. "Keith reacted quickly and forcefully. He screamed as loud and long as any child can. And everyone inside the chapel rushed out to come running."

"Surely your husband led his guard in pursuit of these dastardly knaves?" Comlan tried to tame the mockery filling his question but, fearing he had failed abysmally, quickly asked another more pertinent. "Since you know the identity of these *human* villains, why have you come to me?"

Comlan saw no need to assure Lissan that her visit was infinitely more welcome than another of the audacious summons which her husband had dared issue to the king of the Faerie Realm. The inhabitants of his world had deemed that action taken by a human lord, not even a king, to be an example of the worst in mortal temerity and a ridiculous presumption.

"Because . . ." Hildie took a deep breath and began. "As was true with the failed attempt, nothing is as it first appeared."

A stern smile and slightly arched brows were Comlan's wordless demand for a more specific and detailed explanation.

"A brooch bearing the Shanahans' family pattern brought the weight of blame down upon them after the failed attempt . . . but that brooch disappeared in a way inexplicable to humans. Now the depth of their guilt in this most recent taking is muddled by equally odd happenings."

Comlan's half smile deepened with wry approval. The path of his daughter's reasoning was sufficiently convoluted to honor her Tuatha blood. And yet, although these words succeeded in claiming his complete attention, he found it necessary to hide his impatience to hear more beneath the impassive expression of an abruptly donned mask.

"You asked if the culprits were pursued," Lissan continued. "Aye, indeed the Shanahans were pursued and found . . . but not Hildie." She unwaveringly met the power of her father's penetrating eyes. "The Shanahans both swear by all they hold sacred that Hildie simply disappeared."

"She escaped and that worries you? Why?" Amused by knowing more than Lissan of the likely explanation, Comlan grinned.

"Escaped without leaving a trail?" To her mother's delight, Lissan promptly snapped back. "How? How, without fairy interference?"

"Ho! Fairy *interference*, is it now?" Comlan laughed, taking contrary delight in his daughter's fiery spirit.

Not bothering to hide irritation from the father who, even without resorting to his amazing senses, could always read her thoughts with disgusting ease, Lissan demanded, "Will you help?"

"If it were needed, for Hildie's sake, I would." Comlan hid a smile behind a solemn mask. "But my help isn't necessary. Kieron already has that matter firmly in hand."

While his daughter sat back to consider the likelihood of his claim's truth, Comlan pondered the dire prospects she'd unknowingly roused with her talk of fairy interference.

Comlan feared that the events Lissan had reported were the result of an ominous threat growing stronger. The loosening of restraints over chaos might easily cause the bending of fairy spells into unintended results. And if that were true, anything could happen. For that reason, he was alarmed by even the faint possibility that Lissan's tale was actually a further portent pointing to a terrifying escape of dragons.

Once freed, the Dragons of Chaos would wreak devastation upon his world and, did the humans but know it, the mortal world as well.

Recalled to the present by the reassuring touch of Amy's gentle hand brushing his arm, Comlan reluctantly acknowledged that the time his grandmother had warned would come had now arrived. The time had come when he must share the legend with his daughter. He must share and ensure that she understood its import well enough to carry the warning to her world.

While descending the stone stairway from her bedchamber, Hildie wished she had some clear explanation of recent events to give family and friends gathered in the great hall. She paused in shadows beneath the arched opening into that vast chamber and took quick stock of the waiting scene.

Trestle tables had been disassembled. Their tops rested against stone walls with benches bracing them upright. Her father sat in a massive chair drawn near the central hearth, leaning forward over an improvised layout of the day's unsatisfactory quest while near the full measure of Ailm Keep's garrison crowded around to intently watch.

"There—" Rory jabbed toward the trencher representing a forest glade. "That's where we overtook the Shanahans only to learn my daughter had been taken from them as well."

"What next can we do to see Lady Hildie safely returned?" Grady's earnest concern robbed his amiable face of its usual pleasant smile. "There must be some action we can take?"

When her father's attention shifted to the speaker, Hildie knew by the grim expression on his face that it was time to alleviate their fears on her behalf and hastened into the hall.

"Worry no more for me, Papa." Hildie's quiet voice easily carried through the hushed hall.

Rory's gaze instantly flew to the plainly weary but unharmed young woman gliding across the floor swept clear of rushes to facilitate the crude map's creation. The next moment he strode forward to welcome her home with open arms.

Anxious to soothe his concern, Hildie responded to the hug with the strength of unmistakable love for her father.

As the two separated, guardsmen and houseserfs crowded around to enthusiastically greet their lord's miraculously returned daughter. Hildie was warmed by the earnest affection radiating from the core of these actions and responded with a gentle smile and solemn gaze encompassing them all.

Once the noisy excitement inspired by Hildie's return settled into the hall's more common dull roar, Rory motioned for her to lead the way up winding stone steps to the family's private solar.

Halfway up the first flight, the hall's din faded and steadily ascending footsteps became the only identifiable sound. Watching his daughter move gracefully upward, Rory reminded himself not to allow gratitude for her safe reappearance to dim awareness of the unabated and looming threat of a war.

Rory was all too well aware that Hildie's return in no way negated Lord Morven's ominous promise to wreak destruction for an imagined slight. The vicious Lord of Dunbarrough Keep was so deeply intent on a quest for vengeance (though for humbling defeat in a long-past conflict rather than a rejected suitor's feigned insult) that he would never back down.

Only as Hildie stepped into an oddly deserted solar gone chill for the lack of its usual cheery fire, did she think to wonder about her mother's absence. Why hadn't she been present to greet her daughter's return either in the hall below or here. Before Lissan could ask, her father drove the question from her mind by recounting the fearful events which followed her failure to appear at the betrothal.

Seeing an expression of dismay deepen on Hildie's face with his each succinct word, Rory took his daughter's hand and led her to sit across from him at the small table. Only then did Rory conclude his tale with the most alarming fact of all.

"Lord Morven will, of a certainty, return." Two pairs of midnight dark eyes locked in solemn agreement. "And, backed by the great might of his sovereign's armed troops, he will follow through with his threat likely to see both Connaught and Munster ravaged and drenched with blood."

"But I didn't intentionally fail to appear for the betrothal." Hildie was emphatic in stating this fact despite an uncomfortable suspicion that it could mean little.

"I am certain that Lord Morven is as well aware of that truth as you are . . . but it matters not at all." Because Rory knew how sharp were Hildie's wits, he was not surprised by her immediate nod of agreement. "Lord Morven has won what in reality he sought . . . an excuse to invade Connaught."

Hildie was relieved that her father not only saw the nature of Lord Morven's actual intentions but accepted her innocence—if not of a wish to evade the betrothal, then of the deed.

"It was I who led the search party that overtook the Shanahans. And it was I who consigned the pair to languish deep down in Ailm Keep's dungeons."

With a half smile and wry humor Rory sought to ease the strain while moving on to a different yet equally important matter and questions that also needed to be asked.

"But who took you from the Shanahans? Can you describe that knave?"

Hildie had dreaded this moment since being stolen from a father and son only to be deserted in a luxurious prison without portals. The answer was a truth no more sensible or useful than the response given to another query nearly the same. She'd had no better response after the failed attempt by the two faceless foes who had tried to spirit her away from Grady's protection on a return from Tuatha Cottage than she had now. But still she must try.

"I was left leaning against the trunk of a fallen tree while the Shanahans drank from a nearby stream." Resigned to performing this unavoidable task, Hildie gave a concise account of the most recent experience. "Then in a single instant I was swept up. In the next I was deposited inside a strange abode lacking either windows or doors."

Hearing the faint toll of a warning bell echo through her mind, Hildie abruptly paused to nibble her lip while more cautiously choosing her words. She'd come shamefully close to unintentionally revealing a secret visit by comparing her prison to the hill-home of Prince Gair and his wife, Mae.

"But never once"—with these emphatic words Hildie focused her father's attention on a more important subject—"did I catch the faintest glimpse of the one responsible."

Rory grimaced, gaze gone to black ice. As he had suspected, clearly these events were the doings of an otherworldly being.

"But how did you get from that 'strange abode' back here to Ailm Keep?"

"Kieron rescued me." The warmth of Hildie's smile and immediate response was more revealing than she would have knowingly allowed. "Just as he's done many times since I was a child."

Dark brows lowered into serious scowl. "And are you certain it wasn't Kieron who took you from the Shanahans?"

Rory had never been comfortable with the mercurial Tuatha, particularly not the mocking and too charming Kieron. And, considering the recent strange events threatening his daughter, Rory felt he had even less reason to trust Kieron now.

Hildie bit her lower lip harder. Twice in a depressingly brief period of time she had nearly babbled of facts far better kept to herself. Any hint of her true feelings for the magical Kieron would only increase her sire's distress—the reaction she least desired. And yet she had nearly assured her father that it couldn't possibly have been Kieron who stole her away from the Shanahans because she would've instantly recognized his embrace.

Focused on the difficult task of untangling

snarled strands of logic behind the likely unintentionally intertwined schemes of several culprits,
Rory failed to see that his next penetrating query
oddly soothed Hildie's uneasiness.

"After coming to you in the 'strange abode' that
served as your prison, did Kieron immediately
bring you back to the keep?"

Hildie suppressed a smile. Her father clearly
feared for her virtue while in Kieron's company.
Although her usual response to his opinions was
honest respect, now her solemn expression was
threatened by not merely a smile but a grin near to
bursting free.

Her father couldn't (and it was best that he
didn't) know the only danger lay in her earnest
wish for some grain of truth to support his suspicions. Nor must he ever learn how gladly she
would trade her chastity for Kieron's love.

"Kieron whisked me free from my opulent
prison home to Ailm Keep in the space of a single
heartbeat." Considering her recent private confession, Hildie was grateful that her father hadn't
asked how quickly Kieron had departed after de-
positing her atop the tester bed. She wasn't overly
confident of her ability to conceal a guilty grin.

With questions posed and answered but few solutions revealed, Rory returned to the hall where
his garrison waited to continue laying plans for the
defeat of Munster. Hildie, however, climbed to the
bedchamber where Amy now lay curled up on a
cot and lost in the deep sleep of innocence.

Lured by the promise of restoring slumbers and too weary to either completely disrobe or carefully put aside the outer gown easily stripped away, Hildie slipped into bed still garbed in the fine linen of her mist green chemise.

Safely unseen, Ardagh patiently waited and watched. While warriors below plotted tactics and strategies for battles to come, Ardagh reviewed the scheme he'd devised for laying false trails.

He was proud of his ploy and confident that a strategically "lost" amulet would mislead both fairy and human pursuers. Yet, not until Lady Hildie settled into slumbers as deep as the innocent dreams which cradled a toddler sleeping in a bed too near, did he again steal away the prize.

CHAPTER 11

In a mood as foul as the overcast morning, Rory swung up into his saddle. And, after accepting an amazingly docile bundle of auburn fur from Grady, he set off through bailey gates thrown wide.

While crossing tilled fields and entering the forest's jade shadows, Rory scowled at innocent green shoots and fresh sprouted leaves. It was assuredly the least destructive way to exorcise his frustration. Aye, frustration and a growing wrath over repeated assaults made not by a warrior in honorable battle nor born of war's animosities but launched against his blameless daughter.

Seun squirmed, demanding Rory's attention. A wry half smile tilted one corner of Rory's mouth. After his little Amy was carried to the morning meal asking where her sister had gone, the poor animal had followed him to Hildie's empty bedchamber. The older girl's absence seemed to have left the fox as lost as his youngest daughter.

Rory glared blindly at the path ahead, so familiar that he was free to concentrate on more important matters. And those two words precisely defined this morning's depressing confirmation of another abduction—the third! Rory deemed these persistent attempts to steal his daughter as a bad, a very bad jest that could only be seen as a viciously timed blow aimed directly at him. And even worse was the unwelcome fact that, as with the previous taking, his best hope for recovering the daughter who had simply vanished in her sleep still lay in the aid of otherworldly powers.

Lissan had yet to return from the visit to her father's Faerie Castle (not surprising since time in that realm didn't march with the measurement of human hours). But unfortunately her absence left Rory with but one remaining path toward his goal ... and it led to Tuatha Cottage.

At his approach, the dainty Maedra stepped through the ivy-covered structure's doorway. Curious, her golden head tilted to one side as she softly called out a welcome to him.

"Good morrow, Lord Rory."

"And to you." Rory's crooked smile deepened when young Eamon appeared behind his mother. Plainly Liam had already departed to take up duties assigned to him at the past night's meeting.

"I'm sorry ..." As Maedra spoke she unknowingly confirmed Rory's assumption. "You've missed

Liam. He has already set off to ensure the bridge's security, as you commanded."

While Maedra spoke, she motioned for her guest (along with his wife's pet fox) to enter into the comfort of a cheery home whose warmth was increased by cushions in bright hues and earthen bowls she'd filled with fresh flowers.

Rory gladly followed his hostess to settle in matching chairs which faced the central hearth. Eamon scooped up a fat pillow to sit cross-legged in the open space between adults while the fox curled into a tight ball of russet fur on the floor at the far side of Rory's seat.

"I never doubted that Liam would be faithful and prompt in his duties," Rory belatedly responded, gazing steadily into the fairy-born woman's lovely face. "But I fear you have misunderstood my purpose for traveling to Tuatha Cottage. It is not to seek Liam's aid that I've come."

Delicate brows slightly arched in a wordless question.

Face expressionless and wishing to simplify a complex explanation, Rory began. "The recent past has been a series of shocks—more and faster than I'd ever have thought possible."

Maedra nodded. "Liam told me about the Shanahans foolish abduction . . . and how their intent was thwarted by another's greater success." Her face went solemn. "He also told me of Lord Morven's threat and immediate departure."

"If it had ended even there," Rory's tone went

as hard and cold as ice, "matters would be less snarled, more easily untangled."

"But if it didn't, what happened?" Eamon's breathless question erupted from a child's bottomless well of curiosity.

"Eamon—" Maedra immediately chided her son for interrupting.

Rory waved a mother's needless apology aside to answer the boy's question with information he'd come intending to share.

"After darkness put a halt to our fruitless search for Hildie, we returned to Ailm Keep. Then while I met with my garrison to make preparations for defeating Lord Morven's threat of violence against Connaught, we were shocked—and relieved—when Hildie calmly descended from her bedchamber to join us."

"How did she get there?" Eamon demanded with a dubious frown. "I mean to her bedchamber without anyone seeing her?"

"Kieron," Maedra said without a heartbeat's hesitation.

"Aye," Rory agreed, steadily meeting her gaze. "Kieron brought her home."

Eamon's hazel eyes widened as he looked from one adult to the other. He had heard the name whispered before but, hard as he'd tried, never had he been able to learn more.

"Unconscious when taken, Hildie never saw her second captor. However, the chamber without portals that she described as the prison in which he left her was clearly no human's abode."

"Tuatha..." The quiet word fell softly from Maedra's tongue.

Rory nodded, oblivious to the boy holding his breath and hoping not to be noticed.

Eamon knew any action that reminded the adults of his presence was likely to bring an immediate end to this intriguing conversation on matters he was certain would never willingly be shared with him. Old tales of fairy magic and rumors of spells and sorcery he'd heard aplenty. Once he and Donal had even asked Lord Rory and Lady Lissan about them.... Donal's father had scoffed while his mother changed the subject.

Eamon's attention was abruptly summoned by the sound of his own mother's voice.

"Milord—" The faint sparkle in Maedra's eyes betrayed her amusement over the query that followed. "If 'tis not for Liam's aid that you have come to Tuatha Cottage, then for whose?"

Dark sapphire eyes held Maedra immobile. "As Lissan hasn't returned from visiting her father, *you* are my closest link."

Eamon's eyes widened. Their lord's wife was visiting her father? The parents of Lady Lissan were only spoken of in whispers and he knew for a fact that Donal had never met his grandparents.

To remind her guest of Eamon's nearness, Maedra gave her head a slight shake an instant before her gaze dropped to the boy.

"Recall the promise you gave your father, Eamon," Maedra said with a feigned sternness lightened by an affectionate smile for her son. "You promised you would and you must have the stable mucked out before he returns."

"Papa won't be home for donkey's years," the boy immediately protested, even though he knew his cause was doomed.

Maedra's scowl of gentle rebuke was sufficient to send Eamon on his way. Still, not until the cottage door closed on the boy's back did Maedra respond to her lord's request for aid.

"What would you have of me?"

Anxious to lose no additional time, Rory promptly answered. "Both Lissan and King Comlan must be told of these further developments. Aye, must be told that Hildie is missing *again* and this time under circumstances even more peculiar, more ominous than earlier attempted abductions."

"I fear your faith in me misplaced," Maedra ruefully confessed, earnestly wishing that it wasn't true. " 'Struth, there is nothing I would not willingly do for either Lissan or Hildie's sake. But, by giving my oath to live a human lifetime without them, my fairy powers were suspended."

Feeling his best chance for a quick end to Hildie's danger slipping away, Rory's face again went as cold and emotionless as granite.

"I can't cast spells." Shaking golden hair with deep regret for the discouragement caused by her words, Maedra began to flatly list her regrettable limitations. "Nor can I either summon or visit any among the Tuatha de Danann."

The fox resting quietly at Rory's feet abruptly rose and gave auburn fur a healthy shake.

A brilliant smile replaced Maedra's wistful expression. This very special animal had waited for the perfect moment to remind her of its own peculiar abilities.

"I have no magic," Maedra repeated, each word clearly enunciated. "But," she triumphantly added, "Seun assuredly does."

Sparks of renewed hope lit Rory's dark gaze while Maedra wasted no moment on unnecessary explanations. Rather, she rushed to open the door and wave Seun out with a confident command.

"Fetch Kieron."

"Seun." Startled, Kieron glanced down at the animal who'd suddenly appeared in the Faerie Castle's crowded great hall and now sat on her haunches within a handsbreadth of his feet.

On returning from his amulet-empowered rescue of Hildie, Kieron had been anxious to share news of that deliverance and, more importantly, the circumstances that strongly suggested Tuatha involvement. But he'd chosen not to intrude on the rare visit between King Comlan and his daughter.

Bending to scratch auburn fur behind the fox's pricked ears, Kieron murmured, "Did Hildie send you to fetch me, girl?"

Responding with a sharp yelp, Seun spun in a

tight circle that ended facing the Faerie Castle's impressive but unnecessary double doors. The fox's actions were an effective demonstration of an anxiety to lead him somewhere.

Had Hildie already been overtaken by renewed peril? A sharp stab of alarm pierced Kieron's usual impervious shield. He calmed this surely unnecessary concern for Hildie's safety with memories of how often she had dispatched the fox to fetch him for a rescue from feigned dangers she could easily have overcome alone. But still . . .

Kieron motioned for the fox to lead the way and immediately followed without pausing to either consider alternatives or take the wise precaution of leaving a message for his king.

All too quickly Kieron found himself standing in the middle of an unanticipated destination—Tuatha Cottage. And, even more disconcerting, he faced the summoner least expected—Lord Rory O'Connor.

"Hildie has been kidnapped." Rory wasted no moment on useless pleasantries.

"Nay—" Kieron's deep gold brows met in a fierce scowl. "I whisked her free and delivered her safely to Ailm Keep well before dawn."

"So you did." The single sharp nod of a dark head added weight to this reluctant confirmation. "But your rescue doesn't change the fact that Hildie was later whisked away . . . again."

"Can't have been . . ." Kieron instinctively refuted the unwelcome statement which not only put

his elfling in imminent peril but threatened to confirm the damning involvement of fairy. Despite
pride in his race's magical strengths, he didn't want
to admit as fact that such powers had been wielded
to hie Hildie from her tower bedchamber.

"Hah!" Rory instantly and vehemently ridiculed
Kieron's refusal to acknowledge this simple human
reality. "Then tell Hildie's baby sister how else it
could be possible that she awakened to find her
sister's bed slept in but empty."

Kieron's scowl was fierce in the fleeting instant
before he vanished.

Rory glared at the vacant space where Hildie's
much admired "hero" had so recently stood—leaving her father bereft of the help he'd come to the
cottage seeking.

"Lady Hildie was here in the dark hours of last
night but gone by dawn?" Lissan gently demanded
of Grady while her heart sank anew.

Having just returned from her father's magical
court reassured that Kieron would easily rescue
Hildie, Lissan found this third (or was it the fourth)
taking of her stepdaughter in so brief a span of
time confusing—and disheartening.

Grady earnestly nodded while repeating his report. "Lady Hildie came down from above and entered the hall to tell Lord Rory to worry no more."

That Hildie had descended from a higher level
in the keep rather than arriving from without

seemed to Lissan certain proof that a being of magic had delivered the girl home.

And yet, how could Hildie have then disappeared as mysteriously? Having never shared her husband's dubious view of the Tuatha de Danann, Lissan didn't want to think any member of that race might be involved in such vile shenanigans, but . . .

"Where is Lord Rory?" Beneath the weight of growing concern Lissan's voice was utterly flat. Though rare for him to linger in the keep during daylight hours, save for regularly scheduled meetings of the lord's court, she felt certain her husband would be actively searching for the trail leading to Hildie.

Perceiving nothing amiss in her query, Grady responded with unusual coolness. "Gone off to Liam's cottage—alone."

Recognizing Grady's disapproval of these arrangements, Lissan sent him a reassuring smile even while questioning his statement.

"Alone?"

"All alone." Grady grimaced but promptly corrected himself. "Alone, save for the little fox that Lord Rory insisted on carrying under one arm even though Seun would have followed him afoot."

Lissan slowly nodded. Although she had just returned from a journey and was certain her horse was likely as weary as she was, it was equally clear that another trip was necessary.

"Pray have my mare led back into the courtyard," Lissan told the young guardsman with more calm than she actually felt.

The simple fact that Rory had taken Seun and ridden alone to meet with the only other being with blood bonds to the fairyfolk was sufficient to raise Lissan's trepidation. It convinced her that she, too, must go to Tuatha Cottage.

"Take me, Mama." Donal had entered the hall and slipped unnoticed to his mother's side. There, certain of her destination, he insistently tugged at her hand. "Please take me? Please, Mama?"

Lissan's loving gaze dropped in an instant to her pleading son but soon lifted in search of her children's nanny—the comfortably plump matron standing just behind the boy. A generation past Maud had looked after Rory and his brother, the first Donal. At Rory's request Maud had returned and Lissan gladly welcomed her help with the newest O'Connor children.

"Where's Amy?" Lissan was inspired by Donal's arrival to ask about her ever-curious but surprisingly absent youngest daughter.

Maud's answer came with a gently reproving smile. "Allowed to linger in the hall with her father, the poor, wee gosling went to bed far, far too late. And yet still she awoke with the dawn." A much valued servant, Maud offered bold opinions . . . but cushioned with affection. "Now, at last Amy is asleep."

Lissan could hardly miss the gentle caution against awakening the child and willingly complied. "Then, Maud, I will happily leave Amy in your good care while taking Donal away with me."

As the older woman nodded, Hildie turned to issue one more command.

"Grady, please have Donal's pony brought to the courtyard, too."

Kieron focused on Hildie's amulet with the full force of his powerful will.

The next instant he found himself on the edge of a woodland path where the branches of ancient, gnarled trees entwined overhead to severely limit sunlight. Holding himself invisible to the human guardsmen already there, Kieron watched as their leader sank to his knees and reached out to retrieve an object sparkling even amidst the forest's dense, green gloom.

"Saints!" the guardsman gasped in amazement while studying the ring plucked from a thick carpet of tangled grasses. On its delicate band bloomed a golden rose of exceptional beauty. And cradled by petals at the blossom's heart lay the dark fire of a multifaceted sapphire.

Disgust burned in the aqua eyes beneath Kieron's deep scowl. The spell of finding he'd cast over this amulet hadn't failed him. The amulet he had found . . . but not the precious elfling on whose finger it should safely reside!

Clearly the ring had been taken from Hildie and strategically placed here to lay an intentionally misleading trail.

But laid by whom?

Glaring at the innocent vegetation which had pillowed the charmed piece, Kieron irritably acknowledged that the surrounding multitude of green blades remained undisturbed. The only sign of any creature passing near belonged to the guardsman who had bent to retrieve Hildie's amulet.

Kieron's eyes blazed with dangerous fires ignited by this frustrating additional proof of forbidden fairy interference in human matters. He was horrified by the possibility that one of his breed might be responsible for Hildie's abduction.

CHAPTER 12

Though sensing a larger company inside Tuatha Cottage than when he had left, Kieron showed fine disregard for Lord Rory's discomfort with magic by instantly reappearing in their midst.

But Rory was equally unwilling to waste time on trivial matters. He immediately rose to his feet and strode forward to boldly face the newcomer with a harsh demand.

"What did you learn?" Rory wanted to know everything that Kieron had discovered, but he definitely did not want to hear by what mystical means such information had been secured.

True to his mercurial nature, Kieron gave a deep laugh even while providing an answer unwelcome to them all.

"Nothing—I learned absolutely nothing."

Seeing that in response to this announcement her husband's irritation was dangerously near to over-boiling, Lissan quickly stepped forward and moved to his side. By slipping her arm through his, Lissan successfully provided an interruption sufficient to ease the rapidly escalating pressure.

Kieron's expression shifted in a brief instant from its feigned merriment to a frown of honest self-condemnation and deepest irritation for the wretched truth behind his statement. Disgust over that fact grated in Kieron's voice as he added details to his unhappy report.

"I learned nothing save that the perpetrator is a wily foe adept at keeping opponents off stride both by the unexpected haste of repeated actions and the laying of false trails."

Although Rory was limited to a human logic ridiculed by fairy, that much he already knew. His black ice gaze scrutinized the being now proven a disappointment. Kieron a magical creature? Hah!

"Come, Kieron," Maedra sweetly invited while gliding forward to take his hand, determined to aid Lissan's attempt to soothe strained tensions. "Join Liam at table and I'll pour you a mug of ale."

Maedra motioned Kieron to an empty seat at the trestle table permanently set up on one side of the small chamber. She then moved to fetch another mug even though it was most unlikely that Kieron would imbibe of a mortal brew so inferior to his customary beverage in the Faerie Realm.

"We must go." Rory's sharp words sliced through the cottage's air of determined hospitality. He was as annoyed by the inappropriate moods of

Hildie's apparently useless Tuatha guardian as by his lack of either worthwhile information or useful plans to see the girl safely returned.

"Papa—" A young boy's voice suspended hasty preparations for that departure. "Please, may I tarry the night with Eamon?"

Rory's attention immediately shifted to his son. Because the adults in the cottage had been focused on discordant words exchanged between two mature males, they had remained oblivious to the whispered conversation of two boys and were startled by Donal's unexpected request.

Maedra stood holding an ale-bearing pitcher near her husband's right shoulder when the question in Lord Rory's sapphire glance won an immediate response from Liam.

"Donal is always welcome in Tuatha Cottage," he quickly assured his lord.

Comforting himself with the likelihood that the Tuatha visitor would surely soon depart, Rory nodded silent gratitude to the couple abruptly landed with an unexpected overnight guest.

"Once back in the keep I'll make arrangements to ensure that someone will come and fetch Donal home tomorrow."

Though unwilling to confess it aloud, Rory was relieved. Without this distraction, the ever curious Donal would likely pry into matters best left alone. Thus, by leaving their mischievous son behind to be entertained by trusted friends, he and Lissan would be free to focus on methods to see their elder daughter's peril defeated.

After Donal's parents left for Ailm Keep and Eamon settled into a discussion of strange events and pending dangers with Kieron, the two boys huddled on a bench at the room's far side. By earlier sitting still as mice, they'd been permitted to observe inexplicable deeds never before revealed to them. Now while adult voices droned on, the youngsters resumed their own whispered deliberation of other urgent matters.

"Don't you see?" Eamon demanded in an earnest undertone. "Kieron appeared out of nothing just as suddenly as that odd stranger vanished at the cavern's edge."

"Aye, he did, didn't he...." Donal's emerald eyes sparkled in delight.

For a fleeting moment Eamon thought his friend was referring to Kieron's inexplicable arrival but Donal's next words showed him the foolish error of that too hopeful assumption.

"Old knave is a pigeonheart. He just vanished soon as I threatened to tell my father about him." Donal clicked his tongue in a further emphasis of contempt for the stranger's action—cowardly even if a sorcerer's spell.

Despite this unintentional diversion from his goal, Eamon doggedly continued. "I think we must tell Kieron about our discovery and the stranger who tried to scare us away."

Donal cast the other boy a dubious glance. He

was loath to share their discovery with anyone and even less anxious to risk mentioning their encounter with the odd intruder.

"If we tell anyone what we've seen and done, the only thing likely to happen is that we'll be saddled with guardians who would be certain to put an immediate end to our forest adventures."

"But Kieron is different," Eamon argued. "Surely you understand how, since his habits are as magical as the stranger's, it must be safe to share our secrets with him?"

Cautious nature overriding a child's natural urge to boast about exciting events, Donal slowly shook his dark head even though he knew his unwillingness would badly disappoint Eamon.

Eamon was impatient with his friend's avoidance of an obvious subject demanding attention—mystical deeds and ancient practices. He had heard rumors about Lord Rory's strict command that such superstitions never be mentioned to his children—but this was different. This was important.

Intending to challenge Donal's stubborn refusal to question weird events, Eamon attacked the subject directly and with words threatening to rise to a betraying level of volume.

"I think," Eamon loudly hissed, refusing to permit Donal's doubts to bring an abrupt end to their truly important discussion, "that Kieron is part of the Tuatha de Danann."

"You believe in the fairy breed?" Donal asked in mock horror.

Eamon immediately scoffed at the answer. "Are you saying you don't?"

Donal shrugged, unwilling to flatly answer this blunt question one way or the other. For long moments the two boys stared steadily into each other's eyes, neither ready to yield.

"I suppose we've got to tell Kieron," Donal at last allowed. "Leastways, if he is Tuatha, he'll know how to banish that horrid stranger."

"And," Eamon added with a meaningful glance, "if that odd intruder had some part in your sister's disappearance . . ."

Donal grimaced. His friend had put into words the fear he had kept carefully and firmly suppressed but now perversely welcomed for the glimmer of hope it provided.

"Surely, if it's true," Donal whispered, "Kieron will be able to force the wretch to see Hildie safely returned."

Though the boys had finally agreed upon an action, the chance to put it into motion didn't arrive until after Liam departed to resume his duties and Kieron settled into quiet conversation with Maedra.

Then, still straddling the bench shared with his friend, Eamon sent Donal a meaningful glance while tilting his bright head toward two adults seated at the table against the opposite wall.

Donal fully realized the gesture was meant to urge him into accepting that this was the best opportunity to take action that they were likely to be given. And, despite lips tightening to hide continuing uneasiness, he nodded.

"We've made a great discovery," Eamon's announcement cut through the adults' murmured conversation. "Donal and I wanted to show Papa, but he's too busy. Can we show you, Kieron?"

Maedra was surprised but more amused than offended by her son's choice to share this adventure, this discovery he clearly found exciting with someone he hardly knew.

Kieron was just as surprised to have been selected for this honor. Yet because the boys greatly reminded him of the adventurous child Hildie had been, he couldn't resist the temptation. He rose to his feet and with an affectionate smile motioned for the youngsters to lead the way.

Silence reigned while the trio—Kieron flanked by a boy on each side—moved beyond the herb garden which grew outside the cottage door. Indeed, it wasn't until well after they had entered woodland shadows that Donal abruptly divulged the nature of the exciting discovery he and his friend had made.

"There's this crack in the ground—"

Excited and too impatient after lingering so long for the tale to begin, Eamon couldn't wait for his friend to give a sedate explanation.

"And inside it," he broke in, "there's a big, big cave."

Donal flashed Eamon a glance of disgust for the

interruption even as he continued. "We meant to go exploring—"

"And we're still going to do it!" Eamon asserted, so intent on the prospect of this tantalizing adventure that he nearly tripped over a branch wind-torn long ago from a nearby tree.

"Aye," Donal instantly agreed although indignation simmered in his previously cool tone while he added yet another unpleasant fact to this account of their bewildering experience.

"We were in the process of making plans for that adventure when a peculiar stranger tried to shoo us away!" The memory was every bit as annoying to Donal as the actual event.

Eamon dashed forward and spun around to plant himself firmly in front of the wondrous companion who surely must be a sorcerer.

"You've got to tell that vile wretch to stay away from us and tell him not to dare defile our cave by entering it!"

"Tell him?" Kieron's brows arched. "Me?"

"Surely you know him..." Eamon firmly answered without hesitation. "Donal and me were certain that you must."

"Why?" Kieron asked another, equally succinct question while his penetrating aqua gaze steadily scrutinized Eamon until the boy shuffled nervously beneath its power.

"Because—" Donal joined the discussion with a matter-of-fact observation meant to strip away useless queries along with their unimportant answers and settle the matter. "The stranger vanished as suddenly as you appeared in the cottage."

While smiling wry acceptance of the boy's clear reasoning, Kieron made a simple request. "Describe your odd stranger's appearance to me . . . in detail. Elsewise how will I know which of my many acquaintances you would have me warn away?"

The youngsters exchanged a meaningful look before simultaneously launching into the task with remarkable accord.

"He was old," Donal promptly asserted.

Nodding earnestly, Eamon expanded on that simple fact. "And he had lots of long, long, white hair that didn't look like it had been touched by a comb in donkey's years."

Kieron's half smile deepened at this repeated use of the colorful term which must be a favorite of young Eamon's.

"But the weirdest thing about him was his eyebrows," the dark-haired boy solemnly stated. "The outer ends slant upward so sharply that he looks like a demon for true."

This last piece of news put a scowl on Kieron's face, as he motioned for the boys to continue leading the way to their discovery. With the youngsters moving ahead, he was free to ponder a dangerous possibility, nay, an ominous likelihood. The culprit's identity seemed all too clear—and a confirmation of King Comlan's bleakest suspicions.

Before Kieron had devised a worthy scheme to

deal with this newly revealed opponent, an enthu-
siastic Eamon intruded.

"There it is!" The bright-haired boy rushed to the
edge of a crevasse, fairly dancing in his excitement
and brightly grinning.

"Isn't it strange, a big split in *flat* ground." Donal
was quick to point out details difficult to explain.
"It's as if the whole of the earth beneath our feet
was hollow."

In response Kieron neither smiled nor frowned.
Rather, his face went utterly impassive. While for
the boys these facts understandably held the thrill
of unknown adventures, for him they signaled the
increasing strength of dreaded dangers he had
wanted to believe could be forestalled.

To Kieron this split in the earth strongly suggested that a perilous breach had opened between
the human and fairy planes. Worse, this discovery
raised the ominous probability that the Dragons of
Chaos had escaped through the opening to ravage
both worlds. Sinking to his knees at the edge of the
ragged tear, he peered inside—an alarming view.

Kieron stood again, and Seun immediately
slipped between his feet to begin picking her way
down into the chasm.

"Both of you—" Kieron issued a stern order to
the boys. "Go back to fetch your parents and lead
them here with all possible haste."

As Eamon and Donal retraced their path, disappearing into forest shadows, Kieron whisked
himself to the cavern's floor.

Watching unseen, Ardagh exulted in Kieron's foolish mistake. His schemes for revenge were progressing infinitely more smoothly and at a brisker pace than he could've hoped.

In an instant the darkness below had nearly swallowed Kieron. Yet still Ardagh waited. The other's integral golden glow could be dimly seen moving farther and deeper into twisting passages. Not until even its faintest glimmer disappeared did Ardagh quickly move to securely seal the cave shut.

Ardagh found it wryly amusing that he'd a superstitious human to thank for his success with this task. Throughout the ages mortals who both believed in and feared the power of fairy also knew banes able to halt it—and by ancient teachings had woven mats of hazelwood to ward off the Tuatha de Danann.

As fairy himself, Ardagh could neither break nor move such a barrier with his own hands. However, by donning the guise of an elderly human and feigning great fear of the Tuatha, he had convinced a mortal farmer to trade such a mat for two barrels of salt pork. Then, in deference to his seeming infirmity, the fool mortal had even loaded it onto Ardagh's cart.

Standing now on the cart's seat with a forked branch in hand, Ardagh found it a simple chore to shove over one side the mat woven of green hazelwood withes. It landed, as intended, across the breach. Then with a great deal less effort—indeed, a simple wave of his hand—he rolled a massive boulder to lay across both mat and cavern opening.

As a last step, Ardagh wielded carefully strengthened and long refined magical powers to hide any betraying sign of the cave's existence. He seamlessly concealed the blocked opening's position by blending apparently untouched greenery into surrounding vegetation, even creating the illusion that ancient mosses layered one side of the boulder.

A strained hush had held the great hall of Ailm Keep in a tight grip since the return of its lord and lady . . . without their eldest daughter.

While the returning pair removed and hung cloaks on iron pegs driven into a stone wall near the incoming door, Maud watched from a comfortable chair close to the central hearth, cradling the still drowsy Amy in her arms. On their entry she'd cast a darkling glance of warning toward Grady who had looked ready to dash forward and demand news from a lord plainly wrapped in illhumor. Under Lord Rory's deep glower, even houseserfs trod softly and in handling utensils took care not to rattle or clang them together.

Lissan's stress was deepened by this unnatural quiet, and she gracefully turned toward her husband with a simple request.

"I beg a boon of you, Rory." A loving smile lent emphasis and power to the soft plea. "Pray come with me to our solar. There are things I must share with you . . . alone."

While eavesdroppers might've heard intimate promises in Lissan's words, they struck Rory hard with guilt. He had been so selfishly intent only on his own woes and displeasures that he'd spared no consideration for the woman he loved. Even worse, though he had sent Lissan on a quest after Hildie was taken from the Shanahans, he'd failed to ask about results made more important by the latest abduction.

The climb from hall to solar seemed endless to Lissan but she forced her impatient temperament to bide its time until they'd settled into seats facing each other across the small table.

"You saw your father." Rory stated it as fact not question yet waited for his wife to answer.

"Aye." Lissan's quick smile flashed. "And my mother, too."

Rory gave his dark head a brief shake. Though rare, he occasionally caught glimpses of a fairy's contrary nature in Lissan. And this response, which totally ignored the unspoken but obvious question, was assuredly a prime example of that inherited trait.

Lissan immediately repented her unwelcome, obtuse answer and attempted to repair the damage by giving the reply he sought.

"I have news—no, not news—but information that you must hear even though you will likely find it hard to actually believe." Lissan reached across the table to rest her fingertips on one of the hands Kieron had laid palm-flat on the table.

"Unfortunately your hesitation to credit it for the truth that it is will rouse a serious danger, one my father tells me I must try to avoid by helping you understand and accept."

A faint frown drew Rory's brows together. This sounded ominous.

"I followed you to the cottage, anxious to immediately tell you what I learned," Lissan continued.

"But to say anything with the others present would have meant explaining where I'd been and with whom I had talked."

The frown deepening into a fierce scowl on Rory's face validated the solemn truth in Lissan's next statement.

"I knew you wouldn't appreciate having the details of my mission to the Faerie Realm spoken of while both Donal and Eamon were present." Lissan cast Kieron a winsome smile.

" 'Struth." Rory nodded, grateful for his wife's cooperation in upholding even this decision that made her so uneasy. He was fully aware that it was her father's support of the choice which had convinced her of its logic: The next generation would be best served by shielding them from the barrage of uncomfortable questions certain to follow knowledge of the mystical kingdom and its inhabitants.

"And I thank you for that." Rory turned his

hand over to capture the delicate fingers resting above and brush a kiss across their tips.

"So, I waited," Lissan continued with a loving smile. "Waited, even though I feared that if I didn't tell you soon, it might be too late."

Dark brows arched but Rory said nothing to further delay her objective.

Lissan immediately launched into a solemn re-telling of the ancient legend of the Sidhe. She gave special care in describing their struggle to defeat and then imprison the terrifying Dragons of Chaos. It was an amazing tale but so simply told that she feared Rory would discount its devastating importance. Earnest voice aching with her anxious desire for his understanding, she concluded the story.

"And beneath that Circle of Stones sealed by a powerful spell engraved in the near forgotten Og-ham script, the Dragons of Chaos have for centuries remained muzzled, impotent . . . but frustrated and raging against their bonds."

"If Chaos has been so long contained," Rory asked the most logical question, "why did you fear this telling might be too late?"

"The recent trembling of the earth cracked that seal." The corners of Lissan's mouth lifted only slightly with a forlorn smile. "Chaos has begun ris-ing to the surface, threatening both the Faerie King-dom and our world."

It was clear to Rory that Lissan found cause for grave concern in this mystical tale and tried to be sympathetic, yet his disbelief in superstitions and distrust of any supernatural creature left him exceedingly dubious. Besides, it was surely logical for mythical dragons to be easily overlooked when compared to Hildie's very real and immediate danger.

CHAPTER 13

I am brave, I am brave, I am . . . By repeating this litany of desperate bravado Hildie staved off panic waiting in the dark.

Hildie sat on a chill floor of solid rock, grateful for leastways the limited warmth provided by the delicate cloth of her abduction-abused chemise. And though it was impossible to judge time while alone in this eerie prison utterly devoid of natural light, it seemed to Hildie as if she had been here for days and days and days and . . .

With a smile of self-mockery doomed to remain unseen, Hildie acknowledged how impossible that was. Without water she would be dead long before that much time passed. She named herself a fool for permitting the regrettably morbid thought which accomplished merely an increase of her thirst.

"This must stop!" Hildie ordered herself, speaking aloud solely for the comfort of hearing a human voice—only to learn that under her current circumstances it *wasn't* reassuring.

In this apparently vast chamber the sound of her own words was ominously increased by the deep, hollow echo which followed even the faintest noise. It was that echo, together with the pervading musty odor, which pointed Hildie to an eerie possibility. She strongly suspected that she had somehow been delivered to either the same cavern or another very like the one containing the Ogham inscribed Circle of Stones.

Mind filling with memories of their visit to that mysterious site, cherished as was every moment spent in Kieron's company, Hildie earnestly wished for the comfort of his presence now.

In the next instant a familiar bark seemed to echo. Wishful imagination? Hildie quickly tamped surging hope down with the likelihood that this was no more than an illusion inspired by thoughts of the beloved male who had given her the magical fox.

A soft, warm bundle landed on Hildie's lap—a wiggling bundle of fur that surely must be Seun. Despite the black void of her surroundings, Hildie's gaze instinctively dropped to the animal. To her amazement and delight, she could make out the faint outline of her treasured pet.

Hildie's dark eyes lifted to peer through black gloom and focus on a faint and distant source of light—Kieron's gently glowing aura. The warm smile on her petal soft lips bloomed ever brighter as with every step he drew nearer.

"Ah, there you are—" As Kieron dropped to his knees at Hildie's side, the vision of sweet temptations inadequately covered by flimsy and too revealing garb instantly struck him, hard, with an aching awareness. To temper this response, he quietly teased, "Playing hide and seek again?"

Though elated by the arrival of her hero, her rescuer, Hildie was at the same time slightly annoyed that the first action Kieron took wasn't to sweep an imperiled lady into a fervent embrace but to tease her. She answered his foolish banter about silly games, likely aimed at safely consigning her to childhood, by launching a mild counterattack.

"If you intend to ask, as you did last time, how I arrived at such a destination . . . don't."

Kieron was pleased by his elfling's undimmed spirit and threw back his head to heartily laugh. Because Hildie rarely reacted as most humans would, he found her a constant delight.

In his resounding amusement Hildie found a warm encouragement vastly unlike the icy alarm earlier inspired by the echo of her own words.

"I won't," Kieron wryly assured her. "It would be a sorry waste of our attention since the way you arrived is far less important than devising a method for how we both escape."

A startled Hildie demanded, "What do you mean, *how we* escape?" Seun had led Kieron to rescue her so often that she'd assumed . . .

"As I explained once before—" Kieron's deep voice took on a rare serious tone. "I cannot safely whisk even myself, and far less you, to freedom through walls of natural stone."

"Then I was right." Hildie found an unexpected boon in this confirmation of at least one assumption. "I thought this must be the same cavern where you brought me to view the Circle of Stones."

Kieron's mocking grin seemed to flash the brighter for surrounding darkness. "In that you were both right and wrong."

Certain that this apparent riddle was yet another example of the Tuatha's delight in all things unpredictable, Hildie cast Kieron a reproving glare but patiently waited for the explanation she was confident would follow.

"'Struth," Kieron added, shifting to comfortably sit rather than kneel at her side. "We are in the same maze of caves but not, I fear, anywhere close to the Circle of Stones."

"Maze?" Hildie frowned against an uncomfortable bewilderment.

"Aye, this"—Kieron absently waved at their surroundings—"is all part of the vast labyrinth of caverns first inhabited by the Sidhe. It's this network of passageways which the Sidhe later imbued with sufficient power to form a secondary layer of confinement meant to thwart any possible escape by the Dragons of Chaos."

With this reminder of the dragons a terrifying

thought struck Hildie. "If our first visit to this sub-terranean world wreaked havoc on the restraints controlling Chaos, will our current intrusion fur-ther weaken those bonds?"

"Aye." Kieron reluctantly nodded, wishing for Hildie's sake that he dared completely flout the rule of Faerie which commanded that all honest human questions be truthfully answered. "Further weaken them we surely have."

Hildie recognized the sincerity in Kieron's an-swer but an unfamiliar, darker tone in his deep voice increased her concern and inspired a further question, nay, a quiet demand.

"What are you hiding from me?"

Silent moments passed while Kieron gazed steadily off into endless shadows, plainly unwilling to answer. But, proud to be just as stubborn as he was, a determined Hildie persevered.

"I already know that Munster means to soon in-vade Connaught in punishment for my choices." Hildie reached out to clasp Kieron's strong arm, strengthening her entreaties for him to provide a thorough response. "Is there more?"

"Aye." Again Kieron nodded, turning his full and potent attention to the gentle colleen tempt-ingly near. "The war spawned by Munster's false pride is as nothing compared to the devastation threatening to soon overtake us all."

As if she'd been granted a faint reflection of his magic by her love for this male possessing exceptional powers, Hildie clearly heard and understood what Kieron had yet to say.

"The Dragons of Chaos are slipping free of their bonds." Kieron laid a powerful hand reassuringly over the dainty one still resting atop his arm. "They have already begun to move unfettered between your world and mine."

Hildie firmly bit her lower lip but even that action couldn't successfully stifle the moan of regret for her part in seeing this wickedness set loose to ravage all she loved.

Kieron moved to lift Hildie into his lap and wrap her securely in his arms. He wanted to absorb Hildie's every pain and ease her every distress by bearing it in her stead.

As powerful arms closed about her, Hildie welcomed the fierce excitement of this longed for embrace and with a revealing sigh melted closer against Kieron's broad chest. In complete trust, Hildie snuggled nearer and nearer still until beneath her ear she heard the pounding of his heart. Its cadence was almost as rapid as the beating of her own.

Knocked off-kilter by the sweet colleen's unexpected and very likely unintended sensual assault, Kieron shuddered. Attention seized by his reaction, Hildie glanced upward.

Kieron's intense aqua gaze moved slowly over his elfling like a whisper-light caress. Thick masses of ebony hair framed her heart-shaped face while unblinking fascination filled equally dark eyes so steady that it seemed certain they would burn a brand of possession into his soul.

Here within the circle of his arms lay a small and tender wrong, a forbidden temptation from which Kieron knew he should yet couldn't look away. The lovely woman clad in the inadequate garb of her abduction was far too enticing. His teeth clenched tightly against Hildie's innocent allure.

In instinctive comfort, Hildie stroked trembling fingers over Kieron's rigid jaw. Yet, even while being cradled within the magical fire of her beloved's strong embrace, she was absolutely certain that all too soon he would attempt to set her aside like a child or, worse, a sister.

Desperate not to lose this precious opportunity, Hildie scolded herself to fight his rejection. And toward that end she recklessly dove headlong into the hungry blaze which only he could so easily ignite and lifted her mouth as an offering for the ravishment of his.

A deep groan rumbled up from Kieron's depths but rather than accept the gift freely surrendered, he laid a searing trail of tantalizingly slow kisses. With his lips he traced down the elegant arch of a throat bared by her uptilted chin until he reached the vulnerable dip at its base.

Dazed by the wild sparks erupting beneath Kieron's lips, Hildie's head fell back over his arm. When his mouth first brushed the tip of her chin and then moved to torment her with a succession of brief caresses at the corners of her lips, her hands curled over broad shoulders. She was deeply aware of restrained power in the iron thews beneath his tunic's incredibly fine weave.

Kieron lifted his head and from a breath above gazed down into Hildie's sweetly flushed face. He took a terrible delight in the unshielded hunger in passion-dark eyes.

Shivering uncontrollably, a small moan escaped Hildie. That wordless plea for the deep kiss withheld won from Kieron a slow and dangerously potent smile which in turn summoned from her heated memories of their previous embrace—hot, exciting, and a pleasure near too deep to be borne.

Deaf to the fading call of a good conscious perilously close to defeat, Kieron bent to taste anew the berrywine of Hildie's mouth. He gently brushed across her lips, gradually enticing them to open for the heat of joining.

By twining dainty fingers into a golden mane, Hildie sought to hold Kieron's mouth steady and claim the firestorm of his devastating kiss.

Kieron answered the call by fitting his mouth completely to Hildie's, deepening their kiss to a hungry feast even while gently shifting the delicious curves of her form to lie stretched out against the long length of his powerful body.

Gladly releasing the last shred of reality, Hildie welcomed this stunning embodiment of her every dream and sank into a mindless haze of desire. She flowed more fully against him like water downhill. Wild excitement trembled through her as she arched into his strength and helplessly shifted to brush lush curves across muscles she could feel rippling in answer to her desperate movements.

Kieron crushed the tender prize closer and for feverish moments gave her the unrestrained ardor of his devouring mouth. But the liquid fire coursing through his veins demanded more. He wanted to touch every texture, taste all of her honeyed sweetness, and swallow her into the endless possession of his arms. While never relinquishing the delights of her mouth, Kieron's hands tangled in the insubstantial cloth of the chemise barring him from his goal.

Lost to sensible thought amid a vortex of blazing hunger, Hildie recklessly yielded to the hot pleasures of caressing hands. They slowly pushed her lone covering upward, shifted her until in one smooth motion he pulled it off over her head and cast it aside. His hands then returned to lay a searing path up her sides from the gentle swell of hips to the sensitive flesh beneath arms clinging to him.

Kieron feared they had already gone too far into forbidden delights. But, although deeply aware of the wrong in his actions, he couldn't prevent his hands from smoothing down Hildie's graceful back to curve over her rounded derriere. He urgently lifted and tenderly fit her softness intimately into the changed contours of his own body.

Caught in a dark, welcome whirlpool of unfamiliar, stormy sensations and dangerous, aching hungers, Hildie innocently writhed against his throbbing need. At the same time she pressed un-tutored but passionate kisses on his throat and over the fine-spun cloth covering his chest.

When Kieron went as utterly motionless as only one with magical powers could, Hildie's heart sank. It seemed that by her inexperience she had blundered. Hildie's lips moved in a silent cry against this defeat in her quest for a desperately sought prize.

In the next moment Kieron sat up and with one fluid motion stripped off his own tunic. Stunned by the magnificent view of his powerful torso, breath caught painfully in the back of Hildie's throat but burst free in the next instant as he lay back down at her side and pulled her close again.

With a curious, honest passion, Hildie slowly moved her mouth across the tempting planes of the massive chest rising and falling heavily beneath the hesitant touch of her lips. Then, though sensing a potent danger growing, she grew bolder.

Kieron permitted Hildie's exploration, cradling her in his powerful arms yet restrained the urge to crush the teasing siren urgently to his aching body. But when her tongue found a flat, masculine nip-ple, a growl rumbled from his throat. He could bear no more and rose above her supported by one arm. The aqua flames of heavy-lidded eyes burned over a tempting form, desperately studying the delicious, yielding colleen innocently offering all of heaven.

This was wrong. Kieron's brows met in a golden

scowl. Its blot on his honor was bad enough but the irradicable stain left on hers would be infinitely worse—and something one with his powers should have sufficient control to forestall.

Steadily meeting his gaze, Hildie reached up to again wrap her arms around his strong neck, twining her fingers into cool gilt strands. She gently tugged until with a harsh groan he lowered his head to renew their devastating kiss. Filled with aching hungers for an unknown end, she savored the texture of his back's hard planes while his lips moved to her throat and from there, at an agonizingly slow pace, trailed sweet torment over breasts that swelled to meet them.

All too soon Kieron recognized in the pliant, sensuous body twisting against his own painfully taut form a plea for the surcease that only he could give. And all his proudly held control fell to ashes before her tender demands.

Still, though prey to a desire more powerful than any he had known, Kieron was determined that this woman beloved suffer no pain to mar the memory of this, likely their only forbidden moment of piercing satisfaction. He deeply regretted a rare limitation. Anywhere but here he could in an instant have provided a down-filled mattress and silken bedcovers worthy of the treasure Hildie was. And anywhere but here he could've rid himself of the last unwanted garment as quickly. Instead he had to withdraw his arms and pull away long enough to physically divest himself of impeding chausses.

Kieron restrained his own wildly insistent need to trace with fingers and lips the incredibly soft and nearly luminescent skin of lush curves. With stinging pleasure he teased her every sense until every line and curve burned beneath his touch.

Hildie moaned but with pleasure as Kieron slid one leg between her silken thighs. And when he shifted to lie full atop her slender length, she welcomed this new and exquisite intimacy, dove headlong into the raging flames of a hungry fire.

Rising on one forearm, Kieron watched a face passion-rosed and ebony-framed for the first hint of discomfort as with his free hand he gently tilted Hildie's hips to make possible a tender joining.

Desperate to be carried deeper into the consuming blaze, Hildie instinctively clasped Kieron's hips nearer. And as his body merged with hers, the accompanying flash of pain seemed to her merely a natural part of passion's fiery fury.

Glorying in the feel of Hildie sweetly trembling beneath his desperate hunger, Kieron rocked them both deeper into an ever hotter conflagration. Hildie clung to the source of tormenting delights while he carried them both beyond sanity to the point where storm and fire converged, crashing together in an explosion of searing sparks.

Resin-soaked torches lit the way as two boys led a small party through the night forest's gloom. It hadn't been a simple task to obey Kieron's order. Even the call for the Lord of Ailm Keep and his wife to come back to Tuatha Cottage had been time-consuming. Added to that was the time necessary for their return. But with perseverance the pair proudly led their parents toward the site of the great discovery only to come to an abrupt halt on finding a most unpleasant sight.

"Where did that come from?" Eamon demanded, aghast and distressed.

"How did it get there?" Donal echoed his friend's consternation but with a broad streak of suspicion.

"Is this, this boulder your great discovery?" Rory asked, trying to hide his annoyance over so foolish a demand for time already in short supply what with necessary preparations to meet the looming invasion. It was that threat which made necessary the full contingent of warriors who had accompanied them here, though holding back to lend two families privacy.

"Nay!" Promptly denying guilt in the stupidity of such a deed, Donal's dour expression was a remarkable duplicate of his father's. "Our discovery lies below where that monstrous rock now sits . . . but didn't only hours past."

While Rory skeptically met his son's earnest gaze, Liam stepped closer to the obstruction and, holding a firebrand near, studied the ancient mosses covering one side. That the lichen spread in a natural pattern up one side alone was surely proof that it had stood here for eons.

" 'Struth, Papa." Eamon trailed his father to the boulder. "A peculiar chasm lies on this very spot, below that massive stone. 'Tis a gaping split in the earth which opens into a vast cave."

Donal picked up the tale. "After we led Kieron and Seun here, the fox promptly found a path down. Before Kieron followed, he told Eamon and me to fetch our parents to this place."

"And now we're here," Rory flatly stated. "What would you have of us?"

"We thought Kieron would be waiting to meet us," Eamon forlornly answered for his friend. "But with our cave sealed by that wretched boulder, he's likely trapped beneath."

Maedra moaned softly . . . a quiet sound but enough to win the attention of her companions. The boys couldn't know how sadly probable was their assumption. Although in part descendants of fairy, they had been shielded from knowledge of the Tuatha. Thus they didn't know how easily fairy powers carried that breed through hollow hills. Even less would the boys understand that this cavern of their great discovery, if of natural stone, would be impenetrable to Kieron.

In response, the other three adults exchanged glances which spoke wordless volumes. They all recognized the serious dangers implied by these developments. Even Rory, although he had never wanted to believe, knew enough of the Tuatha de

Danann's magical powers not to discount the tale so earnestly believed by the two boys who had related it.

Rory slowly stated a deeply regretted fact. "There seems nothing we can do here ... not tonight ..."

Silence uncomfortably reigned, as no one was willing to yield against inexplicable forces.

After endless moments Rory proposed the only viable action. "I suggest we return to our homes. Then on the morrow with sleep-refreshed minds we'll meet again to consider this ill and its possible cures."

Rory didn't say it aloud, but he also wanted private time to consider what impact these strange happenings would have on the looming threat from Munster.

CHAPTER 14

Kieron looked down into his slumbering elfling's winsome face, intense gaze lingering on lips bright as sun-kissed cherries and just as sweet, only witness their slightly swollen curve. Her head was pillowed on the cape of an extraordinary hue which he had rolled into soft comfort. And although the ebony satin of her hair was a complete antithesis to his kind's standard of golden beauty, it was far lovelier to him.

Summoned from dreams spiced by heated memories, Hildie slowly became aware of an unaccustomed warmth pressed against one side and a weight wrapped about her midriff. While tantalizing scenes from recent events seeped into conscious thoughts, she wiggled nearer to this inexplicable heat's source with a contented smile of happiness.

Hildie's thick lashes lifted, allowing eyes of midnight blue to caress the fantasy come true and lying heart-stoppingly near. Though his wretched oath would assuredly prevent him from confessing its reality, Kieron's expression betrayed all the impossible emotion she craved.

Slowly turning to fully face Kieron, Hildie wrapped her arms about his strong neck and reached up to press soft kisses against his jawline before nuzzling his firm throat.

Not even Kieron's strong willpower was equal to the task of curbing an immediate response, and he brushed his lips across the top of Hildie's dark, tangled curls. But, by the lesson learned from his recent dishonorable actions, he inwardly acknowledged the imperative need to raise a firmer shield against any further betrayal of his oath. Toward that determined goal, he quietly reminded his far too beguiling love of their still waiting challenge.

"We must find our way free."

This quiet admonishment, gently spoken though it was, thrust Hildie back into the chill world of harsh reality. Her family was in danger—a danger loosed by her misdeed, a danger that she must strive to see securely contained once more.

Helplessly gazing into the sweet face of a forbidden love, Kieron couldn't help but notice that his words had abruptly extinguished the sparkle in sapphire eyes. He wanted to instantly undo the damage, but couldn't. Not while the need to begin and succeed with their search was so vital.

The sight of Kieron's expression going solemn

worried Hildie. Had her fears spread to him like some vile plague? Hoping to prevent even the possible threat of further contamination, she hastily asked, "How did you get here?"

"Tch, tch." Kieron cast her a stern look of mock censure. "I thought we agreed never to ask that question."

"Nay." Dreary spirits lifted by his teasing words, Hildie's lips also tilted upward. "*You* agreed not to ask."

"No matter." Kieron smiled, pleased to see at least a flicker of Hildie's fire revived. "I am willing to answer and share an odd story of the trail that led me here."

Despite having been obliquely chided, as if she were a child, Hildie took no offense. How could she be annoyed with the lover whose recent passionate embrace made it impossible for him to ever again claim that he viewed her as either a child or a sister. And now she had that memory to cherish against the future rejections she feared would inevitably follow.

"So," she cheerfully inquired, "tell me just how you found me?"

Sun-bright hair brushed Kieron's broad shoulders as his head tilted to one side. "Eamon and Donal shared a tale with me, the story of a 'great discovery' they'd made."

Wielding the gentle whip of a slight frown, Hildie prodded Kieron to move on toward the direct explanation she sought.

"The boys were anxious to show me their find," Kieron teased with cryptic words and a wryly amused half smile.

Hildie's frown deepened and Kieron relented.

"They led the way to a ragged split in the earth's surface . . . truly a remarkable discovery." He chose not to mention the strange figure who had tried to shoo the boys away.

"It was your pet fox who promptly found a path down." Kieron cast a quick glance toward the small animal stretched out and dozing beyond their feet. "I whisked myself to the cavern's bottom and from there Seun led me to you."

"If Seun and you descended through a *split in the earth*—" Hildie immediately identified what seemed to her an obvious solution for what he'd led her to believe would be a serious problem with no simple answers. "Then to claim our freedom surely all we need do is retrace your path."

Meeting her hopeful gaze with a peculiar half smile, Kieron slowly nodded in agreement. "After we have found that opening, I should be able to whisk us both back through it."

Kieron chose not to point out that it was exceedingly unlikely to be as simple as that. First, he feared any retracing of his own steps through the complicated maze wouldn't be easily done. Second, he had a bleak suspicion that they'd been deliberately trapped here with all exits blocked.

Hildie beamed, unwilling to peer too closely into the details of this earnestly desired boon. Reaching for her pale green chemise, she gracefully rose and quickly pulled the delicate garment over dark, passion-tangled hair. She spared but a single rueful thought for the once lovely garment's current sad state.

"Ready, milady?" Having donned his clothes while she dressed, Kieron formally proffered Hildie his arm as if prepared to escort a grand and beautiful queen into a royal gala.

Resting dainty fingertips atop the fine azure linen of his sleeve, Hildie gave a merry smile while, to sweep an elegant curtsy, she lifted the tattered skirt of the undergown now her only gown and poorly treated in the abduction.

"Let's away."

Thankful for Kieron's glow which provided sufficient illumination to their journey through ominous shadows and down uncertain paths, Hildie admonished herself not to let growing thirst or hunger dampen the dauntless spirit of adventure.

With Seun in the lead, they made remarkably few false turns into passages going nowhere. Yet Hildie had silently begun to suspect their quest doomed even before a frustrated Kieron announced that they had reached their destination.

"There it is . . . or was."

Sapphire eyes followed the wave of Kieron's hand to focus on a pile of rocks plainly fallen from above. She peered up to the rubble's undeniable source—an odd and unwelcome sight.

It seemed that a mat of loosely woven wicker

was performing an impossible task. The flimsy webbing appeared to support a massive granite boulder rolled across to block Donal and Eamon's great discovery—a "split in the earth."

"The opening is closed," Hildie acknowledged, "but it's plainly not solid, natural stone." She paused to send him an arch smile. "Surely you can whisk us both through it?"

"Nay." Disgust coated Kieron's response. "The knave responsible for closing this breach chose the elements of his barrier well."

While striving to hold a growing sense of hopelessness at bay, Hildie cast Kieron an inquiring glance which miserably failed to hide her dread of a disappointing answer.

Kieron responded to his elfling with a grim smile. Though he desperately wished it were possible to reassure Hildie with easy solutions, such lies would all too quickly be exposed.

"Neither I nor any other of my race can move, break, or pass through hazelwood."

Hildie's attention immediately lifted to the barrier overhead. Though not obvious to her, Kieron clearly knew that the wicker mat had been formed by interlacing withes of hazelwood.

While she studied the obstruction Kieron continued, "We're trapped."

Shocked sapphire eyes immediately flew to the speaker, earning an explanation. "I can't pass through the wicker and you can't possibly move the massive boulder beyond."

Slow grin blooming, Hildie made a suggestion. "But what if I break the wicker? With it in pieces couldn't you either move the boulder or simply whisk us through it?"

Kieron's brilliant smile reflected the delight he took in the sharp wits of his sweet love. She had quickly and rightly identified the parameters of their best opportunity.

"We can certainly try." Wrapping large hands around Hildie's tiny waist, Kieron easily lifted her high above his head. But even with her arms stretched up as far as she possibly could, Hildie wasn't able to reach the wicker matting.

Recognizing the only alternative, Kieron took one pace forward and slightly to the side before lowering Hildie's feet to rest on a base of questionable stability partway up the pile of rubble.

Hildie immediately realized what she must do and cautiously began to climb, careful to test each foothold before trusting it to support her weight as she moved on to seek the next. When at long last able to wrap fingers around hazelwood withes, she tentatively started to pull and then vigorously tug in earnest. Unfortunately, thin branches green when cut and woven remained pliable and not easily broken.

It required much time along with a good many scratches and harsh bruises to soft skin for Hildie to succeed in pulling the first few pieces apart. And considerably more time passed before the edges of the still boulder-obstructed opening were fringed with splintered strips and ragged fragments of once woven matting.

After Hildie jumped safely down into Kieron's waiting arms, she wrapped her own about him and gazed triumphantly at her handiwork above.

"Now you can whisk us free."

With an equally delighted grin of quiet praise, Kieron nodded. He then buried her winsome face against his throat.

Hildie expectantly waited to be transported in an instant. Waited ... and waited a little longer ... and longer ...

Brows lowered in a disgusted frown, Kieron glared up at the shadowy surface of charcoal-hued granite. He found himself caught between rage and the horrible shock of being unable to either transport them through or move the barrier.

Although the atmosphere of the labyrinth itself imposed restrictions upon the Tuatha de Danann, *this* inexplicable limit of powers *shouldn't* be possible. And yet it clearly was.

"Sire." A startled Rory hastened forward to greet the young man stepping from the entry tunnel's shadows into the great hall.

"Cousin—" Before Rory could drop to one knee in homage to his king, Turlough affectionately swept him into a hearty bear hug. "Welcome me not as your sovereign but as your student, as the pupil you taught both how to rule and how to protect our kingdom's peace through military might."

"Plainly I failed in the most basic of those duties." Taking a step back, Rory feigned sternness to chide this much-loved apprentice. "You have already forgotten the first lesson I toiled so hard to teach: Do not merely accept but demand the oath of fealty from *all* subjects . . . no exceptions."

With the last word, a determined Rory knelt and bowed a dark head to this cousin, once his young student but long since become a man and battle-tested warrior. He respectfully renewed his honorable allegiance to Turlough, King of Connaught.

"Fealty accepted," Turlough announced, resigned to yielding against Rory's stubborn will now as so many times before. "That done, can we turn our attention to the infinitely more important issue of the kingdom's defense against invasion?"

Even more anxious than this king to waste no further moment, Rory promptly responded. "I have assigned rotating patrols to ride our border with Munster both day and night."

"And what news did their most recent report bring?" Turlough plainly sought reassurance that he had arrived in time to aid in building adequate defenses to block the threatened attack.

"Several advance incursions have been made but little damage done. . . ." Rory's gaze went hard and glittered like black ice as he added, "Save for the abduction of my daughter."

"What?" Turlough's own eyes narrowed to dangerous slits. "The wicked knaves dared to make off with your daughter?"

"Someone did," Rory flatly stated, inclining his head while giving a slight shrug, as if it were possible to dislodge that uncomfortable burden.

"Someone?" Turlough settled on this strangely ambiguous wording. "Do you actually doubt the source of these blackhearted villains?"

After pausing for a long moment, wondering at this hesitation from the cousin so rarely uncertain, Turlough gently probed further. "Surely you have no enemies among your own?"

Though giving his dark head a quick shake, Rory's smile was tight. "I am positive that the villains rise not from among mine nor any other of yours. However, I also fear 'tis possible that they are not from Munster either."

Turlough's fierce scowl deepened. He didn't like riddles, never had, and assuredly not while serious threats loomed all too near.

"I swear that my lord husband is not being as intentionally obscure as it seems," Lissan softly promised their king while stepping forward to drop a graceful curtsy. " 'Tis only a matter of Rory's continuing reluctance to address the issue of my father, his kingdom, and subjects."

As uncomfortable with the topic of the Tuatha de Danann as Rory, in the twelve years since Lady Lissan's inexplicable arrival, Turlough had nearly succeeded in putting it from his mind. Not that he wished to in any way denigrate the wondrous and most effective aid Rory's wife had provided to bring an abrupt halt to that last threatened invasion but . . .

Rory was dismally aware of the hall filled with too many eavesdroppers anxiously waiting to hear every revealing word and quickly proposed a retreat to the family solar's privacy.

Once inside the cozy chamber warmed by a small blaze stoked and waiting each evening, the two men immediately settled at the small table. Before joining them there, Lissan brought a smoldering twig to light the array of wax tapers placed on a silver platter which would reflect their glow.

Turlough lost no time in posing a simple but most important question. "Which of your two daughters was taken?"

"Hildie," Rory responded, appalled by recognition of his own witless failure to make this pertinent point crystal clear.

With a grim smile, Turlough acknowledged the fact that he had already assumed to be true. Indeed it had seemed obvious considering that the coming confrontation had been precipitated by Lady Hildie's long delayed choice of bridegroom.

"You can see that," Rory continued, "if the arrogant lord from Munster were responsible for Hildie's disappearance, he would be unlikely to return with an armed demand for blood retribution to repay the insult of his suit's rejection."

"Except," Turlough calmly reasoned, "as you pointed out in the letter sent to inform me of this threat, the impending invasion seemed Lord Morven's intention from the outset."

Rory warily nodded.

"Then," Turlough continued, "what is there to prevent the wretch from taking a greater satisfaction in seizing both the blood of battle and the woman his people will believe is its cause?"

" 'Struth, what you suggest is possible," Rory agreed yet went on to explain why and what made it less likely. "But deeds have been done which cannot be easily accounted for in human terms."

Turlough's brows arched. Again they had returned to the subject of involvement by one—or perhaps many more—of the Tuatha de Danann. Was it more probability than mere possibility?

"Let me list for you the strange events," Rory began. He spoke of the mysteriously disappearing brooch, faceless abductors who moved without touching the earth, and a monstrous boulder appearing from nowhere to seal a vast cavern.

"Lady Lissan." A solemn Turlough spoke directly to his hostess. "Has your father any explanation to offer for these strange deeds?"

"I spoke with him before this last and only successful abduction. He assured me then that Kieron would always rescue Hildie no matter the nature of her takers."

"Kieron?" Turlough's single word was a query which Rory hastened to answer while Lissan firmly bit a bottom lip, annoyed with herself for having spoken the name without explanation.

"Kieron is the Tuatha guardian who King Comlan chose and assigned to protect my daughter Hildie, his human niece."

Though completely unfamiliar with the tale of a human niece, Turlough remained focused on the core issue to ask a further question.

"Then this Kieron failed?"

"Kieron . . ." Rory's voice was ice-cold. "Is missing, too."

Seated on a golden throne with his wife at his side, King Comlan's brows met in a fierce scowl while he gazed across the uncommonly quiet crowd in his Faerie Castle's great hall. He was worried, deeply worried . . . an emotion nearly unknown and extremely uncomfortable for any member of his race to endure.

Unfortunately, worry was but one among the myriad of nasty symptoms caused by a new and devastating affliction proven contagious and rapidly spreading its ghastly infection throughout his realm.

Comlan's subjects had flocked to him, expecting a simple remedy to heal what had weakened and restore that which was lost. But, although Comlan knew the cure's source, neither he nor any among his subjects possessed the necessary ingredients to blend and distill that desperately longed for elixir.

"I beg you, sire—" An adolescent male threw himself to the marble floor at his king's feet, unwilling to believe the most powerful among them couldn't repair whatever had gone wrong.

"Tell me, I beseech you, what spell to cast able to undo all the harm I've caused my own family with my folly."

Golden head tilting to one side, Comlan studied the earnest youngster, one of his favorites. Perry was an excellent example of fairy ambiguity what with his contrary choice of interests. The youth still caught between child and adult was equally known for his joy in silly pranks and the beautiful melodies he composed and skillfully coaxed from his harp.

"What action did you take that needs to be undone?" Comlan solemnly inquired, hoping with dubious confidence that the nature of Perry's problem would prove less difficult than it sounded.

"I intended no ill, truly." Sincerity glowed in Perry's bright gaze. "I acted only to secure leastways a brief span of solitude in which to work out chords and rhythms for a new melody."

"You're a fine tunesmith, Perry." Amethyst softly praised the rarely serious boy gone solemn. "The whole court, in truth, the entire realm looks forward to hearing the songs you create."

With a stern inquiry Comlan returned the conversation's focus to the boy's dilemma. "To secure this coveted solitude, precisely what actions did you take?"

"I banished my pesty brother and two little sisters to the Ivy Maze. . . ." An uneasy shrug accompanied the confession. "But I only meant to leave them there for a little while ... asides, they like playing games of hide and go seek among the maze's ivy draped walls."

"So, you whisked your siblings to the Ivy Maze?" Raised brows demanding an answer, Comlan waited until the boy nodded a response before requiring another. "But now you have discovered it's no longer so simple to bring them home again?"

Golden hair whipped about a young face as Perry fervently nodded. "Please tell me what I must do to safely transport them back?"

"Do you know where the Ivy Maze grows?" Comlan quietly asked.

"Of course." Perry cast his sovereign a doubtful glance for this surely odd logic. "How else could I have taken them there?"

"Ah, but—" Comlan began while his wife's lips gently curled. Amy strongly suspected the point her husband meant to make and wasn't the least surprised when it was confirmed by what next he asked.

"Can you *physically* move between this site and that ... without magic?"

"I suppose." Perry scowled. "But why waste the effort?"

"Necessity," Comlan flatly stated, no hint of humor in his steady gaze. "And because, if you are sincere in the wish to undo your harm, 'tis that action you must take. Go of your own self to fetch and lead home those you sent away."

With this statement Comlan rose to his feet and by that action instantly commanded the hall's full attention while his somber expression spread a hush over all. Because he had no cure for their malady, he had postponed further demoralizing his subjects with bleak facts. But now by this most recent ailment, Perry's lost powers, he realized it must be done.

"The time foretold has arrived." Deep words held an ominous ring. "Upon us now has fallen the perilous time of darkness and restless chaos."

The final word spawned a quiet storm. Gasps of alarm joined gusts of denial to erratically sweep through the great hall. Comlan permitted an unimpeded roll of rash ridicule for the ancient legend to jostle against daunting terror and fearful worry for its cause.

Only after he was again the focus of his subjects' silent and unwavering attention, did King Comlan clearly state the nature of their peril.

"Too many among you have dared to doubt the truth of ancient legends." He slowly looked from face to face and found a depressing number of sheepish gazes dropping, unable to meet his eyes.

"Our shield against catastrophe has been sorely weakened by failure to respect and guard its strength." Under the weight of this criticism for an undeniable wrong the audience was mute. "The Circle of Stones has cracked and the bonds our ancestors imposed upon the Dragons of Chaos are disintegrating."

"But then they'll escape!" Perry gasped.

Comlan's smile was bleak. "They have already begun slipping free."

"No!" Perry's desperate denial was quickly echoed by many others.

"It's too late to dispute undeniable realities." Cynicism lent Comlan's lips an unusually deep twist. "We have all seen and experienced proof that by the Dragons of Chaos's very nature control is lost."

The dubious expressions on the faces of too many made it plain to Comlan that the pride his race took in ambiguity had blinded them to the sad truth that Chaos would as readily steal their powers . . . a wicked feat already begun.

"With the courage of our ancestors, look deep into the ever increasing tide of recent unpleasant events." With all the power at the heart of his important message, Comlan sternly admonished the crowd. "Bravely admit that you have felt the dismal effect of our powers beginning to erode."

By the sharp-honed wits of their ancient breed those gathered acknowledged that the peril had become very real in its erosion of fairy control. It was that loss of command which had caused a cascade of dangerously unpredictable results. All too many spells and bindings had ended in embarrassing examples of negligible strength or had demonstrated a disastrous potency twisting into completely unintended results.

Although the Tuatha de Danann had ever cherished things never of a certainty one way or another, that most definitely did not apply to the mastery of their own magical abilities.

"What can we do to seal the breach in the Circle of Stones?" An elder fairy whose powers were already weakened by advanced age, and had now been seriously diminished by spreading chaos, moved to join Perry in facing their monarch within two paces of his throne.

"Even had we the ability to mend that crack, as Perry earlier asked, why waste the effort?" Comlan's question was met by scowls of determined misunderstanding, forcing him to repeat himself in simple terms which the dullest feeblewit wouldn't dare misconstrue.

"For what reason would even a *mortal* farmer close the gate after his cattle had escaped?"

Though Comlan's statement was hardly encouraging, others steadily stepped forward to directly approach their sovereign, desperate hope glowing in eyes pleading for a solution.

As unofficial spokesman, the boldest among them addressed the king. "But if it was our ancestors, the Sidhe, who subdued and imprisoned the Dragons of Chaos, surely we are capable of capturing and seeing them again safely restrained?"

"*If* it was?" Scalding disgust bathed Comlan's terse response.

The errant speaker immediately dropped to his knees and in wordless remorse bowed so low that his forehead nearly touched the floor.

"Rise," Comlan commanded, annoyed that his own loss of self-command had permitted the sort of harsh ridicule he had always despised. With threatening gloom tightly leashed he issued a flat statement. "Regret for your doubt is no more useful than would be penance paid by even the whole of the Faerie Realm."

As bid, the one kneeling rose to his feet but, despite an obvious uneasiness, tentatively pursued his goal . . . the goal of them all.

"Then tell us, sire, what we can do to mend our wrongs and defeat the menace freed."

Penetrating eyes firmly holding his questioner's gaze, Comlan responded with a cheerless answer. "Neither you, nor I, nor any other among the Tuatha de Danann possesses that power."

Born in many throats an anguished sigh rose up against this deplorable fact.

"The dragons learned from past mistakes," Comlan felt compelled to explain. "And by experience with the Sidhe, their instincts cautioned that to remain free the fairy powers which first leashed them must be diluted, sapped and withered into feeble impotence."

"Then we are truly doomed?" Perry gasped, even the resilience of his youth wavering against this bleak prospect.

Rather than answering directly, Comlan simply said, "Only the legendary Seunadair, wielding magic not of fairy born, can save us from destruction."

CHAPTER 15

Mounted on a powerful black steed halted amidst a hilltop glade, Liam gazed wishfully toward the eastern horizon. Though the hour of dawn was upon them, thick, dark clouds hung so low that their gray mists defeated the bright hues of sunrise . . . an ominous start to the new day.

"I can hardly believe that Lord Morven would actually dare to attack Connaught." By the uncertainty wavering beneath the bravado of Grady's bold statement it was clear that in his heart he knew the lord from Munster would gleefully launch precisely that dastardly assault.

"Of course he will." Liam cast the younger man a look of long-suffering patience. " 'Tis only a question of when he'll appear."

Grady's shoulders sagged, not that he had expected a different answer from his lord's most trusted knight . . . but a flickering glimmer of hope had survived. Now even that faint spark had been snuffed out by Liam's flat statement that the long-strained and tenuous relationship between king-doms had truly degraded to such a dangerous level.

As a child during the struggles of the last major conflict, Grady's skills had never been battle tested, and he feared they would prove unequal to the challenge. His self-doubts made the prospect of im-minent war disheartening and more.

"Nay." Liam shook sun-streaked hair in disgust while continuing his gentle lecture. " 'Tis our awareness of Lord Morven's ability to easily con-vince King Muirtrecht that the time is ripe for an-other invasion which makes it so vital that these patrols along our border be seriously undertaken." Liam's hazel eyes held Grady's full attention. "Aye, undertaken and continually, relentlessly pursued."

"But what can the knaves from Munster possibly expect to gain?" Grady rashly asked though he al-ready knew the dismal answer to his own mono-tone, rhetorical question.

Liam sent Grady an incredulous glance. True, his companion on this patrol had been a mere boy when, more than a decade past, Munster had launched its previous attempt to invade Con-naught. But how could even a child have missed the lethal purpose behind that fearsome confron-tation?

"Oh, I know." Grady hastened to correct the un-intended impression that he was in sorry truth a complete and utter witling. "I know they mean to humble Connaught under Munster's rule but do they really think the people of our kingdom will meekly bow to their control?"

"Not merely bow to their control." Again Liam shook his head. "Rather, they want to see the whole of Connaught fall victim beneath the swords and arrows of Munster."

As if in proof of those words came the zing of an arrow shot from the dense woodland shadows behind. And with its deadly force knocked Liam from his horse's back.

"Liam!" Grady screamed, instantly swinging down to belatedly throw his body as shield across the fallen leader.

A glum Hildie gazed up beyond the highest rock atop a haphazard pile of rubble to the tattered shreds of matting she had toiled so hard to rip apart . . . to little good purpose. Determined cheer threatened by looming discouragement, Hildie nibbled her lips to cherry brightness.

Gaze rarely staying far from Hildie, Kieron couldn't help but see her resumption of this nervous habit and worried that it signaled deepening despair. Cradling the alluring colleen nearer, he rued the limitations this mystical site imposed on powers which elsewhere he could wield to distract her.

Holding Hildie safe in a strong embrace, Kieron settled down on the cavern's stone floor and leaned back against a solid granite wall with her draped across his lap.

"Don't fret," Kieron gently admonished his tender elfling. While fighting to see Hildie returned to her family he yet dreaded the victory which would put her beyond his reach—and rightly so. Kieron dutifully worked toward that end by trying to rekindle the spark of her fiery spirits.

"We *will* find our way free."

"I fear for my family." Hildie turned full into Kieron's embrace, wrapped her arms around his neck and mindlessly nestled closer against his broad chest while gazing up with earnest concern.

"Because of me, war looms over them . . . and the prospect of famine and death hovers above the whole of Connaught."

"You are not—" Kieron began, intending to remind Hildie that Munster's threat was nothing compared to the infinitely more powerful menace of Chaos restlessly moving unchecked across the land.

Delicate fingertips pressed his lips to stifle further words. And, after even that instant of further thought, Kieron was grateful for Hildie's action. She had prevented him from repeating his warning that the mortal kingdoms faced a hideous and far more serious danger than simple human warfare. No matter that it was a certain truth, Kieron would protect his elfling from that greater fear for as long as he could.

Having thoroughly misinterpreted what Kieron

had meant to say, Hildie had acted to forestall an expected but useless assurance that she wasn't solely responsible for those looming dangers. And to prevent him from again addressing that same topic, she rushed on with her own arguments.

"*Yes*, war will come because of my stubborn refusal to wed a human rather than the incredible, golden being I love." The aching softness of heartfelt emotion lay revealed in Hildie's midnight blue eyes by Kieron's natural glow.

Kieron was awestruck by the purity in this vision of love. That it was backed by his precious elfling's open declaration was a temptation too powerful for Kieron to withstand. Not only did her assertion of love scatter words of comfort from his thoughts but it completely overmastered his honorable resolve not to further compromise her virtue.

Hildie saw Kieron's jaw go tight. Was he offended by the declaration of love from the mere human he had so often warned was forbidden to him? Fearing he would withdraw cherished comfort to immediately set her aside, she snuggled even closer.

Determined to savor every moment of this stolen embrace, Hildie's thick lashes descended to tightly close sapphire eyes. By this action Hildie was freed to drink in the intriguing masculine scent beckoning her nearer still to the big body doing thrilling things to her senses.

Knocked further off-balance by the feel of Hildie's delicious body melting against his, Kieron took terrible pleasure in her willing surrender. And, even while scorning himself for a fool, he willingly surrendered to the temptation of the delicious but forbidden fruit that she undeniably embodied.

Sweeping one hand down the long arch of Hildie's back Kieron saw them both slide sideways to lie facing one another on the cavern's smooth, cool floor. He pulled her tighter into his embrace and aligned her hips more intimately against his. Combing his fingers through the luxuriant, black satin of her hair, he cradled Hildie's head to hold her mouth steady as he took a kiss, long and slow and hard.

Beneath his sensuous assault, Hildie moaned. And at that wild sound, Kieron deepened their contact into a sweet torment. Hildie clung to the center of this fiery whirlwind, curious hands savoring the strength of his broad back.

Kieron's mouth shifted. First he brushed hot pleasure tantalizingly over her cheeks and then found the sensitive hollows beneath her ears. When Hildie's head dropped back, laying her long, tender throat vulnerable, Kieron was no more able to resist this innocent invitation than he'd ever been able to refuse her plea for any boon.

Tongue tip trailing fire down to the dip at the base of her throat, Kieron savored skin like rose petals and took wicked delight in the wildly accelerated pulse beneath.

Gasping at hot sensations beyond bearing, Hildie

was overcome by the liquid heat flowing through her veins and wound small fingers into Kieron's golden mane, urging him nearer still.

"Although I might honorably hesitate to intrude upon tender intimacies shared between a lawfully wed husband and wife . . ." The taunting statement trailed into silence.

Chill words splashed over the passion-tranced pair like cold water fresh from the icy North Sea. Kieron instantly sat up, shifting Hildie to lie across his lap with her blush-brightened cheeks tucked into the curve beneath his chin. His aqua eyes, gone more piercing jade than soft azure, narrowed on the sneering being newly arrived.

"When, Ardagh, have you ever in your exceedingly long existence hesitated to take any wretched action that you believed would suit one or all of your many ill-begotten goals?"

"You wound me, Kieron." A mocking frown tilted Ardagh's oddly slanted brows even farther askew. "And after I came, at no small pains to myself, to issue a well-intentioned warning to the tasty morsel who is your . . . companion."

Having recovered leastways some small measure of her usual composure, Hildie found herself host to a strong desire to view the source of this unpleasant voice. To win this goal, she pulled just far enough away from Kieron to glance over her shoulder. Her curious sapphire gaze settled on a peculiar figure with flowing white hair and devilish brows.

In silence, an impassive Kieron coldly stared at

their obvious foe, refusing to yield Ardagh even the limited satisfaction of hearing him question the reference to a warning.

Ardagh plainly intended to compel his audience's complete attention as he stepped forward. By this action he fully entered the circle of Kieron's pale glow and allowed his gaunt and oddly angular figure to be more completely revealed.

The elder male's movement startled Kieron with the realization that this long-banished member of the Tuatha strangely lacked the same luminescence. Indeed, Ardagh seemed less substantial even than the very real human colleen at Kieron's side— almost as if he were merely a specter, a wraith.

Did Ardagh lack the physical aura of magic by choice, as when a fairy takes on a human guise to walk unnoticed through the mortal world? But, no, that logic couldn't apply here. No, not here in the presence of another member of his race. . . .

"Milady," Ardagh addressed Hildie. "Your fears for family and friends, while commendable, are utterly useless."

Fanned by Ardagh's warning with its proof that the fiendish cur had lingered near and unnoticed long enough to eavesdrop on a private conversation, Kieron's ire flamed higher. Kieron gritted his teeth as the temper set to simmer by knowledge of a spy, reached fury's boiling point with recognition of a further and more dastardly wrong. The wretch had carelessly mangled the tenuous shield Kieron had begun building to protect Hildie against unpleasant truths.

Ardagh ignored the younger male's raging animosity to focus the ice storm of his full attention on the dainty Lady Hildie.

"The Dragons of Chaos, which *you* loosed"—Ardagh's oddly intense gaze drilled into Hildie—"soon will consume the earth and all that it holds . . . your family, your kingdom—and you."

"And you, as well!" Kieron instantly snarled in return.

Although Ardagh quickly slipped through shadows into anonymous darkness, his wicked laughter seemed to echo endlessly, trapped in the black labyrinth's chambers and corridors.

As Kieron glared after the departing figure a further curious puzzle arose. The Ardagh he remembered from the past had delighted in unexpected, dramatic arrivals and departures ever accompanied by swirling scarlet robes. Strangely, the man just gone wore garb so drab that Kieron couldn't now describe it to anyone. Moreover, though Ardagh's arrival had assuredly been unexpected, his departure—actually *walking* into the shadows—was far from dramatic. Why?

Concerned for her companion's vile mood, Hildie took a cue from her half sister's habits in an attempt to distract Kieron.

"I'm thirsty," Hildie plaintively stated, gently tapping against a masculine cheek where an anger-knotted muscle throbbed.

Startled, Kieron glanced down into serious sapphire eyes that failed to hide the silver glitter of humor glowing in their depths. He laughed and the sound was reassuring to Hildie despite its dark chord of self-mockery.

"Anywhere save here in this cavern—" He shook his head in feigned disgust with her request. "I could wave my hand and in a single moment produce for you buckets of the purest, most refreshing water or flagons of sweetest ambrosia."

Hildie's brilliant grin flashed. She'd spoken only to distract Kieron from his obvious fury and plainly she had succeeded. Not that she wasn't thirsty because she was. She really, really was.

"Here the best I can do in an instant to quench your thirst is promise you that throughout these caverns small streams flow into vast rivers . . . and I know how to find them."

Despite the large number of people gathered in the great hall for the day's last meal, tension held the level of conversation to a dull monotone. Seated next to Rory at the high table, Lissan gazed morosely at the wooden trencher they shared. It was piled with savory foodstuffs . . . but unappetizing. Instead she reached out to lift her goblet and slowly take a sip of wine.

This was their second evening meal since Hildie's abduction and the whole of Ailm Keep was demoralized by a complete lack of clues to aid in the young woman's rescue. Spirits flagging, Lissan gave little notice to two loosely joined discussions unintentionally clashing for preeminence. On the one side new plans for pursuing Hildie's freedom were reviewed and discarded while weighed on the other were strategies to best meet the looming invasion from Munster.

"My lord—" The distress in this ragged call instantly won and closely held the entire hall's attention.

Rory's penetrating gaze moved just as quickly to settle on the young guardsman late for the meal yet rushing past lines of food-laden trestle tables to bow before him.

"What is it, Grady?" Rory calmly asked, eyeing the guardsman he'd last seen departing well before dawn to ride patrol with Liam. "What drove you here—not to join but to interrupt our meal?"

Grady's face, already haste-brightened, went an even more alarming red as he straightened to mutely face his frowning lord.

Fond of the clearly flustered guardsman, Rory dryly provided him with a choice, confident that the answer must be one or the other.

"Have you good news of my daughter?" Rory absently motioned to the right and then to the left. "Or a bleak report on our enemies' approach?"

"Neither," Grady gulped out, hands twisting awkwardly together.

This response was the last thing Rory had expected and his dark brows furrowed while beside him Lissan shifted uneasily.

"I accompanied Liam to Tuatha Cottage with all good haste," Grady earnestly announced, moving a pace closer. "But after seeing him safely under Maedra's care, I knew it was my duty to immediately return and report the foul deed to you."

"Foul deed?" Rory brusquely demanded. "What foul deed?"

"It was almost dawn when Liam and I stopped at the crest of a hill to look down across the quiet forest stretching out below." Returning calm steadied Grady's voice and inspired both the faintly relieved smile that warmed his eyes and his expansive descriptions of that morn's panorama.

"But what happened that needs to be reported?" Patience having never been Rory's strongest talent, he prodded the one too easily distracted from direct answers to refocus.

At this sharp reminder any tendency for wordiness deserted Grady, and he flatly said, "An arrow was shot from the woodland behind."

The grim statement instantly earned two simultaneous questions.

Lissan anxiously inquired, "Who was the target?"

"From whose bow was it shot?" Rory demanded to know.

"The arrow knocked Liam from his saddle," Grady told Lissan, confused by the question when surely the answer was already obvious.

"And," Grady continued, shifting full attention to his lord. "Because I had to choose between chasing the knave and tending Liam's wound, I have no notion who shot it."

"But where is the arrow now?" Rory's voice was strained.

"I brought it back with me," Grady answered, grateful for Liam's wise counsel in urging him to take this precaution.

"But *where* is it?" Rory persisted and added a second, more important query. "Has the fletcher given it distinctively hued vanes?"

A bright rush of color betrayed Grady's embarrassment over having foolishly left the pertinent object with his packed saddle. Thus, he gladly seized upon the second question, relieved that leastways he had the answer for it.

"Of its three feathers two are yellow and one is brown."

When Lord Rory's eyes turned to black ice, Grady heartily wished for the courage to ask his leader what was meant by this particular pattern completely unfamiliar to him.

CHAPTER 16

Having departed Ailm Keep with the dawn, Lissan had only just arrived at Tuatha Cottage. Not wishing to disturb the patient or wake his possibly resting wife, she gently eased the door open a mere crack to cautiously peek inside.

Maedra was awake but Liam wasn't.

While Lissan watched, Maedra dipped a small cloth square into the basin full of chill water which Eamon had drawn fresh from the well outside. As she folded and placed the cool pad across her injured husband's forehead, deep anxiety cast its bleak shadow across azure eyes normally clear and bright.

"Welcome, Lissan," Maedra quietly greeted without glancing behind.

Lissan wasn't surprised that Maedra's extraordinary senses had already announced her presence. However, she was surprised to find the valiant guardsman lying on a back she had thought arrow-pierced during the unexpected assault.

"Where was Liam hit?" Lissan gently asked when within two paces of her worried friend.

Maedra turned to face her visitor, "The wretched arrow struck the bone that lies below the ridge of Liam's left shoulder."

"His scapula." Lissan nodded, her knowledge of the science of anatomy, carried back through the centuries from a lifetime begun far in the future, now stood her in excellent stead.

"The wound seemed of little real danger when Grady brought Liam home to me," Maedra said in a quiet tone that betrayed a serious concern and the ache of self-blame. "Although the injury bled profusely when the arrow was removed, I thought the flow would be easily stanched and foolishly remained unworried."

"But . . ." Maedra's gaze returned to her patient as she took the pad from his head and dipped it back into chill water. "No matter the treatment employed, his bleeding hasn't lessened."

"What actions have you taken to soothe pain and mend flesh?" Lissan softly inquired, anxious to help but also quite certain that even her learning from the era of science wouldn't be as effective as Maedra's healing talents.

Lissan knew that although Maedra had forsworn her fairy powers, those abilities were unnecessary for other skills which she had learned in the long ago. During the past decade and more of their friendship, Lissan had discovered how carefully Maedra had been taught to successfully wield a natural magic. She'd been trained to know not merely which of the plants growing wild possessed healing properties but the most effective methods for their application.

"For pain and healing I've repeatedly given Liam a tisane of bitterroot blended with seeds from the yellow wort," Maedra responded while again laying the folded cloth across his forehead. "And I have repeatedly applied a poultice of thyme and plantain intended to staunch blood and cleanse flesh of poisons."

Lissan solemnly nodded approval, pleased that even during this early year in earth's history the Tuatha were already familiar with the importance of, if not the term for, antiseptics.

"But Liam all too soon became entirely lost to clear wits," Maedra continued, left unaware of Lissan's reaction by having remained focused on her injured husband.

"And, no matter how often I coax him to lie face-down, Liam constantly throws himself over on his back." Bewildered, Maedra slowly shook a golden cloud of disarrayed hair gone uncombed for more than a day. "With that action he has repeatedly dislodged the poultice, rendering it utterly useless."

Maedra turned the damp pad over to tenderly reposition it. "I blame that misdeed, in part, for the fact that during the hours since his attack Liam has only gotten worse . . . until by dawn this morn he'd fallen into this unnatural sleep."

Lissan nodded, faintly recognizing these symptoms. She was fairly certain that her nineteenth-century medical texts had blamed a similar condition on some kind of poison in the blood. This recognition only increased Lissan's depression for there was assuredly no cure for such a malady in this century.

Maedra had been warned how fragile humans' bodies were and how easily maimed, but this was her first experience of pain in the prospect of a beloved human's demise. She wished with all her heart for lost powers and their ability to mend this cherished mortal she feared slipping from her world.

Lissan's soul wept for her friend, so in need of what she no longer possessed—Tuatha powers assuredly able to mend Liam with ease.

As she hadn't intended to speak aloud, Lissan didn't realize that her last phrase had been audible until Maedra wistfully answered.

"Your father warned me of the anguish I would suffer when human limitations prevented me from wielding the abilities I'd long taken for granted."

"Although you have temporarily set aside your healing powers, the Faerie Realm is crowded with many who still possess them," Lissan gently reminded her friend. "We have only to seek their aid."

"I can't leave Liam," Maedra regretfully argued.

She appreciated her friend's honest desire to help but knew too well the boundaries imposed and which she had accepted in exchange for her selfish goal of a human lifetime shared with Liam. "Nor would I be welcomed by the king who cautioned me about the price I must pay."

"Nay, on that you are wrong." Lissan firmly shook ebony locks. "Where humans are concerned, I promise you that my father has a much softer heart than he dare reveal to his subjects."

Maedra didn't answer but a spark of hope brightened the azure crystal of her gaze.

"Good, then it is decided," Lissan firmly stated and began gradually backing toward the door. "You must stay at your husband's side while I go to my father and beg his healing aid on Liam's behalf."

"*Your* husband won't approve," Maedra anxiously renewed her arguments. "I fear Lord Rory will be greatly displeased if you steal attention from the vital search for Hildie to ease my woes."

"Not true," Lissan instantly denied the suggestion. "Rory is truly fond of Liam. And when we departed the keep this morn, he was pleased that I planned to offer you my support this day while he oversees the strengthening of border patrols and organizes the renewed search for our Hildie."

Lissan could clearly see her friend's quiet desperation and knew that, however reluctantly, in the end Maedra must agree to the plan. Yet, wanting to ease the burden of Maedra's inevitable feelings of guilt for accepting the boon, Lissan sent her a conspiratorial glance and added more.

"Besides, carrying your plea for Liam's healing will give me a fine excuse to make another journey to my father's realm."

The next instant Lissan hoped that Maedra had missed the reference to "another journey." Already carrying the weight of serious worries, Maedra didn't need the added burden delivered by suspicions of fairy interference in Hildie's abduction.

As Liam shifted on the bed and groaned in pain, Maedra immediately shifted her unwavering attention to him.

Once her friend was fully absorbed in performing loving duties, Lissan lost no moment in departing on her mission. With dark fears for Liam's health goading her onward, she climbed the hill behind the ivy-covered cottage with amazing speed. At its crest, Lissan stepped into the magical ring of forever blooming flowers and expectantly waited to be escorted in an instant to the Faerie Castle.

Kneeling on wet stone, Hildie again reached down and with cupped hands scooped up cool, refreshing liquid. But this time, rather than greedily gulping, she slowly swallowed, savoring its crystal purity as it trickled down a parched throat.

Kieron had kept his earlier promise by leading the way straight to this swiftly flowing, underground river. And now, with desperate thirst quenched by his thoughtful action, Hildie could more easily ignore the grumbling sounds of growing hunger.

"Thank you," she quietly said while settling back on her heels.

The sweet appreciation glowing in sapphire eyes was more than sufficient gratitude to please Kieron. He lay stretched out, half reclining with weight supported on elbows and forearms.

"Now that the most immediate need has been met, we should choose our course of action. What direction do you think we should take?" By tilting a golden head, he indicated the various tunnels intersecting at this river crossroad.

Hildie was mildly surprised that a male—not just any male but one of exceptional powers—deigned to seek the input of any woman on an important decision. Beyond her father's respect for Lissan's opinions, Hildie was well aware that most males held the feminine intellect in low regard.

A rueful smile bloomed on lips Hildie had nibbled to berry brightness. She ought to be ashamed of herself for even momentarily thinking no better of her beloved than that. Now if only she could offer a useful suggestion to justify his faith in her. . . . Sadly, in this utterly unfamiliar place, she had none.

For long moments the dark cavern's silence was disturbed by naught but the steady ripple of flowing water barely seen amidst heavy gloom lessened only in the circle of Kieron's aura.

"How did Ardagh leave this place?" Hildie eventually asked. The next instant a nasty question rose to mock her words. "He is gone, isn't he?"

"How?" Kieron's white grin flashed in response to Hildie's first question. His elfling had instinctively struck the target dead to point!

"Down here where there are limits to my fairy powers, it is clear to see precisely which of we two is truly magical."

Initially startled by this high praise of which she knew herself so unworthy, Hildie was even more surprised when Kieron sat up to brush a fleeting kiss across gasp-parted lips.

"Although assuredly unintended," Kieron continued, "our vicious jailer has leastways provided us with proof that there *is* a way out."

Lissan nodded, realizing that although the question she'd posed in response to his query was no answer in itself, it had stoked the faint spark of hope into a healthy fire.

"Ardagh obviously knows a way to navigate through this labyrinth to freedom," Kieron quietly explained his reasoning. "And if he can do it, then we can find that portal, too."

What Kieron didn't mention to Hildie was the likelihood that the wretched Ardagh would've blocked his own point of exit as securely as he had sealed the site of Kieron's entrance.

Although Kieron's observation remained unspoken, Hildie's wits were too sharp to fail in recognizing that bleak probability for herself.

A morose silence settled its uncomfortable weight over the pair while, too uneasy to meet the other's gaze, they blindly peered toward surrounding areas of particularly dense blackness, each indicating the opening to a tunnel.

Eventually Seun padded over the uneven, damp rock surface bordering the river's edge and lapped up more of its bounty. That gentle sound lured her companions from their reveries.

"Let's set off on our task," Kieron said, striving to sound more positive about meeting the challenge they faced than he actually felt. The mere fact that Ardagh knew a way free provided no hint as to which of several shadowed paths dimly seen to converge at this point they should pursue.

Anxious to calm the uneasiness Hildie valiantly fought to hide, Kieron firmly made a suggestion. "I believe our most logical action would be to follow the river's course."

"Aye," Hildie agreed. "Waters moving with such speed must exit somewhere." Wearing an equally thin mask of confidence, she gracefully rose to her feet and stepped closer into her beloved's reassuring circle of golden light.

Kieron safely tucked Hildie's small hand into the crook of his arm and started forward to trace the route of the river. At the outset, and most places after, their journey was easy with a pathway broad and flat. But in several spots it narrowed dramatically and in those instances the resolve to proceed required considerably more care.

In those places they were forced to exercise both patience and skill either in maintaining balance while crossing narrow ridges or single-minded determination to scramble up and over the series of rock piles blocking their way.

Their chain of valiant successes abruptly met with bitter defeat.

"But where does it go?" Hildie asked while, steadied by Kieron's strong arm wrapped firmly about her waist, she leaned forward to peer down a sharp drop. Rushing waters cascaded over the sharp precipice into impenetrable darkness.

Disappointment having frozen all emotion from his expression, Kieron flatly replied, "Where it doesn't go, is to freedom."

Hildie pulled back from the edge to rest securely against the support of his powerful form. Turning her face to the side, she gazed upward.

By the ice in Kieron's distant gaze, Hildie recognized the depth of his frustration and ached for him. Yet, having no solution to mend his wound, she waited in patient silence.

"Clearly we have journeyed in the wrong direction," Kieron said at last. He drew a deep, calming breath before adding, "The only option now is to return to our starting point and from there track flowing waters to their source."

Hildie promptly nodded and started back the way they had come. But while wordlessly retracing their steps, she remembered his earlier statement that this river was composed by many streams joining together. If that were the case, she wondered what hope they had for making the right choices to find "its source"? Surely each stream had its own?

Their journey back seemed to take infinitely longer than the trip which had led them to a waterfall and dark abyss. Hildie's soft lips twisted into a wry smile as she acknowledged the reason for this fact: The first had been made with high hopes while the return was burdened with discouragement.

By the time the two of them at last stood on the same spot where they had knelt to drink refreshing waters, Kieron had devised a different and, he earnestly hoped, more successful strategy.

"I fear our best and perhaps only hope lies at the site where our troubles began." Kieron hated to venture even this oblique reference to the Circle of Stones, knowing how likely any reminder of her destiny was to depress Hildie. And yet it truly was their most promising course of action, one he should've recognized at the outset.

Hildie gave Kieron a bleak smile. His mention of their initial wrong and its fearsome price was disheartening with its implied reminder that both her world and his might depend upon her dubious ability to perform the magic of a Seunadair. But since even Ardagh named her as responsible for bringing about such disastrous events, Hildie accepted the duty of doing all possible to see the

Dragons of Chaos recaptured and again imprisoned.

"Aye," Hildie agreed with Kieron's assessment. "After we find the Circle of Stones, we might be able to go through the Faerie Castle's portal and climb the steps beyond to freedom."

"We can try," Kieron responded and with a flashing smile motioned her toward a path leading away on the right.

As Hildie started down the route he'd chosen, she was struck by an uncomfortable memory. Kieron had used almost exactly the same words before escorting her to the site of his arrival only to find that opening blocked by a hazelwood mat and massive boulder. She feared this quest as doomed.

Kieron hadn't wanted to dampen Hildie's enthusiasm with the sorry truth that seriously weakened powers might not be equal to the need. He still saw no useful purpose to be served by worrying her. And she would be concerned by an admission that he wasn't likely to be any more successful in opening the doorway allowing entry to the Faerie Castle than he had been in moving the stone blocking the exit earlier visited.

While they made their way into the tunnel's shadows, they were watched.

Ardagh was relieved that they hadn't chosen the one in which he'd hidden since shortly after their confrontation. While walking away from the pair he'd gleefully trapped, a most unpleasant shock had struck. Thanks to the uncertain nature of the beasts he'd set free, he was unable to become invisible even to the human female. And worse—far, far worse—thanks to the Dragons of Chaos he couldn't escape the maze of caverns he had intended to be Lady Hildie's last abode.

He was trapped down here, eyes blinded by total darkness and able to move only by exercising well-honed senses. How could this wretched development happen now when, without constant attention, his schemes to ensure the destruction of all living things might fail? Or, even more unpleasant, they might succeed while he remained snared in this cavern. But the nastiest possibility lay in the prospect of the trap he had built for others thwarting his wicked dream of standing in the midst of chaos, savoring revenge in the vicious delight of utter devastation.

Unseen in the darkness, Ardagh's smile flashed. His ambiguous fairy nature found perverse pleasure in the strange fact that his only chance for winning freedom lay in following the path of his captives' successful escape. And he knew that possibility was real as, while hiding in shadows, he had overheard them decide to seek the Circle of Stones, hoping that from there they could enter the Faerie Castle.

Ardagh very much doubted Kieron any more likely than himself to win freedom so easily, but . . . He would follow their path, just in case. Oh, he wouldn't risk revealing himself by trailing close behind. There was no need for that since he knew these tunnels well and could reach the Circle of Stones whenever he chose. If they found a way free from there, he would follow.

Counting her blessings where she found them, Hildie chided herself to be glad that this path at least remained flat and wide with no impeding piles of rocks to be surmounted.

Although intersected by other, smaller tunnels, Hildie and Kieron continued down the broad route, and by the ever louder echo of footsteps on stone were encouraged to think themselves moving in the right direction. When those hollow sounds began to reverberate and the light of Kieron's aura no longer reached a ceiling, they knew they'd entered the main cavern, the site of the Circle of Stones.

On recognizing this vast chamber, Kieron gladly welcomed the confidence it revived. Wrapping an arm around Hildie's shoulders, he turned them both halfway about and unhesitatingly escorted her forward through the dark.

Hildie could only see as far as Kieron's glow pierced the darkness but, trusting him completely, she moved where he directed. Within a few paces she could faintly make out the silhouette of a legendary site proven very real. As they stepped closer Hildie saw that a once small crack had widened and spread fully across the Circle of Stones, splitting it in two distinct halves. Proof the original wrong had been compounded.

A strong tremor of dread passed through Hildie and wanting nothing more than to move away from this confirmation of a dangerous folly, she immediately turned to Kieron with an unnaturally bright smile and hopeful reminder.

"Surely we should lose no time in checking the portal?"

Kieron responded with a rueful shrug and put his hand in the small of Hildie's slender back to urge her toward their goal. They came to a halt on reaching the seemingly solid stone wall which had blocked their way when first Kieron brought her to the labyrinth. Hildie watched as he slipped the fingers of one hand into the nearly invisible crevice that had shifted the obstruction aside last time.

It didn't move.

Golden brows met in a fierce scowl as Kieron's arm dropped back to his side. It was, as he had feared, impossible for him to perform even this simple feat of magic. His powers were severely impaired, more so than could be blamed on his current position amidst caverns of solid, natural stone. Even his most inherent trait, his aura, had begun to dim.

By a love more potent than fairy powers, Kieron sensed concern in Hildie's worried gaze and sent her a slight, encouraging smile.

"Don't stew." Kieron gently tapped the tip of her nose. "The Circle of Stones itself holds the key to freedom."

Responding to his gently teasing action, Hildie

grimaced in mock distaste for again being treated like a child by the lover who assuredly knew better. Yet, while Kieron led her back to the ominously marred monument, she struggled with inner trepidations. Would the strange script say the Seunadair held this key, as well as confirm the awesome responsibility for correcting all the hideous damage done.

Bending nearer to the inscriptions, Kieron heartily regretted not paying more heed when taught these secrets in his youth. That lack of attention made the task of now deciphering their meaning more difficult—and time-consuming.

"By magic, the magic becomes," Kieron mused softly. When no immediate interpretation of its purpose suggested itself, he moved several paces farther around the circle's outer edge.

By magic, the magic becomes, Hildie silently repeated the cryptic phrase. What did it mean? Though not easy to admit, she had the uncomfortable feeling that it was intended for the Seunadair. Hildie earnestly wished for any vague understanding of the purpose for this mysterious but clearly significant clue.

As if to confirm Hildie's fears, though unintentional, Kieron read additional phrases. "Magical powers not of fairy born, and wielded not from the lifeless circle of boundaries broken but from a circle of unending life . . ."

Hildie's stillness shook Kieron from his absorption with statements of uncertain purpose. He glanced up and caught a glimpse of apprehension joined to valiant determination on Hildie's face. Instantly concerned, Kieron moved to sweep his elfling up into the security of his arms.

Refusing to heed the wise caution of his conscience, Kieron settled on the cold stone floor with Hildie again dangerously draped across his lap. He foolishly closed his mind to insistent reminders of the damage done his oath and her virtue the last time they'd been in such intimate proximity.

Amidst the labyrinth's darkness there was no way to mark the passage of time in mortal hours yet Kieron knew that Hildie, as a human, must sleep. He allowed himself to justify their embrace with the lie that her need for rest made it safe. To that folly he added the already thoroughly disproved claim that his self-control was strong enough to see his too enticing love left undisturbed while slumber restored her valiant and fiery spirit.

Thick lashes dropped to hide midnight eyes while with stunning haste Hildie fell under the thrall of Kieron's devastating nearness. She could prevent neither the soft whimper of immediate surrender nor the motion of hands lifting to curl around his neck.

Hildie's headlong response caught Kieron completely unprepared to withstand the sweet, wickedly tempting assault. No matter his duty as guardian to tame forbidden hunger for the tender elfling, he gently shifted her alluring form to hold inviting curves that had already laid their brand on him tight against the power of his body. Then a mouth, hard and warm, brushed lightly across her lips.

Her lover was very strong and their embrace bruising but with the flames he had so easily reignited again coursing through her veins like a river of fire, Hildie arched helplessly nearer. Glorying in his masculinity, his size, his strength, she wanted only to be closer still.

Tempted by his, Hildie's tongue ventured forth to taste him. Kieron instantly responded by seizing her mouth in a long, slow, devastating kiss.

Reveling in the searing heat of their embrace and the liquid fire in their veins, soon any obstruction that prevented an erotic feast of flesh against flesh to feed the sensuous delight of ravening hungers was unbearable. Thus, when Kieron pulled a whisper away, Hildie immediately and urgently tugged at the unwanted barrier of his garb while he hastily rid her of an interfering chemise.

Once both were free of impeding cloth, Kieron laid her gently back. Then one masculine hand gradually laid a searing path up her side, over hip and narrow waist until slowly, slowly outspread fingers gliding over skin the texture of rose petals found the first gentle swell of her breast.

While wild shudders of excitement shook Hildie, Kieron watched in satisfaction. He watched as she twisted sensually under the pleasure of his tantalizingly light touch on her breasts, watched her drag in a deep, anguished breath as his mouth came down to nuzzle their softness.

Lost in smoldering need, Hildie tangled her fingers into cool, golden strands while he savored the addictive delicacy of her creamy flesh. Trembling under flashes of wildfire, Hildie tugged his relentlessly teasing mouth closer until at last came the whisper-light brush of his lips across the peak. And even then she wanted more. She arched against his mouth until his lips opened to draw the tip inside.

Overwhelmed by the shocking cascade of fiery sensations, a tortured moan escaped Hildie's tight throat. Plunging deeper into the dark fires of wickedly delicious sensations and wandering through passion's dense smoke, she instinctively enticed, writhing against Kieron's hard body.

The deep, velvet growl coming from his throat sent a shiver of desire through Hildie. Far beyond rational thinking, Kieron gazed down at the exquisite creature while moving his powerful body fully atop her slender length.

Drowning in blazing sensations, Hildie welcomed the heady intimacy and, shaking in an agony of desire, pressed even closer as Kieron's hands slid, palms flat, down to her hips. She clung desperately to the burning source of delicious torment while in an exciting action well remembered, he cupped her derriere and tilted it to ease their slow joining.

Twining her silken limbs about Kieron in welcome, Hildie gladly surrendered to this most intimate embrace. She yearned upward and held tight to Kieron as with a rhythm that grew wilder and ever wilder, he swept her into the delicious torment of the firestorm. Whirling higher and higher, desperate for more, they rose on anguished need.

Crying out, fearing she could bear no more, Hildie found herself carried to the pinnacle of the highest blue flame and hovered there until came a mighty explosion that launched them up into the smoky clouds of sweetest satisfaction.

Uncounted moments later Hildie drifted on soft clouds of blissful contentment, savoring every instant of forbidden intimacy she'd no doubt would too soon be lost to her.

While his beloved snuggled closer, Kieron cradled her tenderly near and in a velvet baritone voice sang her into dreams too long delayed . . . a honey-sweet delay he couldn't regret.

CHAPTER 17

The first mists of twilight had begun gathering at the base of woodland trees when Lissan led her father into the small ivy-covered cottage that had been her home after an unexpected and inexplicable fall through time more than a decade past.

At first sight of anxiously awaited guests stepping into her home, Maedra rushed forward. She dropped to her knees in homage to her king and from that humble position made her own fervent plea.

"Sire, I beg you to heal my husband. I have employed the many cures Queen Aine taught me from her vast knowledge of medicinal herbs, roots, and flowers . . . but Liam only gets worse." The desperate tears leaving a silver trail down silken cheeks was more than adequate proof of her sincerity.

Acknowledging Maedra's mention of his departed grandmother with a rueful smile, Comlan quietly said, "I will do all that I can, but—"

Maedra recognized the slight shake of his golden head for the ill-boding it was meant to imply. She said nothing in response yet the dark clouds of hopelessness near blocking the azure brightness of her eyes spoke volumes and prodded Comlan into giving more of an explanation than he'd intended to share.

"*Our* powers have both weakened and become ominously unreliable."

"Chaos," Maedra woefully murmured. "I have sensed the Dragons' unruly powers growing ever stronger while reaching out to spread violence and confusion over all in their path."

Comlan was surprised that this colleen who'd set aside her powers for the length of a human lifetime was able to sense anything so momentous. But then, perhaps that was but another symptom of Chaos's ambiguity.

"Let us waste no more precious moments but see if I've sufficient control over my own powers to see your husband restored."

Maedra instantly rose and led the way to Liam's bedside.

As King Comlan bent to focus his full attention on the injured man, Lissan moved forward to wrap a supportive arm about her trembling friend's waist.

Faith in her father's ability to wield magic had urged Lissan into beseeching of him the same boon Maedra sought. To her surprise, for the very first time, King Comlan had tried to refuse his daughter's request with warnings of an odd malady playing havoc with fairy powers. Still, though reluctant, he had accompanied her to Tuatha Cottage and she watched while he tried to grant their request.

Time passed and Comlan's brows lowered into an ever fiercer scowl as darkness fell. Despite his many spells cast and actions taken, Liam's condition remained unchanged when the cottage door burst open.

"Is Papa well yet?" Eamon demanded as he pulled his hand from Rory's and rushed across the room.

"Not yet," Comlan responded, turning to catch the impulsive child before he could fling himself across the wounded father.

"How can that be?" Rory asked, deep voice a burr of dread for the answer and concern for his favorite guardsman.

Although Grady was certainly capable of performing the task, Rory had welcomed the excuse of returning Eamon to his home. It justified this visit too long delayed by the duty to join King Turlough in devising strategies and overseeing the troops building defenses to meet an expected invasion. Since the attack on Liam, never had any further sign of intruders from Munster been spotted within Connaught's borders . . . but troops were massing just across the river which defined the boundaries between kingdoms. And no one doubted that an assault was imminent.

Brows arched inquiringly, Comlan cast his daughter a penetrating glance.

"I told Rory," Lissan promptly assured her father in answer to his unspoken question but at the same time glanced toward the husband who had so abruptly arrived, accompanied by two young boys. "He has heard the legend of the Dragons of Chaos."

Emerald eyes gone wide, Donal glanced between his parents and then to Eamon. Dragons? Real dragons? The promise of something so exciting quite put to shame their great, but dismally lost, discovery.

"Are you claiming that your dragons carried my daughter away?" Rory's voice was scathing.

"Nay," Comlan calmly denied. "If it were that simple, it could be as easily corrected."

"Then *what* is it?"

"The Dragons of Chaos can disorder, weaken, or steal the Tuatha de Danann's powers. That, in turn, makes any spell either dangerously unpredictable or utterly ineffective.

"The Dragons didn't steal Hildie, but they are doubtless responsible for preventing Kieron from immediately rescuing her from whoever did."

"It was that wretched stranger," Donal said, tugging urgently at his father's hand.

"Must have been," Eamon promptly supported his friend, an action taken while still held in the powerful arms of a golden figure never before seen.

"What stranger?" The demand for explanation

issued simultaneously from both Rory and Comlan.

Voice aching with regret for not having spoken of the peculiar figure earlier, Donal immediately told about the odd intruder who had tried to shoo him and Eamon away from the cavern of their great discovery.

"Before Kieron went down into the cave, we told him about the wretch," Eamon earnestly announced.

"What did this wretch look like?" Comlan asked with deadly calm.

Between them the two boys repeated the same description they'd given Kieron, and it earned from the glowing visitor the same dark scowl and cold smile of wry disgust that had appeared on Kieron's face.

Wrapped in a warm blanket of happiness, Hildie floated on the pastel mists of pleasant dreams undisturbed until the most melodious voice she'd ever heard began calling her name.

"Hildie . . . Hildie . . ."

Adrift in her fantasy world, Hildie spun about lightly as a feather on the summer breeze. Her curious sapphire gaze settled on a figure familiar . . . and yet not. Although this delicate creature was the image of her stepmother, Hildie could see through the form as insubstantial as a wraith.

"Hildie . . ." Gentle amusement glimmered in soft words. "Have you failed to recognize me as the fairy from whom you descended?"

"Are you . . . ?" The speaker's welcoming smile beckoned Hildie nearer.

A cloud of golden curls glowed as a dainty head nodded. "I am the Lissan whose shed powers created the fairy ring you know so well. Yes, I am King Comlan's sister and the one for whom he named his daughter, your stepmother."

The statement drew a tentative question from Hildie. " 'Tis from you that I inherited the lopsided heart on my nape?"

Never had Hildie questioned King Comlan's confirmation of the magical ancestry that as a child she'd been told was hers by the mother too soon *gone to sing with the angels*. Still, because of her dark hair and eyes, she'd never been able to completely quell doubts about the astounding claim that she was descended from the golden Tuatha de Danann.

The ethereal Lissan moved closer to the dark colleen, not walking but floating even while sweeping masses of gilded hair aside to reveal the same mark on her own graceful nape.

"And now"—Lissan straightened to gaze steadily into Hildie's solemn eyes—"if you believe that I've come to lend aid and are willing to grant me your trust, I have secrets to share with you."

In answer to this tender appeal, Hildie nodded earnestly, heart pounding while hopeful curiosity lit sparks in the midnight blue of her eyes.

"You are born of my direct bloodline, which enables me to relay important truths—mere morsels but vital to the whole."

Hildie anxiously nibbled her lip, aware in quiet depths that this was a dream, a mere fantasy and yet desperately praying she wouldn't awaken before mysterious messages were revealed.

"The portal closed against entry into the Faerie Castle is the first challenge to be overcome," Lissan calmly stated.

" 'Tis a secret simple and easily solved: Impenetrable to fairy but open to you. The stone wall is naught but a powerful illusion to be broken when, with closed eyes, you step through and beyond."

The distress dousing sparks in Hildie's midnight eyes betrayed her horror over even an oblique suggestion that she ought to seek a personal escape accomplished while leaving behind the one who had rescued her from so many past dilemmas.

A teasing grin flashed across Lissan's face as she calmed Hildie's distress. "Once you have broken the obstruction by stepping through it, it will be open for Kieron to follow."

Hildie's brilliant smile blossomed with appreciation for this reassurance of Kieron's route to freedom ... and the faint hope that this apparently simple feat was the only feat of *magic not of fairy born* to be expected of her. The latter hope was promptly crushed by Lissan's next statement.

"There is another secret, one that you must accept." Emerald eyes locked with Hildie's gaze, Lissan recognized and soothed the trepidation in their depths. "You are the Seunadair."

Hildie instinctively clenched her eyes shut against this confirmation of a secret she really, truly didn't want to accept.

"Clearly," Lissan said with a gently mocking, half smile very like the one so common to the lips of her brother Comlan, "you already know the title and the grave duties it entails."

Certain any denial would be instantly recognized for the falsehood it would be, Hildie flatly stated, "I know that the Seunadair is by legend foretold to wield a magic not of fairy born. With that power the Seunadair is destined first to halt the destruction of the Dragons of Chaos and then to see them confined with unbreakable bonds."

Lissan nodded, wry smile deepening while approval glowed in emerald eyes.

"But I have *no* magic," Hildie argued with a heat stoked higher by frustration when Lissan continued her revelation of secrets without pausing to acknowledge Hildie's denial.

"The place from which to imprison dragons and renew guardian powers against chaos is not the lifeless circle cracked but the ring of unending life."

Hildie shook her head at this repetition of the message already delivered when Kieron had deciphered the Ogham inscription. Her lips parted to seek further unknown answers. Most importantly, Hildie wanted to hear specific instructions for how she was to secure the magic she lacked.

"Go back," Lissan said, putting an abrupt halt to Hildie's unspoken words. "Go back and lead Kieron to freedom."

As she spoke, Lissan seemed to drift farther and farther away.

"Stop the destruction." With this command she dissipated into the mist, leaving behind only the faint echo of a final admonishment: "Remember, by magic, the magic becomes."

"No-o-o-" Hildie cried out against abandonment while so many questions remained.

A gentle shaking forced her back to the dark world of reality.

"Hildie, Hildie—" This voice was a velvet thunder vastly unlike the last to call her name . . . and yet in its resonance similar, too. "Wake up, sweeting, wake up. Whatever ill distresses you so is but an unpleasant dream."

Thick lashes half-lifted, permitting Hildie to peek up into Kieron's concern. How could she truthfully explain when, save for her beloved's company, their waking reality was far more unpleasant than the fantasy world inhabited by her ancestress.

Hildie rose without speaking, slipped on the green chemise, and immediately reached for Kieron's hand. She was anxious to test whether or not her dream revelations were truth.

Gazing curiously into the determination on Hildie's winsome face, Kieron allowed her to induce him into standing. He dressed as rapidly as she had. And he would have asked his elfling for her purpose had she not already begun urgently pulling him toward the solid granite wall once a portal, one his weakened powers had been unable to move.

Heart thumping with an uncomfortable mixture of hopeful anticipation and dread of failure, Hildie moved straight across the vast chamber. She was grateful for Kieron's oddly dimmed glow to light their way to the Faerie Castle's closed entrance.

Firmly clasping a masculine hand, Hildie closed her eyes and, to Kieron's utter amazement, easily stepped through solid stone while pulling him to follow behind her daring action.

Kieron glanced back over his shoulder to verify that the apparently unfazed barrier remained intact at their backs.

"How did you do that?" Kieron moved a pace forward to look down into Hildie's face. The fiercely trembling colleen's eyes were still clenched shut. He instantly wrapped her in the reassuring strength of his embrace, whispering his next query into the raven-dark curls atop her head.

"How did you know that you could?"

Hildie was grateful for Kieron's support in this moment when unanticipated, overwhelming waves of shock at the success of her feat threatened an uncommon weakness and possible collapse. Snuggling closer against the comforting warmth of his powerful chest, she shared the nature of her incredible dream and the secrets revealed by the first Lissan.

With one forefinger, Kieron tilted her face upward until their eyes bonded. "And now you accept that you truly are the Seunadair?"

Giving her head a slow shake, Hildie started to protest but Kieron stifled the words with gentle fingers pressed to her petal-soft lips.

"Don't claim again that you have no magic," he cautioned with a tender smile. "Not after passing through the granite wall I couldn't move."

"But I don't know how to fight the Dragons of Chaos," Hildie earnestly argued, "far less how to see them again imprisoned."

"When the time comes you will," Kieron confidently assured the tender elfling clearly alarmed by the prospect of such a formidable task ahead.

The further denial forming on again parted lips met a far more welcome end in a kiss light and tantalizing. When Kieron's mouth withdrew, Hildie felt bereft and rose up on tiptoe seeking more.

Temptations intensified by burning memories of recent passionate embraces, fiery and sweet, were too great. Kieron's lips brushed Hildie's again.

Hildie's sigh came out an aching moan. The sound was more than Kieron could bear and his arms tightened about the tender prize whose gentle curves melted against him without thought of denial. When his mouth settled over hers, the searing whirlwind that seemed his to command returned and swept Hildie deeper into the flaming vortex of devastating desire.

When moments later she writhed against him in

helpless response, Kieron recognized his wrong in having allowed this sweet delight at a time so purely wrong. He abruptly broke their kiss and gently tried to set Hildie aside.

Hildie desperately clung the tighter to her beloved for knowing that once they left the labyrinth behind and returned to their respective worlds, the barriers between them would, of necessity, rise again and likely higher. Almost would she surrender everything, endure anything to remain always near Kieron . . . but she couldn't force others to pay the price for her happiness.

Nay, she was the Seunadair and must attempt to fulfill that destiny no matter whether the outcome be for good or for ill.

Stepping back from Kieron, Hildie resolutely turned toward ascending steps. With equal parts dread and anticipation the two of them dutifully climbed the long stairway slowly winding ever upward toward the freedom they both believed would doubtless see them parted forever.

On the top tread, they exchanged a last, lingering look of love unshielded. Kieron then shoved open the heavy door that normally opened without need for force. Once that portal was unblocked, entry into the Faerie Castle was granted.

The pair stopped, instantly alarmed by an ominous difference. The brilliant light natural to King Comlan's home was vastly weakened. Jaw gone taut against this unwelcome proof of powers far more seriously eroded than expected, Kieron hastily led Hildie to the archway that opened into the great hall. The changes here were even more dispiriting. The vast chamber lacked its usual endless sprightly music and bright entertainments. Worst of all, the ever cheerful, laughing inhabitants now seemed too weak and morose to take delight in even the simplest of pleasures.

Plainly the Dragons of Chaos were close to winning their victory in a complete destruction of the Tuatha de Danann.

Amidst cavern shadows in the depths far below, Ardagh perched on a lone boulder to one side of the portal seemingly closed by granite and pondered a mystifying puzzle. Since he hadn't cast the spell creating this illusion of solid stone, by whose power had it been wrought?

Ardagh had followed his erstwhile captives through the barrier once already. But, on discovering that within two steps the self-absorbed pair indulging in yet another disgustingly passionate embrace were blocking his way, he had quickly retreated.

But surely, Ardagh decided as he nimbly leaped down, by now sufficient time had passed to safely make his own escape.

CHAPTER 18

At midmorn the Faerie Castle's great hall was unusually quiet and the small chamber branching off from it abnormally chill. And yet, the moment a mysteriously appearing fox led two unexpected beings into his dispirited realm, King Comlan had motioned them into its privacy.

"Ardagh." King Comlan surprised Kieron by flatly agreeing with his announcement. Voice as cold as the frigid green ice of his eyes, Comlan explained. "Two youngsters reported Ardagh's involvement to me, but how did you discover the identity of the wicked perpetrator of crimes against Hildie?"

Standing uncomfortably in front of a cold hearth never before lacking warming flames, Kieron immediately answered.

"Together Hildie's small brother and Maedra's son told me about an odd stranger who tried to shoo them away from their *great discovery*—a split in the earth which opens directly into the Sidhe's always hidden and long sealed labyrinth."

"You recognized Ardagh from so little as that?" Comlan asked in mock amazement.

"Nay." White grin flashing, Kieron gave his head a slight shake and hastened to correct the misunderstanding caused by his haste to respond. "It was their description of a gaunt being with sharply uptilted brows and an ability to vanish in an instant that brought Ardagh to mind."

Comlan acknowledged the younger male's helpful clarification with a strained smile.

"I apologize for not being the first to bring this news to you." Bending from the waist, Kieron gave his sovereign a brief half-bow of remorse. "Unfortunately, I had no opportunity to share my suspicions since, shortly after the boys made their confession, I whisked myself down into the cavern they were so proud of having discovered."

"And that's where you found Hildie?" Comlan quietly asked.

"With Seun's help." Kieron nodded and even the chamber's limited illumination rippled a glowing path over his bright hair.

Turning his attention to Hildie, Comlan gently asked a most important question. "Was Ardagh responsible for all the attempts to abduct you?"

"I don't know," Hildie answered truthfully. "I had never heard of Ardagh, neither did I see nor overhear any trace of him, until after Kieron and I found ourselves thoroughly trapped in the labyrinth's endless maze of tunnels and caverns."

"But," Kieron quickly and firmly stated, "it assuredly was Ardagh who took measures to see us sealed inside that trap."

"Sealed you in?" Golden brows met in a faint frown as Comlan asked, "How did Ardagh do that? And with what?"

Having never doubted that unflinching honesty was the best answer to any query, Kieron suppressed disgust for facts flatly shared with his king. "A wicker mat was carefully laid across the gaping gash through which I had entered the cavern."

Comlan's frown deepened into a fierce scowl, silently urging Kieron to provide a further, more detailed explanation.

"Though seemingly an impossible feat, that flimsy wicker webbing supported a monstrous boulder of granite positioned to lay atop the whole . . ." Kieron's voice trailed off with an irritable shrug.

With justified pride for a difficult achievement lighting sparks in sapphire eyes, Hildie shared her role in the ultimately failed action.

"After Kieron explained to me how he could do nothing to remove the wicker barrier, I pulled, tugged, and ripped at it until eventually I broke and shredded it into pieces."

"But then, to my shame," Kieron picked up the narration to tell his part of the event, "I was unable to move the boulder beyond."

Comlan solemnly nodded but promptly asked a pertinent question. "You saw Ardagh while confined in the labyrinth?"

"Aye, Ardagh came to gloat." Kieron's loathing for the man was clear. "He told Hildie that she is responsible for loosing the Dragons of Chaos to consume both her world and ours."

When this restating of the wretched fiend's words sent a shiver through Hildie, against the phantom foe Kieron's jaw went taut and he wrapped a protective arm firmly around her.

In a voice carefully held flat Kieron reported, "Only knowing that the action would be useless, possibly dangerous, kept me from rejecting Ardagh's logic with the certainty that as the Seunadair, Hildie is the only one who can halt that devastation."

"Seunadair?" the king echoed, emerald gaze instantly moving to scrutinize Hildie more closely as a faint half smile slowly curled his lips.

" 'Struth." King Comlan nodded, wryly amused by this odd twist of fate. "The Seunadair."

With the repetition of this title, the last tint of color faded from Hildie's soft cheeks. Kieron immediately sought to lessen her extreme uneasiness by diverting his king's attention.

"My liege, I accept it as my duty to publicly confess culpability in the tragic wrong, initiated at my hand, which opened the barricades for the destruction of us all."

To assess both the wisdom and sincerity of this

offer, Comlan held Kieron's unblinking gaze for long moments before delivering his decision on the proposed action.

"You are right." Comlan was pleased that Kieron had offered, unasked, to perform this ancient duty. Confessing transgressions and accepting punishment was a necessary step in the maturing process even for one of the fairy race. "It behooves every errant member of the Tuatha de Danann to stand strong before the assembled whole and confess wrongs."

Within a very brief time Kieron stood, with Hildie at his side, before a hastily summoned crowd of many friends—and at least one enemy.

Ardagh stood concealed in shadows at the back of the vast chamber and curiously listened while Kieron set out to regale his audience with all that he had earlier reported to Comlan.

Kieron began by admitting his serious misdeed in taking Hildie to the Circle of Stones. Anxious to see Hildie judged innocent of his wrong, he earnestly accepted blame, stating it was his fault alone that the Dragons of Chaos were free to wreak their terror on two worlds.

When a rustling breeze of accusing whispers and muttered threats swept across his hall, King Comlan stepped forward. He motioned for the masses to be calm and listen to his words.

"Assign no blame to Kieron for I do not." Comlan firmly cautioned his subjects who were by their very nature ambiguous. "Kieron was by legend destined to that deed."

Kieron was by far the most startled by this royal pardon. A further gale of whispers rose from the masses pondering this possibility until stilled again by their king's voice.

"Besides, Kieron found the cure for this lethal infection which threatened first our powers and now our mere existence."

Fearing the king's meaning, Hildie glared blindly at the once translucent floor gone dark and dull. She wished, oh, how she earnestly wished that what he said next was true.

"Kieron has done what none of us were able to accomplish." Comlan's emerald gaze moved slowly from one face to another. "He has brought to us the remedy, the Seunadair whom legend declares is a *fairy not of fairy born*. . . ."

With these words Comlan motioned the attention of all toward the dark figure in their midst. "Lady Hildie of Ailm Keep."

"Would that I were." Hildie grimaced, alarm making her heart pound so loudly she feared everyone must hear its panic. "For were that true, then I might possess the necessary powers."

Yet another whisper swept the hall, one of desperate, dubious hope.

"But—" Hildie took courage in hand to gently correct the king of the Tuatha de Danann. "The legend doesn't say by fairy not of fairy born but by *magic* not of fairy born. Sadly, I possess no magic."

By the brilliant flash of the king's smile, it was plain he didn't agree and promptly reminded her of an undeniable fact already admitted.

"Did I misunderstand? Or was it not you who stepped through a solid granite wall no fairy could penetrate? And is that not a magic even greater than any we of the Tuatha possess?"

Hildie sighed. Clearly this was a destiny as inescapable as her stepmother's fulfillment of the White Witch's legend. The next moment she was ashamed of herself for allowing fear of being found inadequate to weaken her courage and tempt her to shirk an already acknowledged fate.

"Tell everyone about the visit to your dreams by my sister Lissan, and the mission of secrets revealed that sent her," Comlan gently commanded. "Tell by what magical feat you unlocked the labyrinth's closed portal, winning freedom for both yourself and Kieron."

Despite the considerable discomfort in finding herself the center of attention for these magical beings, Hildie complied with the king of the Faerie Realm's request.

Hildie began her account with the appearance in her night dreams of an ethereal fairy princess. Next, by royal command, she hastened to report the existence of a very realistic illusion and to relate the tale of how a granite wall impenetrable to fairy was broken by a human's blind trust—hers.

However, because Lissan had disappeared before they were heard, Hildie omitted from her narration the final whispered words, *by magic, magic becomes*. She was not convinced they hadn't merely been an echo in her sleeping mind of the Ogham inscription Kieron had earlier read aloud.

Kieron quietly urged Hildie on to speak about the most important revelation. "Share the first Lissan's advice on the site where the Seunadair's spell must be cast."

Hildie's smile was strained as she repeated the cryptic message. "Not from the lifeless circle of boundaries broken but from a ring of endless life." She glanced sheepishly around suddenly bright faces. "Now, if only I knew what that meant."

An immediate clamor of many voices arose in the hall, all crying out their delight that the simple answer was so very, very clear. But it was appropriately King Comlan who spoke for all by asking and answering two basic questions:

"What is the lifeless circle of boundaries broken? That which was cracked and allowed the Dragons of Chaos to escape.

"What is the ring of endless life? The fairy ring of forever blooming flowers created by the messenger who visited your dreams."

An unwelcome flood of rosy color burned Hildie's cheeks. She felt like a witless fool for having overlooked so obvious an answer.

Sympathizing with his human niece's unmistakable discomfort, Comlan promptly offered both praise and the aid most needed.

"Aye, it is undeniable fact that you are the Seunadair. And it is also true that you are most gratefully welcomed in this time of desperate need—for both our worlds." Comlan's sincerity was unmistakable. "I congratulate you for the fine progress you've already made toward success in your task by uncovering two necessary secrets—where the spell must be cast and by whom. . . ."

Comlan paused long enough to see a smile begin to curl Hildie's lips.

"That leaves only one important element to be added—the spell." Comlan's teasing grin prevented Hildie from sinking into gloom. "Be assured, niece, that Gair and I will teach you the arcane words which our grandmother, Queen Aine, taught us long ago in a far distant time."

Hildie blinked at the unexpected sight of Comlan's duplicate suddenly appearing at his side.

"Aye," Gair agreed with his brother. "We will share the words necessary to form a most powerful chant, the chant required to vanquish and reimprison the Dragons of Chaos."

The fact that both King Comlan and Prince Gair had confidence in her ability to do the impossible went far in bolstering Hildie's own. And when she looked up into Kieron's steadily reassuring aqua gaze, she felt ready to tackle even the most dastardly foes . . . and win.

"Our wrong *can* be undone," Kieron murmured,

love lending rich texture to his tone. "As foretold by the Sidhe, you *are* the Seunadair. And with the Tuatha de Danann's aid, you will see the vicious beasts tamed and confined."

Though earnestly striving to believe every word, still Hildie was forced to consciously conquer lingering doubts.

The castle remained unnaturally dim but hope's bright happiness renewed a fading warmth . . . until one of the lesser beings hovering on the crowd's fringes wound his way through to the forefront.

"If the spell must be cast from Lissan's fairy ring," Perry spoke tentatively, "then it will be rather more difficult than expected."

In a fine demonstration of fairy contrariness, the quiet announcement sent a reverse ripple of silence out from the uncomfortable adolescent at the crowd's center until every eye was focused on him.

"Why is that, Perry?" Comlan asked with an encouraging smile. "And how do you know it's true?"

"It was my turn to investigate any human intrusion into the ring." The youth shifted uneasily as he added, "Warriors are massing on its hilltop."

Hildie gasped. "Munster's invaders have already arrived!"

Lightly squeezing her shoulder in comfort, Kieron made a rueful observation. "Establishing a camp there secures for them a fine view of all who approach and a fine position from which to launch an assault."

An ugly cackle utterly lacking the melodious tones of fairy crashed across the assembly.

Listeners turned as one to find an odd sight in the abandoned musicians' loft built high above one corner of the hall. The figure was gaunt with an abundance of white hair, wildly disarrayed, and sharply uptilted brows.

"Ardagh!" Prince Gair harshly identified the erstwhile foe he had thoroughly defeated long, long ago.

"You've missed the point again, Lady Hildie." Ardagh gloated, voice fairly oozing with vicious glee while purposefully ignoring the one who'd called his name.

"Concern for parents and friends matters not at all when you can't stop the Dragons of Chaos's inevitable destruction."

The mood inside Tuatha Cottage was as somber as the overcast sky outside when Lissan had arrived to spend the afternoon lending help and support to the worried, disheartened, and weary Maedra.

When even King Comlan's most potent spells failed to heal Liam, his wife had fallen even deeper into despair. Maedra never left the side of her wounded warrior while he lingered in an unnatural sleep, unaware of either his surroundings or companions.

Burdened with the myriad of honorable duties necessary to see the kingdom's defenses secure, Rory didn't reach the cottage until after the countryside had been enveloped by the ominous gloom of a moonless, starless night.

Soon Rory and Lissan sat in matching chairs pulled close to one side of Liam's bed while Maedra perched atop a stool on the other.

"I thank you most sincerely for inviting Eamon to stay at the keep during this time of woe." While gazing at Rory with honest gratitude, Maedra repeated what she'd earlier told Lissan.

"I couldn't care for my son properly while tending to Liam. Besides, Eamon needs to be somewhere less focused on this disaster in his family." Maedra attempted a smile but it was grim. "And I am certain Eamon is enjoying Donal's company a great deal more than he would mine right now."

"The boys are good company for each other," Lissan agreed, reaching across Liam's narrow pallet to pat hands tightly clenched in Maedra's lap. Not wanting to add to Maedra's worries, she specifically didn't mention that the pair had slipped away once already in search of the great discovery lost.

"Not," Lissan hastened to add, "that Donal isn't concerned for the friend so clearly worried about his father."

"As am I," Maedra softly responded, words aching with the unshed tears of a gaze that rarely left the unconscious figure.

Rory and Lissan exchanged a helpless glance, wishing for a miracle but expecting none . . . not when even the king of the Tuatha de Danann had been unable to perform that feat.

A loud knocking at the door intruded and instantly had the cottage awash in wariness. A visit so late was alarming.

Maedra's already pale cheeks were chalky as she carefully stood and moved to peek through the crack of a barely opened door.

Surprised, Maedra opened it wider. She knew her caller but doubted either of her other guests would. And, while motioning the adolescent hovering on the doorstep into the cottage, still she left the door ajar knowing it hid the others from her caller's gaze.

"Why have you come, Perry?" Maedra quietly asked. Though she'd always considered it a negligible price to pay, as a condition of her contract for the right to remain in the human world, she'd had to surrender not only her fairy powers but all contact with the Tuatha. Thus, she hadn't seen Perry for more than a dozen mortal years and couldn't imagine why he was here now.

"Earlier a messenger (not me) was sent to Ailm Keep with most important news for its lord and lady. They neither of them were there." Perry gave a shrug and rueful grin. "Thus, our sovereign sent me here, hoping that you might help me locate them."

"What news have you to share?" Rory's deep voice startled the youth who by former fairy powers was rarely surprised.

Perry immediately answered the stern demand. "Your daughter, Lady Hildie, is safe within the Faerie Realm's protection."

"Was it Kieron or my father who rescued her?" Lissan curiously asked as she advanced to her husband's side.

"Neither." Perry blushed, yet another of the many uncomfortable firsts experienced since the Dragons of Chaos escaped. "It was your daughter's magic that saved Kieron."

"We thank you for sparing your time to find and give this news." Rory's gratitude was sincere although his smile was tense with unavoidable awareness of the looming invasion Hildie's reappearance was far too late to forestall.

Perry nodded acceptance of the praise but added, "But I have a second message for you . . ."

Rory's face went as cold and emotionless as stone. That the nervous adolescent had started with good news, left him uncomfortably certain the second would not be as welcome.

"What more have you to share?"

Perry took a deep breath and launched himself headlong into the murky pond of unhappy truths.

"Forces from Munster have slipped into Connaught. By moving in a wide circle around the border defenses you've established, they're now camped on the hill behind this cottage where Lissan's fairy ring blooms."

CHAPTER 19

While dusk's dark fingers stretched across the land, the setting sun of even a cloudy day outlined the western horizon's silhouette with vivid pink. Three figures stood in privacy on the parapet of the Faerie Castle's highest tower.

"Don't you see?" Hildie implored in quiet desperation. "I *must* return to Ailm Keep as hastily as possible!"

"Nay," Kieron softly protested. "I see no value in such a deed."

Sparks flared in sapphire eyes and Hildie drew a deep breath to renew her battle but Kieron stifled her words by continuing with his own argument.

"Why waste precious time making your way to Ailm Keep when the site for the Seunadair to work her magic is elsewhere?"

Standing very near and gazing up into Kieron's incredible aqua eyes, it was very difficult for Hildie to deny Kieron anything. Nonetheless, she was certain that she must.

"I know my family is worried about me. And that worry may be a dangerous distraction from other perils now when Munster's armies are so near and already poised to attack."

"But, elfling . . ." Kieron's honest fear for the safety of his beloved lent a despairing edge to the words. "As even Ardagh knew, until the Seunadair's mystical spell is cast and its awesome magic effective in its purpose, there is no safe way for you to journey back to Ailm Keep."

The couple so deeply involved in their gentle and suspiciously intimate confrontation had completely forgotten the presence of their royal companion until he spoke.

"Hildie," King Comlan called, a glint of amusement in emerald eyes. "I dispatched a message to reassure your family the moment you and Kieron appeared. They know you are safe in my realm."

"But—" Hildie turned slightly while shifting her plea for support in the proposed action to King Comlan. "Although Kieron plainly fails to understand my logic, I feel certain you must recognize the wisdom in my prompt return to Ailm Keep?"

Comlan's brows creased and when he looked no more likely to agree with her than Kieron had been, Hildie again restated her argument—more clearly and more fervently.

"Once I am safely within Ailm Keep's walls, I will agree to an immediate union with Lord

Morven which surely ought to bring a quick end to Munster's threat against Connaught."

"Perhaps," Comlan allowed with little confidence. "But only if Lord Morven is willing to give up his excuse for the goal he sought all along—Connaught's subjugation to Munster."

Hildie had already realized that the vile lord from Munster had proposed the marriage for political reasons rather than personal interest—just as nearly every union was arranged for ulterior motives. But still she hoped with her capitulation now to force Lord Morven into retreating for lack of honorable excuse. It was a weak hope but the only one she possessed.

"Most importantly," she drove her argument dead to point with incontrovertible logic, "it is the only strategy I see with any hope of quick success for driving an interfering army from Lissan's fairy ring in time for the necessary rite."

"Lord Morven won't so easily retreat," Kieron flatly stated. "Not after he's rallied not only his troops but his king's to the cause. It would be humiliating and to that the proud Lord of Dunbarrough Keep will never submit."

"I agree with you, Kieron," Comlan said, "that Lord Morven's pride far outweighs his common sense. But, I also agree with you, Hildie. Your plan to empty the fairy ring in time for the rite before it's too late, is one we've no choice but to pursue."

Kieron's face went to frost-coated stone. He dare not challenge his sovereign's authority. And yet, remembering how his king had cautioned him to step back and see Hildie wed to a mortal, Kieron suspected Comlan's approval of her plan was largely influenced by this opinion. Aqua eyes snapped with resentment unhidden now that fairy powers could no longer enforce a prompt mask.

"Then, sire." Kieron turned the same reasoning back on his king to secure approval on a second issue made important by Comlan's response to the first. "As Hildie's sworn protector, you surely will permit me to accompany her on this dangerous journey?"

Always amused by others' demonstrations of nimble wits, Comlan grinned at the younger male's immediate altering of tactics and instantly nodded approval of his proposed action.

Standing between two males caught up in their own negotiations, Hildie gazed out across a landscape peaceful in its silent darkness. The gentle view freed her to take inventory of necessary steps still awaiting action. Winning King Comlan's support of her strategy was possibly the most difficult but definitely not the last hurdle she must overcome in her quest.

"Hildie—" Kieron called to the colleen oddly entranced by a scene below nearly obscured in darkness. "Hildie, King Comlan was speaking to you."

Irritated with herself, Hildie bit her lip as she promptly turned toward the king and dipped an apologetic curtsy met by similar action spoken.

"I beseech pardon for intruding on clearly serious considerations." Comlan gave her a rueful smile. "I merely wished to give a promise before you depart. Gair and I will later this night join you at the keep. There we'll teach you the spell you must invoke once the fairy ring has been opened to you."

Kieron reached for Hildie's hand and tucked it safely into the crook of his arm before turning to his king with a final, pithy question.

"But what of Ardagh?"

Comlan grimaced against this reminder of the wicked fiend who so recently had issued taunts from the musician's loft. But the most troubling aspect of that scene had come when the wily creature completely disappeared at the same instant in which the assembled crowd began an earnest attempt to capture him. That demonstrated ability to disappear had been a baffling development considering the limitations put on the fairy magic of the Tuatha de Danann.

Inwardly Comlan acknowledged how unfortunate it was that his subjects were so unaccustomed to physical activity unaided by fairy powers. By that lack Ardagh's pursuers had proven clumsy trackers and likely had lost their prey in plain sight.

"Ardagh will be found," Comlan harshly stated. "If not immediately, then once the Seunadair's spell is cast in the rite restoring our powers."

As Kieron and Hildie walked alone down the long, broad pathway leading to and from the Faerie

Castle, the utter blackness of an overcast night was lessened only by Kieron's severely dimmed aura. In addition to this deeply resented limitation, Kieron accepted as his duty the burden of warning Hildie about another awkward and inconvenient loss.

"Since the Dragons of Chaos escaped to freely roam the world," Kieron began with a most basic fact already known to her, "the Tuatha de Danann's powers have been devastated."

Hildie nodded, pale face framed in a silken cloud of raven-black hair blending into the shades of night while a gently amused smile curled rosy lips.

"You needn't be concerned by thinking me unaware that it is no longer possible to accomplish any journey in the twinkle of a falling star."

" 'Tis true," Kieron responded with an aqua gaze so warm that anyone who saw it couldn't fail to recognize the deep emotion at its heart. "Our trip will require a depressing amount of time—as well as a good sense of direction. And, unfortunately, that is another fairy power now severely restricted."

"Moreover—" Shaking a golden head bright even in darkness, Kieron irritably admitted another unwelcome lack. "The magical steeds of the Faerie Realm are far too weak to carry anyone."

"Then, as we must walk to Ailm Keep . . ." Hildie heard his frustration and sought to ease it with an immediate plan for action. "Let's move ahead as hastily as we can while wasting no further time regretting what we don't possess but rather make plans to employ what we do have to win victory in our quest."

They hadn't traveled far into the dense forests of Connaught before stumbling upon a small camp where two warriors from Munster were tarrying the night. It was soon clear that these strangers were scouts dispatched to seek information and keep their leaders advised of troop movements and likely tactics. They unintentionally performed precisely the same service for their enemies as the couple unseen in the dark beyond their campfire's circle of light listened with rapt attention to idle conversation.

"Hah! Danger on the fairy ring's hill?" The derisive comment issued from the intruder relaxed and reclining on the fire's far side. "Do you think the fools here in Connaught actually believe in all the Tuatha de Danann legends and tales?"

"You believe in it, don't you?" taunted the second, larger figure sitting astride a fallen tree trunk.

The first answered with a clipped snarl of disgust. "Can't be true or surely the disrespect in our trespassing on their sacred site would've brought the unearthly race out in force."

"I don't fear a fairy attack." Picking up a chunk of scavenged wood lying at his feet, the speaker violently threw it into the flames, setting off a firestorm of sparks. "Why waste time on foolish superstitions when our invasion is nearly complete and a successful surprise attack so near."

The other nodded. "Only do I wish Lord Morven would put a halt to this endless waiting and issue the command to see our battle won."

"Morven won't." The statement was so flat it betrayed deep resentment. "Not until he has King Muirtrecht's permission and that won't be forthcoming until our sovereign's finest forces arrive to take credit for *our* feats." Disgust coated words ringing with the echo of past complaints.

The one reclining sat up to inquire, "Then how soon will Muirtrecht's warriors join us?"

Another piece of wood was flung into the fire before an answer came. "Can't possibly appear before two days hence since the truly elite segment had to be summoned from their posts in Northern Gaul."

"Gaul?" Sitting cross-legged on the ground, callused hands braced on thighs, the source of this curt query leaned far forward to meet his cohort's gaze with shared contempt.

The response was pithy. "Our sovereign has grandiose plans."

"But . . ." Bitter distaste scalded the words that followed. "We're the ones who die to win his goals."

" 'Struth, we've already lingered here too long without acting and we'll lose the element of surprise if we don't move soon."

"Have we no notion how soon the plan is truly launched?"

"Our leader is not a patient man and less so in

this scheme." One palm slapped the rough bark of a fallen trunk straddled. "I doubt he can bear to wait beyond the dawn after next."

The other smirked as he said, "And we already know that Lord Morven always and only attacks at dawn."

When the warriors' conversation descended into less savory topics and bawdy jests, Kieron gently urged Lissan into slipping deeper into shadows and moving ever onward to their destination.

As they moved silently through the dark forest, Hildie bolstered her courage for the challenges ahead with reminders of accomplishments already made . . . or stumbled upon. She told herself that their dangerous journey had already won reward enough by securing this information about King Muirtrecht's still gathering forces and the likely date of the assault.

Hildie knew her father well enough to know he wouldn't be impressed by the legend of the Seunadair and was exceedingly unlikely to believe his oldest daughter capable of supernatural feats. She hardly believed it herself.

However, overheard news of Munster's tactical plans was a gift Hildie could give her father. A gift which she earnestly hoped would accomplish two feats. First, she prayed it would soften him for the prospect of Tuatha royalty coming to his keep to teach her magical spells. Second, she desperately wanted to believe it would help her friends and family defeat their Munster foes, which might be necessary even if she succeeded with the Seuna-dair's spell.

Though Kieron missed his fairy powers, he had learned to use and in the past had taken pleasure in proving he was capable of many deeds on his own. Thus, he was able to lead Hildie almost directly to the forest edge opening onto the very pathway they sought. It led through bailey gates and over a drawbridge to Ailm Keep.

Hildie and Kieron climbed the keep's outer stairway and began moving down the short entrance corridor passing through the thickness of the keep's stone wall. Then, while gazing with anticipation toward the bright opening into the great hall at its end, she saw her parents. They were framed in the arched portal as they removed their own cloaks to hang on pegs driven into the wall on the doorway's either side.

At nearly the same instant that they were seen, Lissan and Rory saw the figures rushing toward them through the corridor's half-light.

"Hildie!" Lissan softly cried out in delight, impatiently waiting to wrap her stepdaughter in a welcoming embrace.

"And you, Kieron." Lissan next greeted Hildie's Tuatha guardian while Rory swept his daughter into a bear hug. "Thank you for rescuing her yet again."

"I am not worthy of gratitude," Kieron announced with an unrepentant grin that Lissan wrongly ascribed to his contrary fairy nature. "It was Hildie's magic that saved me instead."

"So a messenger from your king told us only a short time past," Rory announced, but didn't look in the least convinced.

"You must tell us your tale," Lissan gently demanded, taking Hildie's hand to lead her toward the dais and its high table, leaving the two males uneasy in each other's company to trail behind.

King Turlough and most other inhabitants of the keep had long since retired for the night leaving the hall nearly deserted, allowing privacy to talk while partaking of a delayed repast. Though comprised of cold dishes left from the evening repast, the mortals enjoyed what was served.

Hildie was worried about her father's reaction to the legend of the Dragons of Chaos. Even worse, his likely reaction to her part in its fulfillment. And, having no idea what else he might already have heard, beyond the news of her escape from an abductor, she chose to start her tale near its end by sharing the news gleaned from Munster's own warriors.

"Papa—" Hildie turned to her father and began. "While walking here, Kieron and I overheard the most interesting conversation between two warriors from Munster camped in the eastern forest."

It was Hildie's mention of a walk that first surprised Rory. From childhood, she had related incredible tales about her Tuatha guardian, Kieron, and his ability to whisk her anywhere . . . so why would they walk?

Within brief moments this minor matter was driven from Rory's thoughts by his daughter's report on the overheard conversation of enemies.

"Dawn after next?" Rory flatly repeated. "We'll be ready to meet their attack. We already are." His mouth tilted into a humorless smile. His claim was a little overstated and yet he truly believed that even if disaster were to strike immediately, Connaught would rise from the battle victorious.

"But, Papa," Hildie gently reminded. "In two days time King Muirtrecht's full force will likely have arrived."

"No matter that." Rory's smile deepened with confidence. "King Turlough's full force has been here for days."

This announcement caught Hildie's breath in a tight knot at the back of her throat. It was truly good news for Connaught's victory in the battle between mortal kingdoms . . . but a death knell for the prospect of convincing Lord Morven to accept an alliance with her and retreat from the fairy ring without blood spilled.

"Hildie," Lissan softly called, tired of waiting for the answer she'd requested at the outset. "Tell us now about your abduction, abductor, and how it is that you saved Kieron?"

Realizing that she could postpone the inevitable no longer and—by the need for haste—shouldn't, Hildie obeyed. With the practice of having told it several times already, she went through the litany of events from the strange Ardagh's involvement, inscriptions read, and on to her dream visitor without appreciable pause.

Nor did Hildie's audience interrupt her narrative. At least not until she shared the confirmation provided by both the dream-Lissan and King Comlan that she was the legendary Seunadair destined to halt devastation, restore order, and confine chaos.

"The Seunadair?" Rory looked dubious. "My daughter, a figure of legend?"

Kieron had remained quiet and nearly motionless since taking his seat at the table but now firmly spoke in support of Hildie. He told the part of her tale that she'd omitted. Lending just weight to her amazing feat, he spoke of the secret revealed by the dream-Lissan and how with blind trust Hildie had led him safely through the illusion of a granite wall he'd been unable to penetrate alone.

"Aye, because of Hildie's thus proven magic, we defeated Ardagh's machinations and walked free of the labyrinth's firmly sealed trap."

"Hildie, magic?" Rory questioned, clearly unconvinced.

"Rory—" Lissan insistently laid dainty fingers atop his powerful hand. "Have you forgotten that your wife is the White Witch?"

Midnight eyes gazed into an emerald gaze and softened. "Aye, you *are* magic."

"As well your daughter may be. She is undeniably the descendant of fairy—a fact now proven twice over."

" 'Struth." A deep voice of amazing resonance demanded the high table's immediate attention. "Prove twice and soon thrice."

Two golden figures of incredible masculine beauty strode across the hall side by side.

"Father, Gair, welcome." Lissan hastily rose and moved to step down and greet them both.

"Join us at table?" She politely invited and was as politely declined by two whose palates were accustomed to fare far superior.

"The time is short and we have come, as we promised Lady Hildie, to teach her what she must know to defeat the Dragons of Chaos."

Rory's cynical smile deepened. Comlan noticed and responded with his own mocking half smile. "I see you don't believe in the ancient legend? Unfortunately, in my world, we have incontrovertible proof. And, I'm afraid there are increasing signs of Chaos moving across yours as well."

Gazing at the new arrivals, Rory's dark head warily tilted to one side in question but it was Kieron who responded.

"I noticed your surprise when Hildie told you that she and I had walked here. My inability to whisk your daughter anywhere is but one example of the growing destruction which the Dragons of Chaos have already spread across the Faerie Realm."

Kieron leaned forward to meet Rory's gaze more directly as he continued. "Our powers first became unpredictable and then began to weaken until very little remains."

"I realize," Comlan picked up the warning, "that it is difficult to see any reason to fear for your world when the damage is done in my realm, particularly while you are poised on the blade's edge of war.

"But, though it may be difficult to believe that there is a greater danger, I implore you to spare even a precious few moments to look closely around your own kingdom. Note the changes, slow but becoming ever more confused."

"If you look . . ." Gair listed examples of what could already be seen. "You will find apples growing on berry bushes, streams flowing backward . . . or disappearing altogether."

Rory's jaw was taut. He was growing irritated with claims he firmly believed no more than an example of the illogic of fairy . . . until one of the two houseserfs toiling in the hall piped up from the hearth where she was tending a spitted ox.

"I saw such a thing, I did. It was unnatural and fearsome! The green yew tree has of a sudden begun sprouting the leaves of an oak! Odd, I say." She shook her head in disgust. "Very odd."

"And there was that fish." The other servant straightened from her scrubbing of trestle table-tops. "A big grouper just flew up out of the brook and tried to land on a branch. Truly, I saw it!"

Rory asked, "Where is this amazing flying fish?"

"I ate it, of course." She looked at her lord as if

he were totally daft. "Didn't even have to run traps to catch it."

Rory slowly shook his head over these strange claims. The first had been made by a responsible adult from whom he'd heard nothing the slightest bit strange or odd in the least. The second was not as reliable but . . .

What did it mean?

With Kieron at her side, Hildie led Comlan and Gair up the stone stairway to the family solar where in privacy the brothers taught her the arcane words of an ancient spell.

At the same time, in response to Hildie's gentle insistence, Rory prepared an official document and sealed it with his thumbprint. He'd initially blamed close contact with the contrary nature of fairy for her shocking change of heart. But after Hildie explained the honorable purpose for sacrificing herself in an unwanted betrothal, he reluctantly supported her choice.

Despite the lateness of the hour, since they now knew their foe's precise position, Rory dispatched his courier to Lord Morven. His letter announced Hildie's escape from her fairy captor and readiness to complete the betrothal rite never begun.

However, by the time Hildie and her Tuatha companions descended to the great hall again, a return message had already arrived. As expected Lord Morven refused the offered marital alliance. Indeed, it was phrased as a further accusation suggesting that Rory O'Connor's offer was no more than another attempt to further humiliate Lord Morven with an absent bride.

Rory's anxiety in knowing how few hours remained before Munster launched an assault joined his Tuatha guests' growing stress over rapidly dwindling time to undo a devastating wrong.

Rory and Comlan agreed to unite human and Tuatha forces for the common goal of ridding the fairy ring's hill of violent invaders. Once plans were laid, Kieron and his king went out in search of Ardagh. Unfortunately their weakened powers left them unable even to whisk themselves into the fiend's hill-home and far less able to track him through a world devoid of magic.

CHAPTER 20

Heavy black clouds met and resisted the assault of dawn's first glimmering light while far below an armed host waited at the base of a hill to do battle against an onslaught infinitely more dangerous.

Connaught's two most powerful leaders stood at the forefront of a multitude of warriors they had ordered to assemble in the fields behind Tuatha Cottage. Although a massive force, they stood in complete silence watching for the wordless order to set a carefully devised plan into motion.

With dark brows meaningfully arched, Rory glanced toward his cousin. When King Turlough immediately nodded agreement, they each motioned supporters to move forward into the lower reaches of a dense forest stretching down to the base of the long slope.

The night's rain had subsided but the ground was drenched. Thus sound was muffled by damp sod and thick vegetation as warriors anxious for the fight but trained to hold personal emotions under tight rein moved steadily into place. Each man took up a previously assigned position where he would wait in wooded shadows for Tuatha counterparts to perform their role in this deadly mummers play.

On the hill's far side a far different group began to ascend its slope, moving purposely and relentlessly forward, climbing upward, ever upward.

A dark figure safe in the midst of the Faerie Realm's golden horde, Hildie gazed through predawn's blue-gray haze at a dimly seen oak. She knew it sprouted from the center of the fairy ring eternally growing on the hill's crest—the fairy ring that was both her destination and destiny.

If strategies carefully laid succeeded, then she— a mere human—must soon, very soon cast a most powerful spell.

On the inexorable path, each step taking her nearer to an inescapable confrontation with merciless beasts, Hildie was herself attacked by steadily prickling feelings of extreme inadequacy. Their assault threatened to defeat her before the true battle began.

Hildie valiantly fought their weakening influence by wielding the only weapon she possessed. Like a litany, she silently repeated the arcane words of uncanny power which were a mere human's only hope for triumphing over the Dragons of Chaos.

A thump striking the sodden ground less than a full pace in front of her instantly demanded Hildie's attention.

Very nearly at her feet the limp body of a warrior lay atop a berry bush crushed by his fall. Instantly noting he was brown-haired, not golden like her companions, sapphire eyes quickly darted back and forth, probing into the shadows of thick vegetation for more hidden foes.

Heart pounding and senses sharpened by dread, Hildie was relieved to find no others and heartened to think that with this one rendered ineffective, their approach would go unreported to foes above.

The silent removal of Munster's sentinel guard did nothing to slow the Tuatha de Danann's upward progress. And very shortly after that initial encounter, they reached their goal.

Having stealthily trailed behind the golden army by slipping from tree to tree, Ardagh arrived shortly after. Although robbed of fairy powers and thus reduced to using ungainly physical movement, as if he were no more than a human, he was determined to watch the fruition of his scheme. To achieve that goal while unable to whisk himself into the highest branches of the last towering tree he'd sought for shield, he was forced to literally climb.

Rough bark tore at flesh unaccustomed to harsh toil but Ardagh deemed it but a small cost willingly paid for the pleasure of watching brutal human kingdoms gripped in the savagery of battle while the rampaging Dragons of Chaos rained destruction over all. And, he assured himself, that was precisely what he would see. The human girl couldn't possibly wield magic powerful enough to stop the inevitable end now set in motion, not when even he had none.

While the armies of Munster slept peacefully, oblivious to the nearness of doom to their hopes, they were completely surrounded.

Golden warriors, glow dimmed but still an awesome vision when joined together, noiselessly formed a solid circle, shoulder to shoulder. Of their number Kieron alone remained in forest shadows to stand as Hildie's protection against human weapons.

As part of the bright circle, King Comlan stood with one powerful arm upraised. Once all were in position, his arm dropped.

At that signal, the unearthly roar of innumerable Tuatha voices simultaneously awoke the entire encampment. Dazed and utterly unprepared, Munster's fighting men jumped to their feet and fumbled for weapons. But, despite weakened powers, the Tuatha were still physically much stronger than any mortal opponent.

Very soon the golden warriors successfully closed in on their foes, literally herding them from the hilltop down into the valley below and the waiting weapons of Connaught.

As the last human warrior awkwardly stumbled

from the fairy ring, Kieron escorted Hildie safely to its center.

Hildie took a deep breath for courage, and while looking upward into the strong branches of the young oak overhead began to repeat the ancient spell. Softly, hesitantly at the outset, each repetition gained in strength. And as her voice gained in strength, the earth began to move.

Still gazing upward, Hildie barely noticed as the moon glow natural to the Tuatha, filled the fairy ring and grew brighter while ground her feet no longer touched quaked ever more violently.

Frozen in terror, warriors from both human kingdoms stared helplessly at the brilliant light filling and radiating out from a human maid magically suspended an arm's length above the ground. But while the humans feared, from the Tuatha de Danann an exultant cheer rose with the force of a mighty gale.

Like some vicious beast trapped, held at bay, but snarling at its captor, the ground a brief distance below Hildie's feet heaved and began to buckle. Staring only upward, never allowing her attention to falter, Hildie didn't see the earth open beneath her unmoving form. She didn't see the misty vortex filled with glittering lights swirling toward the chasm's center. She didn't see the figure swept from a treetop into the depths.

"I freed the Dragons," Ardagh screeched, helplessly caught in the spinning whirlwind and railing

against his fate. "You haven't the magic to imprison them or me-e-e. . . ."

Hildie's concentration on the uninterrupted spell
was so strong that she heard neither Ardagh's
words nor the ghastly roar of air swirling around
him, filled with the unrepentant shrieks of the
damned. Though continuing to scream protests,
Ardagh was relentlessly pulled ever downward
and deeper into bottomless depths.

As the vortex drew the last of swirling mists into
its center, it pulled the edges of the chasm together
again, closing the earth. Slowly mighty quakes settled into tremors, tremors into a final few shakes.
Then peace returned, dark clouds parted, and the
sun shone with healing warmth upon a fairy ring
restored to its undisturbed beauty.

Filled with the delighted euphoria of success in
an impossible feat, Hildie's attention slowly
dropped to distant warriors still standing motionless in the valley below.

"Go home." Hildie didn't pause to consider the
difficulty of being heard from so far away . . . nor
wonder at the miracle that her voice carried to
those below as clearly as the tolling of distant ab-
bey bells.

"There will be no battle between the kingdoms
of Connaught and Munster today . . . nor ever in
my lifetime." Hildie paused long enough to see
Muirtrecht motion his forces into a retreat guar-
anteed by warriors her father assigned to see Connaught completely rid of Munster's invaders.

Then, to remove the possibility of similar danger in the future, Hildie added, "Never will I endure marriage with any *human* male."

"Nor should you."

This quiet pronouncement startled Hildie. She turned to find King Comlan at her side and was further surprised when he quietly repeated the one cryptic pronouncement from the Circle of Stones which she had dared to share with no one.

"By magic, the magic becomes." Comlan's smile was mocking but warm.

Hildie shook ebony hair in bewilderment.

"By the spell you've cast," Comlan said, grinning, "you've become as truly fairy as am I."

"And the first with black hair," Kieron observed as he lightly stepped to Hildie's far side. And while wrapping an arm possessively about her waist, with arched brows silently posed a most important query to his sovereign.

Comlan threw his golden head back and heartily laughed. The deep thunder of that sound was filled with a fine mixture of joy, relief, and gratitude for her miraculous cure of the most devastating ill ever to infect his realm.

"Aye, by Hildie's change in being, your oath-sworn barrier is broken." Comlan was pleased that this was true. "And clearly a loving union between you is clearly your joined destiny."

Overwhelmed by the joy of dreams granted, Hildie turned to look up into aqua eyes exploding with brilliant green flames. Rising on tiptoe, she twined her arms about Kieron's strong neck and gently pressed her lips against his.

As thrilled by forbidden wishes granted and heart thundering till he thought the trees would shake with its force, Kieron folded Hildie into his embrace and claimed a devastating kiss gladly returned.

Precious moments later the insistent sound of Comlan clearing his voice interrupted the happily self-involved pair.

"I hesitate to intrude but I am certain Hildie's father is impatiently waiting in the valley below to congratulate her on the success of a task he hadn't thought necessary."

Although there was far more amusement than criticism in Comlan's words, Hildie recognized in them the inescapable importance of promptly descending to meet with her father and his king.

As Hildie turned to leave, Kieron nearly reminded her that with a moment's instruction she could whisk herself down in an instant.

But when Kieron's mouth parted, Comlan sent him a warning look which prevented him from even offering to whisk her there himself.

For all the wonderful events just past, still Hildie's feet dragged as she made her way slowly, very slowly, down the well-trodden hillside path. 'Struth, her father had helped devise the tactics which had made the casting of her spell possible, but she worried that he wouldn't be as thrilled by all its results as she was. . . . Having a member of the Tuatha de Danann for a son-in-law would, she was sure, not please him. And worse was the prospect of him learning that his own daughter had become fully one of them.

King Turlough was first to greet the dainty beauty of amazing courage. "I don't know what happened up there and likely shouldn't but whatever you did was a resounding success!"

"You put our enemies to flight with few blows struck and no blood spilled." Rory swept his daughter into an affectionate bear hug. "Never again will I doubt your heritage."

"I am certain Hildie is pleased to hear you say that, Lord Rory." Comlan had whisked himself to stand only two paces behind the girl.

Rory released his daughter to glance curiously between the Tuatha king and her.

"Yes, Papa," Hildie bravely began, suddenly sure that it would be best to confess all at once. "There was another message inscribed for me in the Circle of Stones: *by magic, the magic becomes*. In casting the Seunadair's spell, I became—"

"Magic," Rory finished the phrase for her.

Anxiety over his reaction to this fact darkened Hildie's eyes to purest black but her father recognized her woe and with the white flash of his smile immediately proved it unnecessary.

When, as had been true of the willful child Hildie had once been, her expression remained blank, Rory knew there was more to be told.

In answer to her smiling father's knowingly narrowed gaze, Hildie instantly stated, "Kieron and I are to marry."

Rory nodded without hesitation. "Then we will celebrate that announcement as well as the victory of Tuatha and Connaught at our feast tonight."

Comlan acknowledged the invitation with an offer of his own. "I and mine are honored to be included at your keep's celebration. And in return for that honor, I beg of you the boon of being allowed to provide the food and drink."

With Rory's supporters joined by Turlough's warriors and visitors from Faerie Realm gathered for a celebration, both Ailm Keep and the courtyard beyond were merrily filled to overflowing.

The people of Connaught had over the past decade begun to believe the Tuatha de Danann no more than a myth. But they'd quickly come to appreciate a race so willing to not only lend aid in repelling intruders but to supply both a great banquet more delicious than anything ever tasted before and ambrosia to drink.

The great hall of Ailm Keep had little need for candlelight on this evening of a battle won almost before it had begun. The vast chamber was for the first time host to a sizeable number of beings able to provide their own illumination to any setting.

Seated at the high table were the keep's lord and lady along with two kings. And yet in the place of honor at its center was a radiant Lady Hildie with a stunningly handsome male at her side.

Elated by the new harmony between human and fairy kingdoms, Hildie beamed. She was garbed in a sumptuous gown presented to her by Amethyst, Queen of the Faerie Realm. It was formed from a soft cloth so delicate it seemed spun of gossamer and shimmered with tones of green ranging from the silvery mist of dawn to that found in the deepest shadows of a night forest.

While the joyous meal progressed, Hildie learned that her father had chosen Grady and the two Shanahan males to oversee the complete retreat of Munster. It was a duty Grady had accepted with pride. Hildie recognized her father's logic in allowing the father and son who had erred to earn their redemption. And after winning free from the sway of unreasoning animosity, that the Shanahans had done by exercising admirable restraint while fulfilling an honorable task.

Midway through the feast Rolan approached the dais and at his father's urging first confessed the crime inspired by his unjustified vanity and begged the lovely Lady Hildie's forgiveness for his foolish wrong. It was a plea she immediately granted, pleased to give others a taste of her happiness.

After the last course of a sumptuous feast had been consumed, King Turlough rose to his feet and gazed down at a dark beauty who blushed enchantingly as he lifted high one of the translucent pearl goblets provided by the Tuatha.

"Twice has Muirtrecht of Munster sought to conquer Connaught. And twice has he been defeated by a valiant lady of Ailm Keep."

The vast chamber went silent while a beaming audience listened intently as Turlough continued.

"The first to wield such power was your White Witch, your Lady Lissan. And now the second to work that magic is the Tuatha de Danann's Seunadair, your lord's daughter, Lady Hildie."

"So, rise." With his filled goblet Turlough motioned to all still seated. "Drink with me a toast to Lady Hildie."

As heads tilted back to drink the toast, Hildie was thrilled to glimpse Liam and Maedra standing behind seats at the near end of a lower trestle table. Had her spell restored fairy powers enough to heal the warrior recently so near death?

At Hildie's side, Kieron followed the line of her surprised gaze and as he sat down again whispered in her ear. "As the spell you cast was finished, Liam arose from his bed, body completely unmarked by the arrow that struck him down."

The king of the Faerie Realm was next to stand.

"I propose another toast to Lady Hildie without whose courageous actions both of our worlds would've suffered unspeakable devastation."

No sooner had that toast been completed than Lord Rory rose to his feet.

"We have two great events to celebrate this night." He waited for the murmur of questions to subside before continuing. "Our victory, Lady Hildie's amazing feat, you already know to be deserving of greatest appreciation and admiration.

"Those of you who reside on my lands also know how long I have waited for my daughter to choose her life's mate." Knowing he held the attention of all, Rory's white smile flashed. "I am pleased to announce that Lady Hildie will very soon be wed to her longtime Tuatha guardian, Kieron."

A split second after the name came a squeal from two young voices again in unison. Rory glanced indulgently between his broadly grinning son and the equally delighted Eamon who was happily seated beside a gratefully restored father.

As Rory sat down, sprightly tunes began. The music of human-played timbrels, pipes, and lutes was lent magic when joined by fairy instruments that lured finished feasters to the dance.

Though Hildie dutifully danced with King Turlough, her father, and King Comlan, she gladly flowed into Kieron's arms when he opened them for her.

So happy she was afraid her heart might burst, Hildie thought being in Kieron's arms was all that she desired until, during one spin of the dance, he whisked her to a magical site, a private paradise meant for them alone.

In the center of an enchanted ring, encircled by forever blooming flowers, Kieron gazed down into his beloved elfling's sweet face and saw the fulfillment of every dream he had ever or would ever have.

"You are magic—" His deep voice purred with unhidden emotion. "The source of all joy and beauty, my life, my love."

His smile held such potent warmth that Hildie felt cradled amidst the gentle embrace of his magic. She snuggled closer and repeatedly whispered her love for him until his mouth claimed hers in a soul-binding kiss that sealed their joined destiny.

Epilogue

Ireland, May Day 1997

In the midst of lush, green countryside a cozy, ivy-covered cottage lies cradled at the foot of a gentle hill. Though very old, it is plainly someone's beloved retreat from the modern world's stressful demands.

Behind this cottage grows a garden filled with abundant delights and out from its back gate lies a well-trod path. This path leads upward to the summit where flourishes a truly ancient oak spreading its protecting limbs across the mysterious circle of flowers which blooms both in summer sun and winter snow.

The locals say that it's here in this circle of blossoms where fairy magic lives on to this day. They happily relate the tale of the fairy princess who shed her powers to be with her human beloved, tell of magical feats down by its power, and whisper of wondrous deeds occurring still.

Some speak about hearing music of a sweetness no human could create. Others report having caught glimpses within the magic ring of beautiful beings who glow with the moon's white light. But only a fortunate few claim to have conversed with and been blessed by the aid of this mystical breed.